— AN ASSASSIN'S CREED SERIES —

LAST
DESCENDANTS

— AN **ASSASSIN'S CREED** SERIES —

LAST
DESCENDANTS

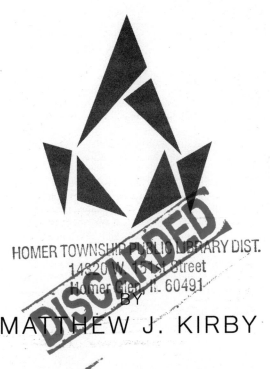

BY
MATTHEW J. KIRBY

SCHOLASTIC INC.

This book was a lot of fun to write, for reasons that I think will be pretty obvious. But the process was made even more fun by the people with whom I had the opportunity to collaborate. First, thanks to Rex Ogle for bringing me on board, and to Michael Petranek for bringing it home. The folks at Ubisoft Montreal have been incredible creative partners, so thanks go out to Aymar Azaïzia, Anouk Bachman, Richard Farrese, and Caroline Lamache. Thanks also to Holly Rawlinson, Andrew Heitz, Samantha Schutz, Debra Dorfman, Charisse Meloto, Lynn Smith, Jane Ashley, Ed Masessa, and Rick DeMonico. With such an awesome team, who needs a Piece of Eden?
—Matthew J. Kirby

Special thanks to Yves Guillemot, Laurent Detoc, Alain Core, Yannis Mallat, Etienne Allonier, Danny Ruiz, Pauline Dutilleul, Marine Gallois, Marc Muraccini, Cécile Russeil, Christopher Dormoy, Yves Lançon, Studio Lounak, Ubisoft Creative Services, Sophie Stumpf, Trey Williamson, Clémence Deleuze, François Tallec, Virginie Sergent, Michael Beadle, Stone Chin, Heather Pond, Andrien Gbinigie, and Stephanie Pecaoco.

Published by Scholastic Inc., *Publishers since 1920*. SCHOLASTIC and associated logos are trademarks and/or registered trademarks of Scholastic Inc.

The publisher does not have any control over and does not assume any responsibility for author or third-party websites or their content.

This book is a work of fiction. Names, characters, places, and incidents are either the product of the author's imagination or are used fictitiously, and any resemblance to actual persons, living or dead, business establishments, events, or locales is entirely coincidental.

ISBN 978-0-545-85551-8

10 9 8 7 6 5 4 3 2   16 17 18 19 20

Printed in the U.S.A.   40
First printing 2016

Art Direction: Rick DeMonico
Page Design: Yves Lançon

For Stuart, who graciously offered his assistance
in the research for this book.

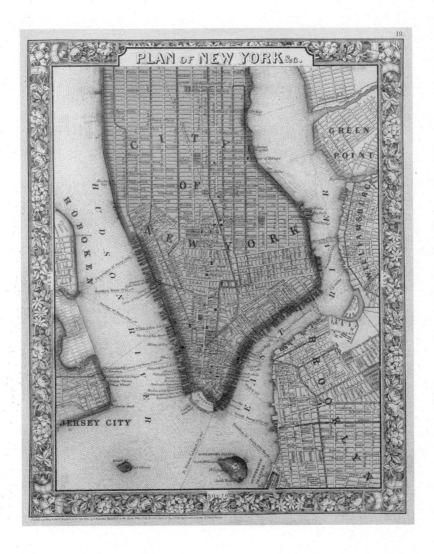

PLAN of NEW YORK &c.

The informant cleared his throat across the dinner table, his long frock coat unbuttoned, his hair greased and curled at his temples. Evening had quickly overtaken the townhouse, and the man had emptied his plate before delivering his message. Boss Tweed had patiently allowed this. His hold over New York had always been rooted in what he could give people, the appetites he could whet, the greed he could manipulate.

"It's true," the informant finally said. "There's an Assassin in the city."

Tweed slurped down another briny oyster. "Do you have a name?"

"Not yet," the informant said. "But someone is working Reddy the Blacksmith to keep the Bowery Boys out of it."

Tweed had consolidated his power and was now the most influential man in New York. He controlled the Tammany Hall political machine, and through it the streets and the ballot box. His network of spies and politicians in Washington had already alerted him to the presence of an Assassin operating in New York. There were rumors the Brotherhood planned to use the ongoing civil war to mount an offensive. It was even possible they had learned of the Templar plan.

"Without the Bowery Boys," Tweed said, "the riots will fail."

"It won't be a problem, Boss—"

"The gangs of the Five Points and waterfront won't be strong enough without them."

"The Bowery Boys are in."

"I trust they are. But we still need to know who this Assassin is, and what the Brotherhood is after."

"I've made inquiries."

Tweed wasn't pleased or reassured by that. It was a mistake to underestimate an Assassin. "Be discreet," he said. "We want to flush the Brotherhood out into the open, not drive them deeper into the shadows." He dragged a bite of roast beef through the brown sauce on his plate and ate it.

"Of course, Boss." The informant eyed the food remaining on the table and licked his lips like a dog.

But Tweed knew true power relied on keeping his constituents wanting more. "That will be all. Return when you have a name and not before."

The informant bowed his head. "Yes, Boss." Then he rose from the table and left the room as Tweed continued to eat.

Out in the street, the informant walked, still hungry, to where he could board an omnibus headed downtown. Though night had fallen, the city carried on by gaslight. He passed the-aters, restaurants, and saloons all crowded with customers enjoying the slight break from the day's heat.

Sometime later, when he reached the gang clubhouse at Number Forty-Two on Bowery, he did so unaware of the eyes watching him, the shadow perched unnoticed on the ledge of a building three stories above the street.

Those eyes were patient, and when the informant left Number Forty-Two a few hours later, staggering a little with drink, the shadow descended and followed silently behind him.

The informant hadn't been discreet enough. A few blocks farther, near an alleyway, the Assassin made his move . . . the flash of a hidden blade, a quick and silent thrust . . .

The body wasn't discovered until morning.

CHAPTER ONE

Owen needed to know.

He already knew, but he needed to know it in a way that could be proven. A way that would convince others, including his own grandparents, of his father's innocence. The justice system had failed, and the public didn't care. His father had gone to prison for a murder he didn't commit, where he had died from a stupid ruptured appendix before Owen could even say good-bye. So now it was up to Owen to find out what really happened the night of the bank robbery.

He thought Javier would understand. They'd been friends since third grade, back when Owen's life went to hell. It was true they hadn't been close for a while now, not since elementary school and junior high, but Owen still thought he could count on Javier.

"So will you come with me?" he asked.

They stood outside their high school, in a courtyard on the side of the building, next to a bank of empty bike racks with chipping paint. Three of Javier's friends, guys Owen didn't know, stood off to the side, watching them, talking among themselves.

"I don't know," Javier said.

"You don't know?"

Javier said nothing. He just stared.

"Come on. You know this tech stuff better than me. Better than anyone." Owen looked sidelong at Javier's friends. "Even if no one else knows that, I know it and you know it."

Javier looked back at his friends, too. He hadn't smiled, he hadn't laughed, he hadn't changed the hard expression on his face at all since Owen had approached him a few minutes ago and explained his plan. The Javier standing there didn't even seem to be the same person Owen used to know, the Javier he'd first met after Owen's dad had gone to prison and his mom had moved them in with her parents. New neighborhood. New school. New bullies beating him up—

"I'll think about it," Javier said. "Now I gotta go." He turned to leave.

"Will you?" Owen asked.

Javier looked back. "Will I what?"

"Think about it."

"I said I would." And he walked away.

Owen watched him return to his group, not sure if they could actually be called his friends, the kind of guys Javier used to protect Owen from. As Javier reached them, they gave him questioning nods in Owen's direction, and Javier just shrugged and shook his head.

Owen had no idea what Javier was into now, how they'd gotten to this point, from best friends to total strangers in the space of a couple of years. It was like that with Owen's mom, too. He would have thought the death of his father three years ago would've brought them closer, but it had just driven their separate islands farther apart. A continental drift that had been gradual, unstoppable, and full of earthquakes.

Owen left school and walked toward his grandparents' house. Whether Javier came through for him or not, he decided he would still go that night. He didn't have a choice. It was up to him.

He needed to know.

When Owen opened the front door, his grandma was sitting in her armchair in the front room watching a game show, the kind that had been on TV longer than Owen had been alive. As he came in, her cat, Gunther, leapt from her lap, and his claws must have dug into her thighs through her housedress, because she yelped and gave a single, slight convulsion. Gunther meowed and strutted over with his tail up to rub against Owen's leg.

Owen bent down to rub behind Gunther's ears. "Hey, Grandma."

"Hello," she said, muting the game show applause. "How was school?"

"Fine," he said.

"How are your grades?"

"Same as they were yesterday."

"You need to bring those up," she said. "Appreciate the value of education. You don't want to end up like your dad."

Owen heard that a lot. It was a freight train of a statement that hit hard and pulled behind it the cargo of every argument, every tear, every hissed conversation, and every shouting match between his grandparents and his mom that Owen had overheard during the trial and since. His grandparents had hated his dad before Owen's mom had married him, and now they hated his memory more. Owen's dad was their "scapeghost," a shade that could be as terrible as they needed him to be, blamed for anything. For everything.

Owen had learned early on not to defend the ghost. But he didn't need to. That wasn't his dad. And soon, everyone would know that.

"I'll bring my grades up," he said. "Where's Grandpa?"

"Out back," she said. "Working on a mower, I think. He could probably use your help."

Owen kept his smirk below skin level. His grandpa never needed help with anything, least of all an engine, which meant there was probably something his grandpa wanted to talk about. Owen dreaded that, but knew he couldn't avoid it, so he nodded and said, "I'll go see."

He walked through the living room, with its old carpet that was either so impervious to stain, or had been so well taken care of, that his grandparents couldn't justify the cost of replacing it, the room's beige, plastered walls hung with his grandma's adequate oil paintings. In the kitchen, he grabbed an orange from a bowl of fruit on the spotless Formica counter, and then he went out the back screen door, which creaked open and banged shut behind him.

The yard, small and manicured to the point of looking plastic, was an amoeba-shaped rug of thick grass surrounded by flowerbeds, shrubs, and bushes. A few orange and avocado trees grew up against the six-foot-tall, slatted wooden fence that marked the border of his grandma's empire.

Owen walked the brick path along the back side of the house to his grandpa's outpost, the shop that had never once been called a garage that Owen could remember, even though that's what it was. Inside, his grandpa bent over an old lawn mower, a single overhead fluorescent dangling above. He wore his old bib, the same kind of denim overalls he'd had since Owen was a boy.

"Is this one to sell?" Owen asked.

"Nah," his grandpa said. "Repair job. The Egertons down the street."

"You gonna charge them?"

"No," he said. "But they'll probably try to pay me anyway."

"Grandma would say she should pay them for keeping you occupied."

He chuckled. "How do you know she doesn't?"

Owen bit the orange rind with his teeth to start it, tasting the bitterness, and then dug into it with his fingertips, dripping juice as he peeled it away.

"Don't get that on my floor," his grandpa said.

Owen always thought a building called a shop would be exactly the kind of place where you could drip juice on the floor, but that was not the kind of shop his grandpa had, where no tool or piece of equipment or chemical bottle could be found out of place.

"Your grandma ask you about your grades?"

"She did."

"So I don't have to?"

Owen dropped the orange rind into the garbage. "You kinda just did."

His grandpa looked up from the mower. "True enough." Then he stood with a part in his hand and walked over to his workbench against the opposite wall, where he tinkered with his back to Owen. "I saw your old friend the other day. What's his name? Javier?"

"Yeah?" Owen ate a wedge of the orange. It was a sweet one, not sour, barely tart.

"Haven't seen him around here in quite a while."

Owen didn't say anything. Just took another bite.

"You still friends with him?" his grandpa asked.

"Sorta. Not really."

"Didn't much like the look of the guys he was with. Gangbangers."

"How do you know that?" Owen asked.

"I could just tell."

"That sounds kinda racist, Grandpa. Javier's not in a gang."

"I hope not. He always seemed like a good kid."

Owen ate the last few segments of the orange, getting juice on his chin.

His grandpa still had his back to him, working on the lawn mower part. "You stay clear of those guys, don't you?"

"Grandpa," Owen said. "Come on."

"Just making sure. This neighborhood isn't what it was when your grandma and I moved here. It was still a pretty decent place even while your mom was growing up, until those last few years of high school." That was when Owen's mom had met his dad, but his grandpa left that unsaid, even though Owen knew he was thinking it. "I'm old and stubborn. I'd never move away from my home. But this isn't the place I would've picked for your mom to raise you. Not anymore."

"I'm not in a gang."

"I know you're not."

"Then why are we talking about this?"

His grandpa turned around, the glow of the fluorescent light bulb reflecting off his bald head. "I just want you to be careful. You're fifteen. I know more about how kids are these days than you give me credit for. It's easy to get pulled down the wrong path. You want to belong somewhere. You start out thinking you can handle it, and before you know it, you're in over your head in a bad situation."

Time with his grandpa in the shop usually went like this. It was as much a chance for his grandpa to work on Owen as it was the engine. Owen knew his grandpa meant well. His grandma, too. But they were also wrong about a lot of things.

"Just . . ." His grandpa shook his head and turned back around toward his workbench. "Just be careful. You got homework?"

"Did it at school."

"Great. Then you can get ahead."

"School is a treadmill," Owen said. "How do you get ahead on a treadmill?"

His grandpa chuckled again. "Smart aleck. Get inside and study something."

Owen smiled and left the shop, returning along the brick path to the back door. Inside the house, he found his grandma had turned off the TV and now worked in the kitchen, slicing carrots on the counter, a large bowl and a pile of uncut vegetables nearby.

"How's it going out there?" she asked.

"Fine," Owen said. "You think I'm in a gang, too?"

"He's right to worry," she said. "Lotta good boys around here have fallen in with the wrong crowd. Hard to forget what happened to your father."

"Yeah, you and grandpa make sure of that." Owen moved to leave. "I'm going to my room."

She put the knife down. "We just don't want that to be you."

Owen said nothing, because if he opened his mouth, he'd just end up in trouble. So he stalked away from her, through the living room, down the hall, to his bedroom. Once there, he kicked some clothes out of the way so he could shut the door and lock it. He stood there a couple of minutes, breathing hard, staring up at the ceiling.

He knew his dad hadn't always been perfect. He'd been in some trouble in high school, some shoplifting and vandalism, but nothing too serious. Nothing that would have stuck to him in a way that made his life hard after the age of eighteen. He'd grown out of all that. The man Owen knew had worked hard, stayed clean, and even without a college degree he'd managed to move his family to a tree-lined suburb with bikes on the front lawns and two nice cars in every driveway. But Owen's grandparents never credited any of that. They only ever saw the high school punk, and after his dad got arrested, the months of the trial were nothing but an extended *See? We were right all along,* directed at Owen's mom.

But they weren't right. Neither were the judge nor the jury.

Owen stepped across the floor to his computer and threw himself into the chair at his desk, toppling a tower of empty soda cans near the monitor. He'd been counting on Javier to make sure the technology was safe and looked right, but if Javier never showed up that meant it would all be on Owen. He smacked the keyboard to wake up his computer, and then did a search online, reading about Abstergo Industries, the Animus, something called Helix, and those crazy-expensive entertainment consoles. But it was all corporate-speak hype, varnished by public relations to the point where it gleamed and said nothing. He got a little more from a few message boards, mostly warnings and paranoid rants about a global conspiracy involving Abstergo. But what multinational conglomerate corporation *didn't* involve conspiracy? That seemed to him to be the nature of the game.

A short while and more fruitless searching later, his mom came home from her job at the copy center. Owen heard the front door, her muffled voice out in the living room talking with his grandma, and then a few moments later, a knock on his bedroom door.

Owen shut his browser. "Come in."

The doorknob rattled. "It's locked."

"Oh, sorry." Owen bounced out of his chair to the door, and opened it. "Forgot."

"Everything okay?" His mom stood in the hallway wearing her blue polo uniform shirt, her hair pulled back, maybe a few more gray hairs than the day before.

"Yeah, fine," he said. "Why?"

"Grandma mentioned you and Grandpa had a talk."

Owen shrugged. "Wasn't really different from any other talk we have once or twice a week."

"I guess seeing Javier really rattled him."

Owen rolled his eyes. "He's not in a gang."

"Okay." She held up her hands, crossed with the short, red lines of a few fresh paper cuts. "If you say so. But it's a good thing your grandparents worry, you know."

"Is it?"

"It means they care."

Owen turned away from the open door and went to fall onto his bed, lying on his back, hands behind his head. "That's not exactly how I'd put it."

She stepped into the room. "How would you put it, then?"

"I'd say they care that I don't go out and rob a bank like my dad."

His mom stood up straight, as if she'd run into an invisible wall. "Don't say that."

"But that's what they're thinking."

"That's not what I mean. Just . . . don't say that."

"Why not? You believe it, too. Or at least, you don't deny it anymore when they bring it up."

"Owen, please. I can't . . ." She glanced toward the door.

"Whatever." He closed his eyes. "It is what it is."

His mom stood there a minute longer, and he listened as she crossed the room, wading through his clothes, stepping on food wrappers, and shut the door behind her on her way out.

Later that night, after dinner and dishwashing, Owen heard his mom go to bed in the room next to his, and shortly after that he heard his grandpa shuffle down the hall. It was another couple of hours before his grandma switched off the laughter and saxophone-heavy music of her late-night talk shows and went to bed. That was when Owen got up, still in his clothes, pulled on a hoodie, and crept from his room. The front door made too much noise, so he went out the back way, careful not to let the screen door bang behind him.

It was a cool night, with a wind that flapped a few newspaper pages down the street. Whereas his grandparents kept their yard and house in postcard condition, many of their neighbors did not. Those that watered their lawns had mostly weeds. Those that didn't had mostly dirt. The sidewalk had cracked and buckled before Owen had moved there, but no one had repaired it since then, and it could trip someone in the dark who didn't know its topography.

Owen had to run to catch the last bus on the route near his grandparents' house, but he made it, and was soon staring through his reflection in the window at the passing streets, heading toward the address Monroe had given him. Although it wasn't an address so much as a location near some factories and warehouses at the edge of the city. He transferred buses twice, fortunately to lines that ran all night, and then walked another mile or so to get there, past graffitied apartment complexes and darkened, gated storefronts.

The section of the industrial park he eventually reached seemed abandoned, with padlocked doors, broken windows, and weeds choking the narrow spaces between the buildings. Infrequent streetlamps smeared the ground with yellow light the color of vomit. Owen was beginning to wonder if Monroe had played him for an idiot, but then he saw the bus parked in the shadows.

It wasn't a vehicle like the ones he'd taken to get there. This bus was old, with distended wheel wells, and between them, a rounded, bulging hood with a wide, angled grill across the front, the kind of model a collector of classic buses would want, if there were actually people out there who collected classic buses. It was painted brown, and the windows were all blacked out, but somehow it didn't seem quite as forsaken as its surroundings.

Footsteps crunched in the gravel behind him, and Owen spun around.

"Relax," Javier said. "It's me." He wore a white hoodie, hands buried deep in the pockets.

Owen let out a breath. "You came."

"I thought about it," Javier said.

"Thanks." Owen nodded toward the bus. "This is it."

"You sure about this?" Javier asked. "Messing around with your DNA? Your brain?"

"I'm sure," Owen said. "I need to know. Besides, other kids have done it."

"That's what I've heard. And Monroe told you this would work?"

"We didn't have time to get into it. He just told me to meet him here."

Javier shrugged. "Then let's go find out."

CHAPTER TWO

Owen walked up to the front-side door of the bus and rapped on it with his knuckles. Then he put his hands in his pockets while he waited, Javier standing behind him. When the door finally squealed open, a cold light that was the blue of a hotel swimming pool poured out around a silhouetted figure in the doorway.

"Glad you could make it, Owen," Monroe said, his voice deep and resonant as a slapped bass guitar. "I see you brought a friend. Come on in, then."

The figure turned away and retreated into the bus. Everyone at school knew Monroe, the network IT guy. Almost everyone liked him, except for maybe some of the teachers. Owen and Javier climbed the narrow stairs into the bus and followed after him.

The vehicle's interior was the opposite of its exterior, completely retrofitted with sleek white paneling, strip lighting, and an array of computer monitors, and it smelled of heated plastic and ozone. An ergonomic padded chair reclined at the rear of the bus. Monroe had gone back to stand to the left of it; he had shoulder-length brown hair and a goatee and wore the same clothes he somehow got away with wearing to work at the school: faded jeans, Converse sneakers, and a flannel shirt over a concert T-shirt for a band Owen didn't know. Owen couldn't quite tell how old he was. Forties, maybe? Early fifties?

"Javier, right?" Monroe asked as Javier came up the stairs behind Owen.

"How'd you know that?" Javier asked.

Monroe snapped his fingers and tapped his temple. "Eidetic memory, man."

"What, is that like photographic memory?" Owen asked.

"No," Javier said behind him. "It isn't. And that still doesn't explain how you know me."

"I spend a lot of my time managing the student database," Monroe said. "I would probably recognize almost any kid from the school."

That answer didn't seem to appease Javier, who folded his arms and looked around the bus. "So what is all this?"

"This?" Monroe spread his arms. "This is you."

"Wow, man," Javier said, his voice flat. "That's deep."

"Relax," Monroe said. "What I mean is, all of this is to get inside you." He pointed a finger at Owen's chest. "Your DNA."

"Yeah," Javier said. "About that. What are you running here? This doesn't look like the Animus entertainment consoles I've seen online."

Owen appreciated that Javier had done some digging of his own before coming here.

"That's because you won't find anything about this model online or in stores," Monroe said. "Abstergo has suppressed it all. This machine is based on the first Animus. But I've made several critical modifications to it."

"So this is the real deal?" Javier stepped forward, suddenly more interested.

"What do you mean 'suppressed'?" Owen asked, remembering how hard it had been to find much in his own search. "What, like trade secrets or something?"

"Something like that," Monroe said. "Publicly, Abstergo markets the Animus as a research tool. Or even a device for entertainment. A very expensive one."

"So what does this one do?" Javier asked.

"In the most basic sense, it's the same," Monroe said. "I take a sample of your DNA, analyze it, and unlock the genetic memories of all your ancestors stored there. Once we have that, we can create simulations of those memories for you to explore." As he spoke, he sometimes looked away, to the side or over Owen's shoulder, not in a way that seemed to be avoiding eye contact, but more that his mind was partially elsewhere.

"So how is this one different?" Javier asked.

Monroe frowned. "Other models can access the memories of anyone with DNA stored in the Abstergo Cloud—"

"But I read that those simulations have been manipulated," Javier said, "by Abstergo."

"Manipulated how?" Owen asked.

"They're more like a reality show," Javier said. "They edit the crap out of them so you don't get the whole story."

"Exactly," Monroe said. "The newer models of the Animus serve the purposes of entertainment and Abstergo's own self-interest. People see and experience history the way Abstergo wants them to. There's no truth to be found there. This model"—he laid his hand on the recliner's headrest—"can only access *your* memories. Uncorrupted. That's the only way to find whatever truth it is you're looking for."

"How'd you get it?" Javier asked.

"I worked for Abstergo," Monroe said. "A long time ago. Any other questions?"

Owen glanced back at Javier, who nodded and said, "Yeah, one more. Why are you doing this?"

"Why are *you* doing this?" Monroe said. "I invited Owen, not you."

"I'm here because Owen's a friend and I owe it to him."

Owen didn't think of himself as sentimental, but he had to admit he liked hearing that.

"Good," Monroe said. "The truth is . . . I'm doing this because I owe someone, too."

By the heavy tone in his voice, Owen knew Monroe wasn't going to elaborate on that, but Javier asked no more questions, and Monroe turned to Owen. "So what truth are you looking for? We didn't have time to go into detail back at the school. Whose memories do you want to explore, again?"

Owen inhaled deeply. "My father's."

"Oh, right. Fathers are important." Monroe nodded. "Anything specific?"

"I need to know what happened to him on a particular night. December eighteenth. Five years ago."

"Oh." Monroe shook his head. "I wish I'd known. In that case, I can't help you."

Owen took a step toward him. "What do you mean? That's the whole reason I came here. You said—"

"You asked if I could get you inside your dad's memories, and I said yes. Which is true. You didn't tell me you wanted to go into your dad's experiences from just five years ago."

"But—"

"It's simply not possible," Monroe said. "Your DNA will only contain your father's memories up to the point when you were conceived, not after. You don't have his genetic memories from when you were, what, ten?"

"He's right," Javier said. "I wondered about that, but I thought maybe he had some kind of new tech."

The bus around Owen seemed to be shrinking, becoming cramped, as his frustration and anger grew. "Then what am I supposed to do? How can I get into his memories from that night?"

"You need a different kind of Animus," Monroe said. "And a sample of his DNA from *after* that night. That's the only way it will be encoded in his genetic memory."

Owen's muscles tensed to the point where they quivered. "But he was arrested that night. They took him away, and he never came home again. I don't *have* his DNA."

Monroe sighed. "Then I'm truly sorry, man."

Owen wanted to put his fist through one of the nearby monitors. He'd come here because this was the only way. The only way to prove his father innocent. The only way to make things right. But it wasn't a way at all. Owen had no way, and he'd only now realized it. He was trapped in this life, listening to his grandparents trash his father, watching his mom surrender her memories of him without a fight.

"If he could get his father's DNA," Javier said, "then could you do it?"

"Absolutely," Monroe said. "With a different kind of Animus, and a sample of DNA from after that night."

Owen felt Javier's hand on his shoulder. "Maybe your mom saved something. Something with his DNA on it. An old shirt, maybe?"

"We don't have anything," Owen said. "We needed money. My mom sold everything to try to keep the house. But we lost the house anyway."

The bus went quiet, except for the gentle whirring of the computer fans, the clicks and whines of hard drives. Owen didn't want to leave, because that would be admitting he had failed, so instead he just stood there amid all that useless machinery.

"Listen," Monroe said. "I've been doing this for a while. Different cities. Different schools. Some kids come to me for the thrill. Other kids, like you, come to me because they want answers. But the thing is, they rarely find the answer they're looking for, and it almost never solves anything. I think you'd do better to ask yourself why the question is so important to you."

"What does that even mean?" Owen said. "My dad went away to prison. For something he didn't do. I think it's pretty obvious why that's important to me."

"Let's just get out of here," Javier said. "This guy doesn't have anything for you."

"What about you?" Monroe asked, looking at Javier.

Javier narrowed his eyes. "What about me?"

Monroe nodded toward the recliner. "You want to give it a try?"

"What about your big speech?" Javier said. "It won't solve anything."

"You're not going into the Animus with a question," Monroe said. "But I know you're curious."

"Don't pretend like you know me," Javier said.

"I've seen your STEM scores," Monroe said. "Pretty impressive. If that's really who you are. That guy would be all over this."

A moment passed without Javier denying it.

"Look," Monroe said, "I'm not trying to force you. Do whatever you want. But you're here, and it really is a hell of a ride to be someone else for a little while."

Javier looked at Owen, and Owen saw a familiar expression there, one that he hadn't seen in a long time. Monroe was right. Back when they'd been best friends, when Javier saw something that made him curious, he got this look of determined excitement, a furrowed brow with a grin. He had that look now, and Owen wondered if that was the real reason Javier had come that night.

"Okay," Javier said. "I'll do it."

"Right on," Monroe said. "Come up and have a seat." Then he turned to some of the consoles and blinking lights.

Javier slipped by Owen and moved past the computer equipment to the recliner, and as he lowered himself slowly into it, Owen felt a surge of anger and resentment. Somehow, his former best friend was doing what Owen had come here to do. Javier was supposed to help him, not take his place.

Javier lay back, his hands up on the recliner's armrests. Monroe sat down on a swivel chair next to him, and brought out a kind of plastic gauntlet connected to the main computer terminal with a tangle of wires.

"Hold out your right arm, please." Monroe opened the gauntlet like a clamshell.

"What's that?" Javier asked.

"This is a scanner," Monroe said. "It sends the genetic reading to the Animus core for analysis. Just hold out your forearm."

Javier pulled up the sleeve on his hoodie, and Monroe closed the gauntlet around his exposed arm.

"You'll feel a pinch," Monroe said, "from the blood draw."

But Javier didn't flinch.

"Good." Monroe spun in the chair to face a computer monitor, and typed away at the keyboard.

Owen moved to where he could see the screen, but none of the windows or text scrolling by made any sense to him.

"Hey," Javier said, his voice low. "Owen."

Owen turned to look at him.

"You okay with this?"

Owen shrugged. "Yeah."

"You sure?"

"Does it matter?"

Javier didn't answer.

Monroe tapped at the keyboard for another few moments. "Excellent," he said. "Very promising."

"What is?" Javier asked.

"Give me a minute," Monroe said. More tapping. More screen flashes. Then he looked up from the terminal toward Owen. "Let's check something."

"What?" Owen asked.

"Genetic Memory Concordance." Monroe pulled out a second gauntlet. "Give me your arm."

Owen folded his arms instead. "I thought you said—"

"This isn't about your dad," Monroe said. "I want to analyze your compatibility with Javier."

"What does that mean?" Javier asked.

"If you both had an ancestor present at the same event," Monroe said, "then your genetic memories will sort of . . . overlap. You can share a simulation. The combined data actually makes the rendering more robust."

"You mean we both go into the simulation?" Owen asked. "Together?"

"Yes," Monroe said. "One of my own modifications. So what do you say?"

Owen was intrigued by the offer, and he kind of liked the idea that Javier wouldn't be able to totally take his place, after all. He stuck out his arm without asking Javier if he was okay with it. "Let's do it," Owen said.

"Right on." Monroe closed the gauntlet over Owen's forearm. Owen felt the sharp pinch of the needle, but tried not to wince. "Data coming in," Monroe said. "It'll just take a couple of minutes to analyze it and then tabulate your Memory Concordance."

Owen stood there next to the recliner, his arm tethered to the computer, watching the screen.

"What if we don't have ancestors at the same place?" Javier asked.

"If you have no concordance," Monroe said, "I can't generate a shared simulation." But after a few minutes passed, and the

Animus core had run its analysis, he announced, "Wow, you . . . you actually have a few really strong intersections."

"A few?" Owen said.

"Yeah. This is extremely rare. Your ancestors have crossed paths several times, at different places and points in history . . ."

He stared at the screen, as if his mind was still working hard on something.

"So are we gonna do this?" Javier asked.

Monroe blinked. "Yes. Right. Okay, while the memory compiles, let's get Owen situated." He went to the front of the bus and brought back a thick yoga mat, which he unrolled on the floor near the recliner. "Not as comfortable as the chair, but it'll do."

Owen lay down on the mat, staring up at the ceiling of the bus, Javier's arm hanging over the chair above him. Owen felt and heard a slight hum from all the animus machinery pulsing through the floor beneath him. Monroe pulled out two black visored helmets, and helped Javier and then Owen put them on. The visor was lighter in weight than it looked and comfortable, dominating Owen's vision with wraparound blackness, while the helmet smothered the hearing in both his ears, disembodying him.

Can you hear me?

Monroe's voice came from inside the helmet.

"Yes," Owen said.

"Yeah," Javier said.

Right on, Monroe said. *Okay, this is how it works. The first thing I'm going to do is load the Memory Corridor.*

"What's that?" Javier asked.

It's a transitional simulation, Monroe said. *You can think of it as the Animus's waiting room. Exposure to a full simulation can be overwhelming, even damaging, psychologically and physically. I need to ease you into it. Once you've adjusted to the Corridor, I'll load the full simulation. Are you ready? This'll be weird.*

"Ready," Javier said.

"Ready," Owen said.

A second passed, and then a flood rushed in, a torrent of light and sound and sensation, like walking into the sun from a lightless place, but Owen couldn't shield his eyes from this. He simply had to endure it until his vision settled, his nerves quieted, and his surroundings came into focus.

He stood in an endless gray void shot through with crackles of lightning. Clouds of mist billowed and heaved around him, occasionally coalescing into geometric angles that hinted at something tangible, the edge of a building, the reach of a tree branch. Owen next looked down and saw that he was not himself.

His chest was covered by a sleeveless chainmail shirt over a heavy, riveted leather jacket. Both were long, reaching almost to his knees. He wore tall leather boots that covered his calves, and leather gloves, while a sword hung in its scabbard from his belt. When he turned his head, a strap under his chin pulled in a way that irritated his skin, and he realized he had a thick beard. The strap held a metal helmet, which had a conical shape, and a slightly downturned metal brim, tight over his head.

"Is that you?" someone asked, just behind him.

Owen turned around. "Javier?"

The figure before him nodded, but it wasn't Javier. Different body, different face, different voice. A middle-aged man with dark skin, wearing a loincloth and a thick, quilted tunic, with bare arms and legs, and sandals on his feet. Stripes of red and white paint covered his face, and he wore a headdress with colorful feathers sticking up in the back.

"You look like the conquistador," the figure that was Javier said.

"You look like an Aztec or something," Owen said.

Not quite. Monroe's voice sounded directly in Owen's ear, and he guessed in Javier's ear, too. *The Aztecs conquered much of Mexico, but not all of it. Javier is a Tlaxcaltec warrior. Their nation was one of several who fought* against *the Aztecs before the Europeans arrived.*

"How do you know that?" Javier asked.

The Animus, Monroe said. *As it analyzes your genetic memories, it extrapolates from them using known historical data. It also tells me that Javier is right about your ancestor, Owen. You'll be in the memories of a conquistador. A soldier named Alfonso del Castillo.*

"Ah," Javier said. "So your people conquered my people."

Again, not quite, Monroe said. *Hernán Cortés did defeat the Tlaxcaltecas, but they eventually allied* with *him against the more powerful Aztecs.*

"Oh," Javier said. "Sorry. I guess your people just gave my people smallpox."

"I didn't even know I had a conquistador ancestor," Owen said.

It seems that your simulation will take place in 1519, Monroe said. *Right before Cortés defeated the Tlaxcaltecas.*

"So we're going to Mexico?" Owen asked. "Hundreds of years ago?"

Technically, Monroe said. *You're not going anywhere. You're still on the floor of my bus. But it's going to feel like you're going somewhere. That's why we're using the Memory Corridor.*

"So what now?" Javier asked.

Now, Monroe said, *I want you to relax. Move around a bit. Get used to being in a simulation of someone else's body while the memories finish compiling.*

Owen took a step, and then another. It did feel odd. This Alfonso guy was shorter than he was, with a different balance, different proportions in his arms and legs. As Javier walked over toward him, Owen pulled his sword out of its scabbard. It had a round golden pommel at the base of a wire-wrapped leather grip, and above that a sweeping hilt that encircled his hand beneath the crossbars. The three-foot blade gleamed like silver.

"Check this out," he said to Javier, and gave the air a slice with it. At first, the sword felt a bit awkward in his hand, heavy and unsteady. But then Owen noticed a tingling on his neck and in his mind that gradually turned into a kind of pressure at the back of his thoughts. As he gave in to the pressure, and let go of his own thoughts, his control of the weapon became more practiced and fluid. He slashed and parried and stabbed as if he'd done so thousands of times before. But he knew he'd never held a sword in his life, and as that thought asserted itself against the pressure, he lost a bit of control.

"Watch it," Javier said, stepping out of the way just as the blade missed his arm.

"Sorry," Owen said, staring at the sword. "That was weird."

What was weird? Monroe asked.

Owen looked up, as if Monroe were somewhere up in the gray void. "The sword," he said. "It was like . . . I knew how to use it."

You do, Monroe said. *Or rather, Alfonso del Castillo does.*

"So that was him?" Owen asked.

You have access to his memories, Monroe said. *All of them.*

"It was like he wanted to take over," Owen said.

In a way, he does, Monroe said. *And in a way, you have to let him. The simulation works by a process of synchronization. To experience your ancestor's memories, you have to kind of take a back seat and let your ancestor do their thing.*

"So we don't have control once we're in there?" Javier asked.

You have some *latitude in the simulation to do your own thing,* Monroe said. *But this isn't time travel. You can't change what happened. You can't change the memory, and if you step too far outside the parameters of the memory, you'll get desynchronized. That'll break the simulation and either drop you back in the Corridor, or even back into the real world. Either way, it's not a pleasant experience.*

"So how do we know if we're about to be desynchronized?" Javier asked.

You'll feel it, Monroe said. *And the simulation will start glitching. But try not to worry about that. You'll learn. Just relax. The whole point of the Animus ride is to get out of the nutshell of your own head and walk in someone else's thoughts for a while. Are you ready for that?*

Owen looked down at the sword and slid it back into its scabbard. "Ready."

Right on, Monroe said. *When I throw the switch, it's going to be overwhelming, much more so than it was when you entered the Memory Corridor. Just take it easy, and it'll pass. And one more thing: When you* go through, your ancestors may not be anywhere near each other, but they're close enough to share the simulation. Don't go racing off to find each other or you'll desynchronize. You can't talk to each other as yourselves, anyway. Just let the memory unfold. Got all that?

"Got it," Owen said.

You ready? Monroe asked.

"Throw the switch," Javier said.

CHAPTER THREE

J avier still wasn't sure if it was a good idea to agree to this. But Monroe was right. Javier had overheard a couple of kids talking about the Animus, and he was curious. Or maybe he really just wanted to get out of his own head for a little while. His own life was so complicated and messed up.

Owen stood there in front of him, in the Memory Corridor. Only it wasn't Owen, it was one of Owen's conquistador ancestors, complete with a helmet and a sword he sort of knew how to use. Javier didn't know how different his own face looked in that moment, but his body felt very different. This Tlaxcaltec ancestor of his was older, with pains in his joints, and the mind trying to share Javier's headspace looked at the world in an utterly foreign way. Javier had taken this Animus ride to get into someone else's thoughts, but his head had only become more crowded.

Here we go, Monroe said in his ear.

The Memory Corridor shattered with an eye-slicing flash of light, and Javier felt a roller-coaster lurch slam his whole body, but more than that, his mind. He gasped and blinked, dizzy, nauseated, as his vision slowly refocused.

He stood in an open field hemmed in by hills, the sun warm and the air cool. The grass at his feet was tall and supple. In his hands he carried a wooden shield, painted and covered with feathers, and in his other he held a kind of wooden sword lined its whole length with razor-sharp, toothlike obsidian blades, which Javier somehow knew was called a *macuahuitl.* Warriors armed and dressed in the same manner stood to either side of him, but many lacked the feathered headdress Javier wore. For a few of them, though, the headdresses were even more elaborate, rising like tall crowns with long streamers. Javier saw one man bearing some kind of branching standard or banner, covered in feathers, rising from his back six feet into the air, and another man wearing what appeared to be a large, long-necked, white bird with wings spread wide above his head.

Javier glanced behind him over his shoulder, and what he saw there stunned him. There were thousands, perhaps tens of thousands of warriors. They filled the open plain, right up to the edges of the forests and the hills. Horns bellowed and voices shrieked what could only be battle cries. This was an army going to war.

And it seemed that Javier was at the front line, with fighting imminent. He looked around again, this time for an escape, feeling panicked. A warrior next to him gave him a confused scowl and said something in a language Javier didn't know.

"What? I don't understand you," Javier said, and immediately felt his perception getting fuzzy around the edges. He lost feeling through his arms and legs, like a disconnect from his body.

The warrior looked even more confused, and even took a step away from him.

Relax, a voice said in his ear. *Let your ancestor do the talking.*

"Monroe?"

Yes. I'm watching your simulation.

That reassured Javier, somewhat.

Let the memory ride, man. Just let the memory ride.

Javier took a deep breath. He tried to shut out the sound of the massive army at his back, the unknown fear of the battle ahead, and relax his mind. As he did, he felt a kind of drumbeat behind his thoughts, an eagerness, and as he listened to that, and even encouraged it, the sound grew louder, and louder, until Javier could hear someone else's voice trying to get out. It felt like the most powerful and disorienting déjà vu, one part of his mind experiencing something at the same time another part of his mind remembered it. The drumbeat and the shrieking voice became deafening, and Javier finally surrendered to the mind and the will vying for control, and as he did, his own voice erupted in a battle cry in a foreign tongue he now understood.

The warrior beside him nodded, seeming reassured, and made a cry of his own. Javier's awareness became honed, his perception clear.

He was Chimalpopoca, a noble *tecuhtli,* a leader of men and warriors who had distinguished himself on the battlefield many times over against his people's greedy and haughty Aztec oppressors.

But now a new enemy had arrived in his people's lands, come from the coast and, if it could be believed, from across the sea. The pale strangers marched toward them even now, astride their towering deer-beasts, armed with their weapons of fire, but here on this ground, this day, the people of the god Camaxtli would capture or slay them all.

"Do you think they are truly *teotl?*" a warrior next to Chimalpopoca asked.

"I don't know," Chimalpopoca said.

"The Totonac and Otomi say they can't be killed. Their arrows and spears counted as nothing but reeds. Their very skin is iron—"

"It is only their armor that is iron." Chimalpopoca stared hard at the line of oak and pine trees ahead of their line. "Beneath it, I wager they bleed."

"So you don't think we should try to make peace with them as the Totonac did?"

"I think we should follow the orders of our war leader."

"But even Xicotencatl's father, the Elder, would have us make peace. I've even heard a rumor that some on the field here today plan not to fight."

"Then they must have been born under a coward's sign," Chimalpopoca said. He had been born under the sign of the first *ocelotl*, which meant he was destined to die as a prisoner of war, a fate he had long since chosen to meet with bravery, but which had so far eluded him.

"Perhaps it is wisdom to refrain," the warrior said. "Not cowardice."

"If that is what you believe," Chimalpopoca said, "then perhaps you should join with the Totonacs and build these *teotl* a city where your farm used to be—"

The conchs bellowed loudly again, signaling the approach of the enemy. Chimalpopoca readied his shield, his *macuahuitl* thirsty for the blood of these strangers. Ahead of him, in the distance, the first of them, these *teotl*, emerged from the forest. They marched in formation with their shields and their giant deer-beasts, their iron helmets and their iron swords. With them came the weapon they called a cannon, which shot stone from its entrails, along with sparks and fire, pulled into battle by traitorous Cempoala collaborators from Totonacapan. At the sight of its black length, Chimalpopoca felt fear, and because of that, Javier felt fear, too.

Javier wondered then what would happen if his ancestor died on that battlefield. He wondered if he would feel the agony of getting run through with a sword or blown apart by a cannon. He knew his body was perfectly safe outside the simulation, but that didn't stop the terror, because his mind was *here*. The realness of the simulation, the smell of incense and the warriors' fear-sweat around him, the whinnying of the conquistadors' horses, the sight of their far superior weapons—he knew how this would go down, and he wanted to get his ancestor out of there.

As Javier entertained these thoughts and asserted himself within his own mind, he took a step away from the front line, and the simulation lost some of its clarity, like dropping from hi-res to low.

You're slipping, Monroe said. *Just let it ride.*

That was harder to do now, with an army of Spaniards advancing with their guns and their swords, against which Javier knew Chimalpopoca's wooden weapon and shield could do very little.

"I'm trying," Javier said.

You can't change it, Monroe said. *It's memory. Just try to remember this already happened five hundred years ago. You can't avoid it. If you try, you'll desynchronize.*

Javier adopted a part of that as a mantra.

You can't avoid it, you can't avoid it, you can't avoid it.

That actually helped him give his mind back over to Chimalpopoca's memories, bringing the simulation back into its fullness of depth.

There were perhaps only four hundred of the *teotl* marching toward them. Against ten thousand Tlaxcaltec warriors. Chimalpopoca smiled with the surety that this battle would soon be at an end, and he wondered if *teotl* blood would feed the gods as well as human blood did, and hoped to take at least one of them alive for the priests to sacrifice upon the altar stones.

The men around him appeared less certain than he, but he rallied them with a war cry, and they echoed it. The valley shook with their voices and the blare of their conchs, and it seemed even the *teotl* quaked before it.

"Camaxtli is with us!" Chimalpopoca shouted to the men under his command. "The signs are with us this day!" To which his men cheered.

When the enemy reached the point of ground Xicotencatl had designated, Chimalpopoca shouted the order to charge, as did the other warriors, advancing on the *teotl* from all sides, completely surrounding them.

Chimalpopoca's men unleashed a volley of their arrows and spears, which fell like rain, but most bounced harmlessly from the *teotl* shields and armor. Some, however found soft flesh and buried themselves. Chimalpopoca grinned as he and his men ran howling across the field, weapons raised high, but before they reached the enemy's line, the fire weapons roared with innumerable cracks of thunder.

Men jerked and fell to the ground mid-stride on either side of Chimalpopoca, bleeding from gaping, mangled holes in their bodies. But he charged on without slowing his pace, leading his warriors through another explosion of fire, and then through a volley of those short, evil arrows that pierced the thickest hide armor. But then the *teotl* rode their beasts into the fray, trampling men and swinging their swords, cutting warriors down and breaking them underfoot.

The first Tlaxcaltec warriors to reach the opposing infantry line hit the enemy's right flank, but only broke their spears and the obsidian teeth of their swords on the iron of the foreigners' shields.

When Chimalpopoca finally reached their forward line, he growled with ferocity and brought his sword down hard enough to stagger one of the *teotl*, but immediately had to dodge the thrust of another demon's sword. That was how it was all down the front. The foreigners kept rank and held tight their line against the attack, taking no chances pursuing any one target. Chimalpopoca's men could only rush and retreat, harrying the invaders without inflicting any real damage, unable to break them, but taking heavy losses in the effort.

Chimalpopoca already smelled the scent that blood makes when it mingles with soil, feeding the earth. If he were to die today, it would be a good death. He leapt forward again, striking the head of one of the tallest *teotl*. The demon's helmet took most of the blow, but his neck bent in a most satisfying way, and he stumbled backward, only to be replaced by another warrior clad in rings of iron. Chimalpopoca met the newcomer's gaze before dodging away, and what he saw in those foreign eyes lit a fire in him.

Up close, the tales were true. These men, if men they were, had pale skin, their faces covered with yellow hair. But Chimalpopoca had seen *fear* in those eyes. A warrior's fear of death. These *teotl* were mortal, after all, if not fully human.

Just then, one of the deer-beast riders charged ahead of the others in his company. The armored beast leapt and kicked, wounding and trampling as the rider's sword slashed and hacked. Chimalpopoca fixed his rage upon them, these false gods, and tossed aside his shield. Then he plowed through his own people toward the rider, raising his *macuahuitl* above his head with both hands. He rushed them from the side, and when he was a rod away he leapt high into the air, flew toward them, and sliced downward into the neck of the deer-beast. The beast did not even find a scream before it crumpled into a heap. Chimalpopoca knew he had broken its neck, for he had felt its bones snap beneath his obsidian blade.

The rider tumbled to the ground, but sprang quickly to his feet, unsteady on one injured leg, swinging his sword wildly. Chimalpopoca wanted to engage him in combat, but before he could, three more *teotl* rushed forward from the line to defend their comrade, and together the four of them folded back in with their force.

"They show loyalty!" Chimalpopoca shouted. "They have that, at least!"

And they were four hundred somehow holding their line against ten thousand. Chimalpopoca surveyed the battlefield, and realized the number of Tlaxcaltec warriors actually seemed to be part of the enemy's success. There were simply too many warriors to maneuver effectively on this plain. But the other went to the *teotl*'s strategy. They appeared less interested in captives than the Aztecs, seeking only to defend themselves, or kill or maim their attackers.

But Chimalpopoca was not fated to die in battle. He examined his *macuahuitl* and found it still had some bite left in it, even after slaying the deer-beast, which his comrades had already begun to butcher so they could carry it away.

He charged the enemy again, and the blow of his sword stunned the *teotl* and shattered the last of his *macuahuitl*'s teeth. Chimalpopoca did not retreat this time, but howled ahead into the breach to break the enemy line. He managed to shoulder his way between two of the iron shields, close enough to smell the vile odors coming off the unwashed demons, and raised his blunted *macuahuitl* for a second strike at their inner line.

But they enveloped him. He felt many hands seize upon him, and though he thrashed and kicked, they drove him to the ground and bound him. Then they dragged him from the battle deeper into their midst, where he was forced to lay there on the trampled earth, staring at the hides the foreigners used to cover their feet, listening to Tlaxcaltec men howl while he could do nothing. That was what caused him to weep into the grass. Not fear, but powerlessness.

For this was his fate. His death was approaching. But to which dark god would these *teotl* sacrifice him, and in what manner?

The battle continued to bloody the plain until Chimalpopoca heard the conchs signal retreat, which could only mean that a high *tecuhtli* had fallen. Within moments, the enemy had him on his feet, and then pulled back their force into the trees even as their deer-beasts and riders charged after the fleeing Tlaxcaltec host. The infantry then marched Chimalpopoca some hundred rods or so through the forest to their encampment, which they had established in a village whose residents had evidently fled. The *teotl* had naturally taken over the temple, which perhaps explained their victory, and showed Chimalpopoca the place of his death. Their god was with them, but which god did they serve?

One of the pale men took Chimalpopoca roughly by the arm, and though Chimalpopoca didn't know him, Javier recognized Owen's ancestor, the man he had seen in the Memory Corridor. His consciousness rushed to dominance. He opened his mouth, about to speak, but that caused an instant fracturing of the simulation, visual glitches, some of the trees overhead blurring into pixels. He remembered that Monroe had told them they couldn't speak to each other as themselves. Owen shook his head, saying nothing, and Javier barricaded his thoughts to prevent them from slipping any further from the memory, slowly restoring his synchronization, but with a bit more of himself maintained at the surface. He wanted to remain aware of Owen, but wouldn't risk desynchronization by talking to him.

The Owen *teotl* hauled Chimalpopoca through the village to one of the houses and threw him inside. He hit the ground hard, and the impact stopped his breath, followed by a few moments of gasping in the dust as the *teotl* walked away.

"Don't fight them," someone said from the shadows, another Tlaxcaltec warrior taken prisoner. "They don't want to harm us. They want peace."

"A very unusual kind of peace," Chimalpopoca said, and rolled onto his back to get a look at the man speaking. He was young, and probably hadn't even captured his first sacrificial victim yet. He knew nothing. He wasn't even bound, but sat mildly on the ground with his wrists propped on his raised knees.

"We attacked *them*," the boy said.

"You think they are not hostile?" Chimalpopoca asked.

"It doesn't have to be this way," the boy said.

"It can only be one way for me," Chimalpopoca said. "It is in the signs."

CHAPTER FOUR

O wen hadn't recognized Javier at first, but he was pretty sure they both now knew who and where the other was, but they couldn't be their real selves within the Animus. They had to play out this shared memory as ancestral enemies, which caused an emotional discomfort that was a bit too close to their present reality, and which Owen had to suppress to get back into Alfonso's mind.

That mind was not a nice place to be. Alfonso had done some pretty heinous, nasty things back in Cuba, and to the Maya in Potonchán five months previously. Though Owen hadn't experienced those memories directly, and didn't want to think about them, an awareness of them had colored the battle Alfonso had just fought and won.

The victory still surprised Alfonso. The sight of those warriors massed on the plain had nearly undone him, but the captain had rallied him and the other men to victory with a cry of "Saint James and strike for Spain!"

That was how it was with Cortés.

Their leader had overcome treacherous governors and mutinies by murderous rivals, and though the expedition's circumstances had become most dire, the men yet believed in Cortés. Even as he'd scuttled their ships at Veracruz, removing any possibility of retreat and stranding them in this feverish foreign land, Alfonso had saluted him in faith, and would do so to the gates of hell. Which was where they intended to march.

Tenochtitlan.

The seat of the Aztec emperor, and the location of his treasury. Alfonso's blood surged at the image of gold in his mind, and the share of that wealth to which he was entitled.

But to reach that fabled city they first had to contend with these natives, the ones Cortés believed it necessary to make into their allies. That was a strategy Alfonso did not and could not understand. He had seen their pagan rituals from afar, the butchery they committed before their idols. These bloodthirsty Indians were not to be trusted, and yet Alfonso did trust Cortés.

"You placed the new prisoner in the house?" another soldier asked from his post nearby.

"I did," Alfonso said.

"Was he wounded?"

"Not badly."

"Good. The captain will be pleased. Bring them some food."

Alfonso nodded and grudgingly went to one of the cook

fires. There he found some of the greasy meat of the hairless dogs the Indians in these parts fattened and ate, and brought that to the prisoners. The younger one, the previous day's captive, accepted it gratefully, but the new one, the older one they had just taken, refused it. That would not last. Cortés would win him over to their side.

Alfonso took up his guard position outside the rough mud-brick house and waited. He was lucky enough to have escaped the skirmish uninjured, so he'd been appointed guard duty. Not that these Indians needed guarding. Well, at least not the first one. The second one they'd just captured, the one who'd killed Juan Sedeño's mare, he needed to be watched. He was obviously some kind of cacique chief, and was neither indolent nor cowardly as so many of them were. Alfonso could almost admire him.

The day passed without any further incursions by the native warriors, the reprieve allowing for the burial of the dead. Cortés ordered these rites performed in secret, beneath the floors of the houses, so that no Indian would see that the *teotl*, as the Indians called them, were mortal.

Toward evening, the graceful Marina came to the prisoners with the priest, Gerónimo de Aguilar. She was the most beautiful Indian woman Alfonso had yet laid his eyes upon, a slave given to Cortés who had since risen to stand at the captain's side. The priest was a shipwrecked Franciscan turned half-savage by his eight years living among the Maya. Between the two of them, they were able to translate the captain's words into the tongue of this region.

Alfonso rose to his full height as the two figures approached, and blood rushed to his cheeks as the dark-skinned woman passed near him through the door, but that fire quickly cooled under the judgmental gaze of the priest, and with a downturned eye, Alfonso followed them inside.

They went to the new prisoner, and Aguilar knelt next to him. The priest spoke to Marina in her language, Mayan, and she then spoke to the prisoner in his Aztec tongue, but Alfonso couldn't understand any of what they said, for none of it was in Spanish. He always felt disquieted witnessing this pattern of exchange, for he could never rid himself of the thought and fear that these peculiars were all conspiring.

After a few words had passed along the chain of tongues between them, Aguilar went to loosen the binds restraining the prisoner.

Alfonso stepped forward. "What are you doing?"

"Cortés ordered it done," the priest said.

"But what if he—"

"Cortés ordered it," Aguilar said again, and that settled it, though Alfonso kept his hand on his sword.

The cacique rubbed his wrists where the binding had bitten into his skin, and where he still had spots of the mare's blood on him, which had dried and now cracked and peeled like scabs. The Indian said something to Marina, sounding angry and belligerent, and she said something to Aguilar, and then they reversed the order and continued in this way for several further exchanges. Marina produced some glass beads and offered them to the prisoner, a bribe presented as a gift.

He refused them in obvious disgust.

"What does he say?" Alfonso asked the priest.

"He will not cooperate." Aguilar rose to his feet. "He would rather we sacrifice him to our god."

"What?" Alfonso said, and beneath his horror, Owen felt fear for Javier. But if he acted in any way on that, the simulation would break. "I . . ." Alfonso said. "I don't understand these savages."

"If they don't give blood to their gods," Aguilar said, "they believe the sun will cease to rise. The world will end. The practice of sacrifice is not cruel to them, but a necessary act of renewal."

"You sound like one of them," Alfonso said, risking an affront.

But Aguilar didn't take it that way. "I have come to understand them."

"Then you must be a savage as well," Alfonso said in a moment and a word from which Owen's consciousness recoiled.

"But you can understand honor, surely," Aguilar said. "He believes it is his fate to die a prisoner. He does not want to run from that. If he becomes our messenger, as Cortés would have it, he believes that will make him a coward."

Through their exchange, Marina remained silent but attentive, as did the prisoners. Owen wished there was some way to talk to Javier within the simulation, but there didn't seem to be, at least not within the model of Animus Monroe had modified. It was difficult to just turn over his mind and body to this conquistador, his own racist ancestor. It was difficult to admit that he had these memories, this man's DNA, entangled with his own.

Marina said something to Aguilar, and the priest nodded as he replied. Then they both strode toward the door to the house.

"Where are you going?" Alfonso asked.

"To get the captain," Aguilar said.

"But he isn't bound," Alfonso said, pointing at the cacique captive.

"Then I suggest you watch him," Aguilar said, and then he and the Indian woman left.

Alfonso took a position before the door, his shadow falling inward along the floor, inflated and huge. The first prisoner, the docile one, shook his head at the cacique, and spoke to him with a harsh tone. Then he went to a corner of the room where he had his sleeping mat and laid himself down with his back to them. The cacique did not reply, but stared hard at Alfonso with a quiver in his rigid jaw that kept Alfonso's sword hand at the ready.

A moment later, snoring emanated from the first prisoner, and Alfonso remarked again to himself on the laziness of these Indians, even as Owen wanted to shut him up. But there was no way to shut up a memory. He had to endure it, unable to talk to Javier about it as the time passed and the tension in the hut rose.

Eventually, voices approached outside. Owen wondered what the Spaniards were going to do to Javier if his ancestor refused to cooperate. If something bad was about to happen to him, Owen didn't know if he'd be able to just sit back and watch it. But for now he did his best to hold fast behind the mind line that divided his consciousness from Alfonso's. Javier appeared to do the same, maintaining their roles as guard and prisoner.

Cortés marched into the house, still wearing his plate armor, the sunlight at his back glancing off his shoulders in blinding flashes that made Alfonso squint. Marina and Aguilar followed the captain into the room.

Alfonso bowed his head. "Sir, beware. The prisoner isn't bound."

"I know," he said. "I am not concerned."

At the sound of the captain's voice and the calmness of his demeanor, Alfonso found he was no longer concerned, either.

"Have you fed these men?" Cortés asked.

"Yes, sir."

"I am pleased." Cortés turned to Aguilar. "You assured him of our peaceful intent?"

Aguilar nodded. "I did."

Owen wondered how that case could possibly be made, considering the battle they had just waged, but Alfonso had no such doubts.

"Do so again," Cortés said. "In my presence."

Aguilar spoke to Marina, a message she then translated for the prisoner. As she addressed the cacique, his demeanor appeared softened somewhat from before, his voice less emphatic in reply.

"The man wonders when he is to be sacrificed," Aguilar said.

"Tell him we will spare him," Cortés said. "And bestow gifts upon him."

Again the pattern of translation followed, as did another offering of the glass beads the captain had been using to entice and bribe the Indians. This time, the prisoner accepted them.

"He says he does not wish to hide from his fate," Aguilar said. "He believes he is to die a prisoner of war. A sacrifice to our god."

"Tell him I have different plans for him," Cortés said. "I want him to carry a message to his king. In doing so, he can be instrumental in bringing about peace between our people. If he puts his faith in me, I will help free his country from the tyranny of Moctezuma and the Aztecs."

Following the translation of this, the prisoner looked up at the captain with narrowed eyes. Alfonso searched the man's expression, watching for that moment when the Indian would become a believer, for Cortés made a believer out of everyone.

A silent interval passed, the captain looking down upon the Indian from the throne of his confidence and power. He stood there resplendent in his armor, gripping the peculiar dagger he always wore at his side, a gift from Charles V, which had come down from Alfonso V, the king of Aragon, given to him by Pope Callixtus III.

Then the moment happened, the prisoner's eyes widened, and he nodded. He spoke to Marina in what Alfonso thought to be a reverent tone, which she translated for Aguilar, and which Aguilar translated for Cortés.

"He will be your messenger," the priest said.

"I am pleased," Cortés said, releasing his grip on the dagger.

What just happened? Monroe's voice shouted into the moment, jarring Owen forward, ahead of Alfonso's memory. *What is that?* Monroe asked.

Owen wasn't sure what he was asking about, but before he could ask or answer Monroe spoke into his ear again.

We have to abort, right now. This might be a little rough. Hang on.

The hut exploded. The world of the simulation blew apart in another mind-splitting flash of light, shredding the figures of Cortés, Marina, and Gerónimo de Aguilar. An arc of pain shot through Owen's head, and he resisted the urge to cry out, clenching his eyes tight until it stopped.

They were back in the Memory Corridor, still clad in their ancestor's bodies.

"What the hell?" Javier said. "Why did you pull us out?"

It's, uh, complicated, Monroe said. *The simulation was about to become unstable. Better to get you out before that happens.*

"Better than what just happened?" Owen said. "It felt like my brain was burning."

Sorry about that, Monroe said. *Just sit tight. I've gotta check a few things . . .*

"What things?" Owen asked.

But Monroe didn't answer him.

"Can you believe that battle?" Javier said at Owen's side. "Wasn't that wild?"

"Yeah," Owen said. "Except my ancestor was a monster."

"He doesn't seem too bad," Javier said. "For a conquistador, I mean."

"You don't know what he did," Owen said, feeling the polished pommel of his sword. "And I don't like thinking about it, so don't ask me."

"I won't," Javier said. "I think I can guess anyway." He looked down at his hands. "Chimalpopoca did some crazy stuff, too."

"Chimapowhat?"

"Chimalpopoca. That's my name—I mean, his name. Starts to get confusing, doesn't it?"

"No. I'm not like this guy at all."

"It's still pretty wild, though, right?"

Owen shrugged inside Alfonso. "I guess—"

Okay, Monroe said. *I'm ready to pull you out of the Corridor. You ready?*

"More than ready," Owen said.

Okay, simulation ending in three, two, one . . .

The Corridor fragmented, but more gently than the simulation had a moment ago. Owen closed his eyes again, and when he opened them, he was lying on the floor of the bus, staring into the empty blackness of the dead visor. He tugged the helmet off and saw Monroe above him, quickly unhooking Javier from the recliner.

"So, how was the simulation unstable?" Javier asked.

"This Animus isn't designed to share a simulation between two people," Monroe said. He finished with Javier and bent down to Owen, unhooking him and pulling him to his feet, his movements rough and hurried. "My modifications can get overloaded. When that happens, it shuts down."

"And you knew that before you sent us in?" Owen asked.

"Uh, yeah, I did," Monroe said. Then he ushered them forcefully through the bus, past all the monitors, toward the door up front. "Sorry about that. I thought it would hold."

"This is messed up," Javier said.

"Hey," Monroe said, "at least you got to experience the Animus for a little while." Then he opened the door to the bus. "But it's time for you to go."

"Hold on," Owen said. Monroe was obviously trying to get rid of them, acting strange. The kids at school trusted him because he was cool, kind of a rebel, and as the IT guy, he'd turned a blind eye to a lot of what they did on the computers and online. He was always laid-back. Now he seemed freaked-out by something. "Seriously, what just happened?" Owen asked.

"Nothing." Monroe shook his head, and gave them both a nudge down the stairs. "Just an adrenaline rush. I got a little spooked there."

Javier stepped down from the bus and hit the ground first. "Wait, were we in danger?"

Owen got off the bus, too, and turned to look back up at Monroe.

He rubbed his forehead. "Maybe. But I think I got you out in time."

"You *think*?" Owen asked.

"I did," Monroe said. "I did get you out in time."

Now Owen felt himself starting to freak out, just a bit, wondering if that machine could somehow damage his brain.

"Just head on home," Monroe said. "Quickly. You'll be fine." Then he shut the bus door.

Owen and Javier stood outside in the gravel. Neither of them said anything. They just looked at each other, and then back at the bus.

The engine started and all the vehicle's lights switched on, the pale headlights and the red brake lights at the rear shining through a sudden cloud of burnt-smelling exhaust. The gears grunted and then the vehicle moved. Owen and Javier stepped clear as Monroe backed it out of the spot where he'd parked it, and then slowly drove away, leaving them alone in the industrial park.

"What the hell was that?" Javier asked. "Where's he going?"

"I don't know," Owen said.

"What was he freaking out about?"

"Before he killed the simulation, he was asking about something."

Javier shrugged. "That was just weird, man."

"Which part? Monroe? Or the Animus?"

"Both. All of it. The Animus. I mean, that was crazy, right?"

"Right," Owen said. "Crazy."

Javier jammed his hands into his pockets. "Well. I better get home."

"Yeah." Owen wondered if this would change anything between them the next day at school. "Me too."

So they parted ways and Owen rode the same buses back, but had to walk a lot farther now that the final line had stopped running until morning. By the time he reached his grandparents' house, the dark sky had just enough light along one edge to say that night was over. But it was still very early. Too early for anyone to be up.

Yet all the lights were on inside.

CHAPTER FIVE

His grandparents and his mom were awake, sitting around the kitchen table. His grandma wore her fluffy, Pepto-Bismol–colored bathrobe, her hair in curlers beneath her hairnet. His grandpa had thrown on some sweats and a T-shirt, while his mom was fully dressed. As Owen came in, they all looked up, and his mom rushed out of her chair to throw her arms around his neck.

"Oh, thank God," she said. "I thought you'd . . ." But she didn't finish.

"Thought I'd what?" Owen asked.

"Where've you been?" his grandpa asked, his voice a lot harsher than it had been earlier that afternoon in the shop.

"Just out," Owen said.

"Out doing what?" his grandpa said.

"Just walking," Owen said.

His grandma sighed, propped her elbows on the table, and rubbed her eyes.

"Just walking," his grandpa said.

"Yeah," Owen said. "Just walking."

"Well, you're home now," his mom said.

Owen tried to smile. "Sorry to worry you."

She gave him another hug and then released him. "I think we should all get back to bed and try to get at least a little sleep. You have school and I have an early shift."

"That would be good," Owen said, relieved and surprised that she seemed so ready to let it go.

But his grandpa sat back in his chair and spread his hands like wings. "That's it? That's all you're going to say about this?"

"Dad, please—"

"No." He shook his head. "No, this is serious. You don't know what he—"

"I know he came home safe," his mom said. "That's what matters."

"That's not all that matters." Owen's grandpa stared him in the eye. "It matters what he was doing out on the streets at this hour. You shouldn't let him just walk away from this. You shouldn't—"

"He's *my* son," she said. "I raise him my way."

"You're under our roof," his grandpa said. "And if you remember, he's not the first kid in this family to go sneaking out at night. I for one would rather not repeat the past."

That stopped Owen's mom, and she seemed to lose whatever it was she'd briefly found in herself to come to his defense. Owen could see he was on his own again.

"You got me, Grandpa," he said. "I was out robbing a bank."

His grandma's hands fell to the table with a rattle of her fingers. His grandpa's eyes opened wide, and his mom sighed.

"Yeah," Owen said, not finished yet. "I just got this irresistible urge, you know? Like when you need a hamburger or something. I just needed to rob a bank, like it was an instinct. But don't worry, I gave the money to an orphanage on my way home. I'm more of a Robin Hood kind of guy."

"Owen, please," his mom said. "You're not helping."

"Neither are you," Owen said.

"Don't you speak to your mother that way!" His grandpa stabbed a finger toward him. "Show some respect."

"Respect?" Owen said. "I don't even know what that word means to you."

"Yes, you do." His grandpa rose to his feet with slight complaints from both the chair he pushed away with the back of his knees and the table he pressed his knuckles into. "Or at least, I've tried to teach you respect."

"How?" Owen said. "By trashing my dad all the time?"

His grandma spoke up then. "We only speak the truth—"

"That's not the truth!" Owen shouted.

"Yes, it is," his grandma said, dropping her voice to a whisper. "Your father had a gambling addiction that none of us knew about. He got a crew of his old friends together and robbed a bank. He shot an innocent guard who had a wife and two children waiting for him at home. Your father was lucky he didn't get the death sentence—"

"He did get a death sentence," Owen said.

Her lips tightened. "We don't expect you not to love your father. But we do expect you to be honest with yourself about him."

Owen *was* honest. That's why he didn't believe any of what she'd just said. There was simply no way his father had done those things. Believing it would be the easy way out. The harder truth was that his father had been framed by his old friends.

"Speaking of honesty," his grandpa said, "I still want to know what you were doing. Don't be a smart aleck. Just tell me. Because at this time of night, I don't like any of the ideas coming to my mind."

Owen decided the only way out of this would be to give them some truth. "I met up with Javier."

"That gangbanger?" his grandpa said. "Why?"

"He's not a gangbanger," Owen said, checking his frustration. "I . . . just had some stuff to talk about."

"What stuff?" his grandma asked.

"Stuff to do with my dad," Owen said. "Stuff I obviously can't talk to any of you about."

That silenced them for a moment or two, because after what they'd just been saying, there wasn't any way they could argue with him.

"Thank you for telling us," his mom said.

Owen shrugged. "Yeah, well. You didn't leave me much of a choice, did you?"

"Next time, just let us know when you're going out," his grandpa said. "I can respect you needing someone your age to talk to. I can respect your privacy. But we need to know you're safe."

"Fine," Owen said.

"And remember what I said earlier." His grandpa came over to face Owen and put a hand on his shoulder. "It's easy to get in over your head. So just be careful. Okay?"

"Okay," Owen said.

After that, he was allowed to go to his room where he never really got to sleep.

Javier was waiting for him outside the school when Owen arrived there later that morning. Owen was a bit surprised, but glad to see that maybe the experience in the Animus simulation had restored some of their friendship.

"Everything okay when you got home?" Javier asked.

"They caught me coming in," Owen said. "I'm pretty sure my mom thought I'd run away. But it's fine."

"They caught you?" Javier whistled. "Man, if my mom had caught me I wouldn't be here right now, I can tell you that. She's so freaked-out I'm going to join a gang like my brother."

They turned and walked together toward the school's main entrance. "How is your brother?" Owen asked.

"Out of jail. Trying to stay out of trouble."

"And your dad?" Back when Owen and Javier were closer, Javier used to talk about how he was never hardworking or tough enough to please his father, who had started life with a lot less.

Javier looked down at the ground. "He's the same. How's your grandpa?"

"The same."

They reached the school doors and passed through them into the main common where students sat and ate breakfast or just clustered together talking before class. A huge banner hung from the ceiling emblazoned with their school's mascot, a

Norseman complete with the kind of cartoon horned helmet that Javier said Vikings never actually wore.

"I want to talk to Monroe," Javier said. "You coming?"

"About last night?"

"Yeah. I want to know why he pulled the plug like that."

They walked through the common, and then up the wide staircase to the second floor. From there they made their way to the school's main computer lab where Monroe had his office. But when they knocked on the door, another man answered, some balding guy in glasses wearing a button-down plaid shirt and khaki pants.

"Where's Monroe?" Owen asked.

"No idea," the man said. "Left a message last night that he quit."

"He quit?" Javier asked.

The man nodded. "Didn't even give two weeks' notice. I'm filling in for now." He looked over his shoulder, back into the office. "Still trying to figure out what he was doing, to be honest. Is there something you need?"

"No," Owen said. "No, we're good."

"Okay, then." The man turned around and went back to Monroe's old desk.

Javier made eye contact with Owen and nodded him away from the door. After they'd walked some distance down the hall, Javier said, "This is getting weird."

"I know."

"How exactly did you hook up with Monroe in the first place?"

"There wasn't much to it. I just heard from this kid he had an Animus entertainment console and he let students use it sometimes. No one else I know has one. So I asked him if I could use it, too, and he told me when and where."

"But now he's gone. And he's got our DNA, along with a bunch of other students'."

"What are you saying?"

"I don't know. But I'm pretty sure he was up to something."

Owen had no idea what that might be, and it didn't seem they would ever be able to figure it out. The bell rang before they could talk any more about it.

Javier glanced around at the students passing by on their way to class, and suddenly he looked like the new Javier again, the one Owen didn't know. "Guess I'll see you around," he said in a final kind of way.

"See you around," Owen said, realizing that maybe things weren't as back to how they used to be as he'd hoped.

Javier walked off. Owen went to class.

The rest of that day he spent wondering what had happened with Monroe. He'd only worked at the school for a year, and who knew what he'd been doing before that? Working for Abstergo at some point. But the way he'd yanked them out of the simulation and then abruptly quit his job led Owen to agree with Javier that something was definitely going on.

The climate back at Owen's house, on the other hand, seemed to have improved noticeably when he walked in. His grandma turned off the TV and offered to make him a sandwich. Then she sat with him in the kitchen while he ate, talking about her gardening, asking about his day. Shortly after that, his grandpa needed to run to the auto parts store, so Owen rode along with him, and they grabbed a milk shake on the way back.

It was as though both his grandparents felt bad about something and they were trying to make it up to him.

"We're going to visit your great-aunt Susie tomorrow," his grandpa said as they reached their block. "She's having a procedure done, and we'll be staying the night with her."

Owen's straw gasped and gurgled as he sucked out the last of his caramel shake. "Okay."

"So you'll be on your own until your mom gets home from work."

"That's fine." He'd been on his own lots of times before now. It seemed that Owen's late-night absence had really rattled them.

"Your mom is working a late shift," his grandpa said.

"I'll be okay."

"All right, then."

Owen's father didn't come up at all that evening, and neither did Owen's grades. But neither did the confrontation from earlier that morning, and they never actually apologized for anything. When his mom came home, she hugged Owen a lot without saying anything, except for the quiet desperation she communicated with her tired, sad eyes, and Owen knew that nothing had really changed. His life was back to what it had been, except now he had even less than what he had thought was his last option.

On the way to school the next day, Owen felt as if someone was following him. He thought at first it was his grandpa checking up on him, but whenever Owen turned to look, he saw nothing but ordinary pedestrians and traffic, and he knew his grandpa wasn't that smooth. But the prickly sensation of eyes on him never lifted from his neck until he reached the school.

Monroe was still gone. For good, it seemed. Owen had to somehow come up with a new way to prove his father's innocence without genetic memory. Before pursuing the Animus, he'd written to all the justice organizations that took on wrongful convictions, but they had all turned down his case. Those lawyers spent their time and energy freeing living clients from prison, they said, not exonerating the ones who had already died there.

Things with Javier were a little better, but not much. When Owen passed him in the hallway after second period, Javier nodded and said hello, but he was with his other friends and he didn't stop to talk. Javier did catch up with Owen after school, though, as Owen was walking home.

"Hey, you hear anything about Monroe?" he asked.

Owen shook his head. "I don't think he's coming back."

"Almost like he was running from somebody."

"It felt like somebody was following me this morning," Owen said.

"I felt that yesterday," Javier said. "What's going on?"

"I don't know."

"I was thinking of going back to the industrial park. Just to check it out a bit more in the daylight. You wanna come?"

"Right now?" Owen's grandparents weren't home. As long as Owen got back before his mom's shift ended, he'd be fine. "Okay, let's go."

So they changed course and made for a bus stop. From there, they retraced much of the route Owen had taken a couple of nights ago, and arrived at the industrial park a short while later. The place looked a little less abandoned during the day than it had in the dark. There were a few more vehicles parked here and there, mostly utility trucks, and some of the warehouses and buildings were actually still in use, at least partially. They found the place Monroe had parked his bus, where its thick tires had flattened the weeds and left tracks in the gravel. They made a search of the area, but didn't find any clues.

Javier kicked at the ground, scattering rocks. "What are we doing here?"

"I don't know," Owen said. "This was your idea."

Javier paced a bit, kicked gravel again. "I want to go back in."

"Into the Animus? Why?"

"To see what he did after."

"Who?"

"Chimalpopoca. My ancestor. He just caved, man. Cortés walked in, and he just rolled over."

"Seems like everyone did with Cortés, he—"

"No, you don't understand." Javier stopped pacing and punched the palm of his hand. "I was—he was full-on ready to die. He was a warrior, he was true to himself. But then he just gave up without a fight."

Owen could tell this was pinching a nerve somewhere inside Javier, but they weren't close-enough friends anymore for him to know what that might be. "Why are you stressing about it? That was hundreds of years ago."

"You think I don't know that? It doesn't *feel* like hundreds of years ago. It feels like two nights ago." Javier shook his head. "Forget about it. I'm going home."

"Javier—"

"See you later." He stalked away before Owen could say anything more.

Owen watched him go, took another look around the site,

and then started toward his grandparents' house. His mom wouldn't be home for a while yet, so he decided to walk most of the way, just letting his thoughts and feet wander the streets until at one point he looked up and realized his path maybe hadn't been as aimless as he'd thought. The bank his father had been accused of robbing was only a couple of blocks away.

Owen detoured to go see it.

He'd only been there once before, and even then, they'd just driven by it, his grandparents and his mom falling utterly silent in the car as though passing near an open grave. The building had somehow appeared sinister to Owen back then, and it still did. It was sleek and modern, all dark glass and sharp corners, taking up the ground floor of an office building, its windows printed with a deep-red MALTA BANKING CORPORATION logo and a banner advertising interest rates.

Owen walked into the lobby, with its grayish marble floors and featureless carpet, the smell of paper and gentle rush of air conditioning. Tellers worked silently behind their counter, customers waited in line. No sign at all remained of the robbery or the slaying of the guard, no echo of the gunshot. Life had simply moved on for this bank, for everyone in there and their money. They went about business depositing and withdrawing as if Owen's life hadn't been completely derailed by the events that had taken place there.

The lobby felt suddenly small and tight, and the cool air tasted stale. Owen turned around and went back outside, where he took a seat on a bench across the street, facing the bank. He sat there studying it, watching the people going in and out, until the bank closed and the guards locked the doors. Then it was 5:17 p.m., the time at which his father was said to have emerged from the bank restroom where he'd been hiding. Then it was 5:24 p.m., the time of the first gunshot, and then it was 5:27 p.m., when the guard died from blood loss. Owen still knew every stop along the prosecutor's timeline, just as he could still recall each frame of the grainy black-and-white security footage of the masked robber. Owen sat there on that bench as evening turned into twilight, replaying the entire sequence of events over and over, searching through them for some discrepancy he had missed. Something the prosecutor and defense attorneys had missed. Something that would have given the jury reasonable doubt.

But he found nothing. Again.

Then it was dark, with only a trickle of foot traffic on the street, and Owen could tell it was late. He'd lost track of time, mired in his own thoughts, and realized he had to get home. He rose from the bench, took a last look at the bank, and hurried toward a bus stop, but just missed the pickup by a couple of minutes. Rather than wait for the next one, he decided to cut over one street through an alleyway and get on a different line that would still get him back to his grandparents' house before his mom.

The side street was narrow and partially obstructed in places by piles of refuse, stacks of old wooden pallets, and bales of wire. About halfway through the alley, Owen felt that sensation of being watched return, as if someone had followed him into the alley. This time, when he turned back to look, he saw the silhouetted figure of a man moving silently toward him.

CHAPTER SIX

Owen thought about running. He thought about calling out to the stranger, demanding to know who he was. He thought about just hiding somewhere in the alley. But each of those choices seemed like an overreaction at that point. It was probably just somebody trying to cut over to the next street like he was. Owen decided to stay calm and keep going, but he hastened his pace to stay ahead of the figure.

Before he'd gone very far, the stranger's footsteps quickened behind him, drawing closer, their echo crawling up his back and over his scalp. Owen broke into an instinctual jog without looking back. The drumbeat of his pursuer rose to match his rhythm, and at that point, Owen knew something was off and sprinted for it.

"Owen!" an unfamiliar voice called. "It's okay! Owen, stop!"

Owen didn't stop, not until he'd made it out of the alley and onto the streetlight-bathed sidewalk of the next avenue. There were several people around here; a pizza place and a liquor store were still open nearby. Owen felt safe enough to turn around and wait for his pursuer, to find out who he was and how he knew Owen's name.

A moment later, the man emerged, wearing a gray suit that bore the smudges and stains of his trip through the dark alley. He looked young, with close-cropped brown hair and roundish features. When he made eye contact with Owen, he sighed and nodded, and then walked toward him.

"Thank you for waiting," he said. "I—"

"Who are you?" Owen asked. "Why are you following me?"

The man looked around, but not at the level of the street. His gaze seemed to be searching above them, the rooftops and fire escapes. "How about we go somewhere and talk privately."

"I'm not going anywhere with you."

"Fair enough," the man said. "Then I'll make this brief. You were recently involved with a man named Monroe, were you not?"

"Who?" Owen said, thinking maybe this had to do with Monroe's disappearance.

"He gave you access to an Animus, correct?"

"What's an Animus?" *How the hell did this guy know so much?* "Who are you anyway?"

"Monroe is in possession of stolen equipment," the man said. "We've been trying to recover it. Your cooperation would be appreciated."

Did this guy work for Abstergo? That could explain how Monroe had the Animus in the first place, but maybe it also explained why Monroe had disappeared.

"Wish I could help," Owen said. He trusted Monroe a lot more than he trusted this guy. "Listen, I gotta go." He turned away from the stranger. "I'm late; my mom is expecting me—"

"I saw you at the bank," the man said, emphasizing the last word.

Owen stopped and slowly turned back around.

"We could help you with your problem," the stranger said, "if you help us with ours."

"Oh, yeah? And what's my problem?"

"You believe your father was innocent."

His words shocked Owen off balance, and for a moment, he didn't know how to respond.

"We could help you find out the truth of what happened that night," the man said.

"What are you talking about?" Owen raised his voice and took a step toward the man. "What do you know about my dad?"

"All will be explained. But you must come with—" The man let out a little gasp. He winced and lifted his hand as if he meant to swat a fly from his face. Then he shuddered, his eyes rolled back in his head, and his body collapsed to the ground, a small dart protruding from his neck.

Owen stared at him for a few seconds in confusion, and then his eyes went wide and he looked up at the buildings around him, their innumerable darkened windows and shadowy ledges. The dart had come from somewhere up there, and Owen was torn between bending down to help the man and dodging for cover.

Just then, a motorcycle ripped around the corner, its engine roaring with an unusual, deep thrum, like a huge insect. It raced toward Owen, sleek and black, and screeched to a halt right in front of him. Then its rider lifted the visor on his helmet, revealing a familiar face.

"Monroe?" Owen said.

"Get on," Monroe said. "Now." He tossed a second helmet, which Owen caught in the stomach.

"But—"

"Now!"

Owen jumped onto the back of the motorcycle behind Monroe, and pulled his helmet on as Monroe hit the throttle. The bike leapt down the street, and Owen watched the buildings speed by. The helmet's visor blinked to life with an internal overlay display showing gridlines, shifting targets, and readouts Owen didn't understand.

Monroe's voice sounded in Owen's ear through an earpiece in the helmet. "Initiate blur."

"Initiate what?" Owen asked.

Then his vision seemed to glitch as though he was back in the Animus. Successive images of the motorcycle cascaded forward ahead of them, and spread out to either side. When Owen looked behind them, he saw an image trail following them, spreading out along the road like the frames of a slowed film.

Blur initiated, said a woman's computerized voice in Owen's ear.

"What is that?" Owen asked.

"Holographic projection," Monroe said, banking around a corner. "To make us harder to hit." He throttled the bike again, and the engine's drone rose in pitch as they shot ahead. "Scan for ghost signals," he said.

Scanning . . . the computer woman said.

"Ghost signals?" Owen asked.

Ghost signal acquired.

"Resolve and sync," Monroe said.

The overlay on Owen's visor shifted, and he glimpsed a glowing figure moving at the periphery of his vision. He turned toward it, and saw the infrared silhouette of a man moving impossibly fast overhead against the city's darkened backdrop. The figure leapt from rooftop to rooftop and seemed to scale sheer walls, following after them.

"How—?" Owen said. "Who is that?"

"I'll explain later. Just keep an eye on him while I try to lose him."

He whipped the bike around another corner, and then another, turn after turn, but the ghost signal managed to stay with them, cutting over the top of whole city blocks. At one point, the figure even somehow got a bit ahead of them, and he paused there. Owen imagined him taking aim at them with the same dart weapon he'd used to hit that Abstergo guy.

"Watch out," he shouted to Monroe.

"I see him. Hold on." Monroe screeched to a halt in a hard turn that almost threw Owen from the bike. Then he spun out and peeled away in the opposite direction, passing the sign for a freeway entrance.

Owen pointed at it. "Could we lose him that way?"

"Worth a shot," Monroe said.

He took the on-ramp and then he really opened up the bike. The front wheel lifted off the ground briefly as they blazed down the road. Owen kept a backward eye on the glowing figure, which gradually fell farther and farther behind them, growing smaller until it finally winked out.

Ghost signal lost, the computer woman said.

"We got lucky," Monroe said. "He could've had his own wheels."

"Who was that guy?" Owen asked.

"I said I would explain later—"

"Explain now!" Owen shouted.

Monroe sighed. "He was an Assassin. You're not safe anymore."

Owen almost laughed at the thought that an assailant would be targeting him. But then he remembered the dart in that Abstergo guy's neck.

"What about Javier?" Owen asked.

"I already got him. We're going there now."

"Where?"

"You'll see."

Owen decided to let it go for now, and instead paid attention to where they were heading. A few exits later, Monroe got on the belt route and took a wide arc around the edge of the city, and then got off the freeway near the docks. They passed a refinery, and then they entered a section of towering warehouses similar to the industrial park on the opposite side of town, except this place seemed in better repair and more frequent use. But it was deserted at this time of night.

Monroe turned off the bike's headlights and brought them to a smaller building nestled between two larger structures, then used a remote control to open a mechanical roller door. He eased the bike through the cavernous opening and closed the door behind them, trapping them in near total darkness.

Monroe killed the bike's engine and climbed off. "Hold tight for a sec."

The overlay display on Owen's visor went dead, and he

waited as Monroe moved away from him out of sight. A moment later, a light switched on overhead, flooding the space around Owen with cold fluorescence. The warehouse was spacious and empty, except for the vintage bus parked nearby that held the Animus. Monroe was walking back toward the bike carrying his helmet. Owen pulled his own helmet off and climbed from the vehicle. Up close, in the light, the motorcycle looked as if it belonged in the air as much as the ground, angled and curved in a way that suggested something designed for total stealth. Owen had ridden dirt bikes with his dad, but this was something very different.

"So," he said, "*this* is all pretty high-tech." He set the helmet on the motorcycle's seat. "I'm guessing Abstergo would have something to say about it?"

"Most likely." Monroe dropped the keys into his helmet and set it next to Owen's. "Come on, let's go join the others." Monroe moved and spoke with an intensity Owen wasn't used to seeing in him.

"Others?"

Monroe didn't respond to that, and instead walked away toward a narrow staircase that climbed up one wall of the warehouse to a door on the second story. Owen followed him, their footsteps clanking on the corrugated metal steps. When they reached the door, Monroe entered a key code on an electronic lock, and the door clicked open.

"This way," he said.

They entered a hallway floored with speckled linoleum tiles, its drywall left plastered but unpainted. Monroe led Owen past a few doors to another locked by key code. When he entered the code and opened the door, Owen felt a gentle rush of cool, ozoned air, and heard the sounds of computers and voices chattering.

"Here we are," Monroe said, stepping aside. He gestured for Owen to proceed.

Through the door, Owen entered a wide, rambling room with several lit spaces scattered through it, and patches of darkness between them. The voices Owen had heard came from a group of sofas and armchairs in formation around a wide coffee table made of black glass. A group of kids roughly Owen's age occupied the furniture, and Javier was among them.

"Let's introduce you," Monroe said as he stepped around Owen and moved toward the others.

Owen followed him, and as they came into the light, the group fell silent and Javier stood.

"You made it," he said, sounding relieved. "You okay?"

"Yeah," Owen said. "I'm okay. What is this?"

"Ask him," Javier said, nodding toward Monroe. "It's his."

Monroe cleared his throat. "Ladies and gentlemen, this is Owen. Owen, you already know Javier. This is Grace and her brother, David." He gestured toward a girl with dark brown skin and a soft smile, her curly hair pulled back, while the younger, skinny boy sitting next to her grinned beneath white-framed glasses. Both wore nice clothes, with designer jeans Owen's mom could never afford.

"And this is Natalya," Monroe said, pointing to a girl with olive skin and somewhat narrow eyes, her brown hair shot with bronze. She wore a plain navy hoodie over a white T-shirt, and she met Owen's nod with a blank expression.

"And finally," Monroe said, indicating a boy Owen had just then noticed sitting in a wheelchair, "this is Sean."

"Pleasure to meet you, Owen," Sean said. He had short reddish hair, pale skin with some scattered freckles, and massive shoulders and arms.

"Good to meet you, too," Owen said. Then he turned to Monroe. "What are we all doing here? And you still haven't told me about that Assassin."

"Assassin?" Javier said.

Monroe held up his hands and kind of stretched his neck. "Just chill out for a minute, okay? I'll explain everything—"

"I don't have a minute," Owen said. "I need to get home. I mean, is my mom in danger?"

"No," Monroe said. "I can guarantee you that much."

"How?" Owen asked.

"She's an innocent," Monroe said. "That would violate a tenet of the Creed."

"What creed?" Javier asked.

"The Assassin's Creed," Monroe said. "But I'm getting ahead of myself. Please, Owen, Javier, have a seat."

Owen and Javier looked at each other, and then slowly took one of the couches.

"Now," Monroe said, "with the exception of Owen and Javier, and of course Grace and David, none of you know one another. You're from different schools, different neighborhoods, different backgrounds. But you have one thing in common. Your DNA. You've all used my Animus, and the truth is that I've been looking for you."

"Why?" Sean asked.

Monroe leaned over and pulled a small tablet out from a slot in the coffee table. He swiped and tapped its screen with his fingers, and a glowing, 3-D image of the earth rose up from the black glass surface, almost as wide as the table. It rotated slowly on its axis, while glowing dots pulsated at numerous locations across its surface.

"Whoa," David said, pushing up his glasses. "*That* is cool."

"Abstergo must be so pissed at you," Owen said.

"Give me some credit," Monroe said. "This table is all mine."

"What are those dots?" Grace asked, leaning forward.

"Events," Monroe said, "throughout history."

"What kind of events?" Grace asked.

Monroe had relaxed back into his normal posture, hands in his pockets. "I'm about to tell you some pretty wild stuff. But you have to go with me on this. I swear it's all true." He ambled around the table, glancing periodically at the image of the earth. "Two factions have been waging a secret war for the fate of humanity since the beginning of recorded history, and probably longer than that. These factions are ancestral. They've been called by many names, but currently they're known as the Assassin Brotherhood and the Templar Order."

"Secret societies?" Sean said. "Are you serious?"

"Look around you," Monroe said. "Does this not look serious to you?"

"So that Assassin chasing us," Owen said. "He was part of this Brotherhood?"

"Yes," Monroe said.

"Why did he shoot that Abstergo guy?" Owen asked.

"Abstergo is a front for the Templars," Monroe said.

Owen thought back to what the stranger had said before the Assassin's dart had struck him down. He'd mentioned Owen's father, and Owen wondered if his dad had anything to do with this secret war.

"These dots," Monroe said, "represent known events, people, or places connected to the conflict between the Assassins and Templars." He lifted a hand and touched one of many dots blinking on the Italian peninsula. As he did so, a second image opened up before it, a man dressed in an embroidered vest, flowing sleeves, and a cloak with a pointed hood shadowing his face. "This is Ezio Auditore, a fifteenth-century noblemen and perhaps one of the greatest Assassins in history. But the Brotherhood can trace its roots in Italy back even further, to the Roman *Liberalis Circulum*." He swiped that window away, took a few steps, and touched a dot in the Middle East. The image that opened was one of a mountain fortress. "This was once the bastion of the Assassin Brotherhood, destroyed by the Mongols in the Middle Ages in an act of revenge for the assassination of Genghis Khan." He closed that window and walked around the earth to touch a dot on the eastern seaboard of the United States. "The American Revolution wasn't just a fight for independence from the English crown. It was a war for the soul of a nation, influenced by these two factions."

Monroe had opened only a small fraction of the innumerable, glowing dots. If each of them represented an event from this secret war, the scope of the conflict was incredible. Almost unbelievable. And yet, Owen couldn't just dismiss it, because he had seen an Assassin in action.

"What are they fighting over?" Natalya asked. It was the first time she had spoken, and her voice was somehow soft and strong at the same time.

Monroe swiped the tablet, and the image of the globe vanished. "To answer that," he said, "let me paint a picture for you. Imagine a society coming apart at the seams. Violent crime is exploding, poverty is rampant, racial inequality, you name it. A society gone to hell. To bring it back from the brink of destruction, there are two possible courses of action. The first is for the people in power to impose order on the chaos. To forcibly shape and guide society toward improvement. The second is to put the power in the hands of the people, to let them decide for themselves what kind of society they want to build and trust in their better natures. Now, which of those paths would you choose?"

No one spoke. Owen wondered if the question was rhetorical, or if Monroe expected an answer. But he soon moved on.

"That's what they're fighting over, Natalya. The Templar Order represents those in power, the ones determined to guide humanity to a better way. The Assassins champion the free will of every individual in a society. Both factions are trying to make things the way they believe they ought to be."

"So they're fighting for the same thing?" David asked.

"They *want* the same thing," Monroe said. "They're fighting over how to get it."

"For hundreds of years?" Sean said.

"For thousands of years," Monroe said.

"Why are you telling us this?" Grace asked. "We don't have anything to do with it."

Monroe folded his arms. "That's where you're wrong."

"How?" Javier asked.

"I've seen your DNA," Monroe said. "I've seen your ancestors. By birth, each one of you here is an Assassin or a Templar." He looked at Javier. "Some of you are both."

CHAPTER SEVEN

S ean looked around the room at the others, wondering if any of them were buying what Monroe had just told them. That Owen kid claimed to have actually seen one of these Assassins shoot someone right in front of him, and assuming he wasn't a liar or crazy, that was information Sean couldn't ignore.

When Monroe had come for him earlier that evening, promising him more time in the Animus, Sean hadn't even hesitated. The Animus got him out of his wheelchair and gave him back his legs, and he would take that anytime. But it seemed Monroe had been hiding an agenda of his own, and Sean wasn't sure what to make of that, or this secret war.

"This is insane, man," Javier said. He seemed like a pretty tough guy, kind of quiet, and maybe not too smart.

"I warned you it was wild," Monroe said. "That doesn't make it not true."

"So what if it is true?" Grace said. "So what if we have Assassin or Templar ancestors way back when? I'm sure lots of people do. That doesn't explain why you brought us here."

"Or what you've been doing," Owen said, "going around to different schools with your Animus."

"Those are actually two questions," Monroe said. "I'll start with the second one, because it's got a pretty simple answer. Basically, I think the Assassins and Templars are both wrong."

"Then what do you believe?" Sean asked. It seemed important to know where Monroe stood, considering he'd been scouring through their DNA. Sean knew how he would answer the question Monroe had posed earlier. He wanted order. He wanted a world where people weren't allowed to drive drunk and ruin others' lives. There was right and there was wrong. People didn't get to choose that for themselves.

"I believe in free will," Monroe said.

"So you agree with the Assassins," Sean said.

Monroe shook his head. "I don't think the Assassins believe in free will. They say they do, but then they demand every member of their Brotherhood swear loyalty and absolute obedience. I don't believe we should give our free will over to any person or faction or creed. The Assassins and Templars need to be stopped, and one way I can do that is by getting to you first. Before they can recruit you."

"Recruit us?" Grace said.

"Sounds like you're trying to take away our free will," Javier said.

"Not at all." Monroe sighed. "You do whatever you think is the right thing to do. Always. My only objective was to make you aware."

"But that's not why you brought us here?" Grace said.

Monroe pointed at Owen and Javier. "I brought you here because of them. A few nights ago, they went into the Animus, and they found something the Assassins and Templars would do anything to obtain."

Owen and Javier looked at each other, and then Owen said, "That's why you pulled us out. There wasn't anything wrong with the simulation."

"No," Monroe said, "there wasn't anything wrong with the simulation. My tech works, and my simulations don't collapse. But I did have to get you out of there."

"Why?" Javier asked.

"A precaution. I've poured through every line of code running the Animus, but I knew it was possible there was something I've missed. And I was right. That's why that Abstergo agent showed up, and why the Assassin is here. They know."

"Know what?" Sean asked.

"That we found a Piece of Eden," Monroe said.

"What's a Piece of Eden?" David asked, leaning forward.

Sean already liked that kid. He was curious, and he seemed earnest.

Monroe hesitated. "A Piece of Eden is a powerful relic from an ancient civilization that predates humanity. They possessed incredible technologies, and some examples have survived to the present day. But they're usually very well hidden."

"The dagger," Javier said. "The one Cortés had?"

Monroe nodded.

"That's what it was." Javier punched his palm. "I knew there had to be something going on. That thing totally brainwashed me—my ancestor."

Owen nodded along. "My ancestor believed pretty much anything Cortés said, too."

"Right," Monroe said. "Each Piece of Eden has a different effect and purpose. It seems the one you found can alter someone's faith and turn them into believers. That may be why some historians think the Aztecs believed Cortés was a god."

Sean didn't like the idea that something could mess with his head that way.

"So if these Pieces of Eden are hidden," David said, "how does anyone find them?"

"Genetic memories," Monroe said. "If the Assassins or Templars identify someone in history who came into contact with a Piece of Eden, they use the Animus to go back through their descendants' memories to locate it. Which is where Owen and Javier come in."

Grace rolled her eyes. "And the rest of us?"

"I believe you are *all* essential to finding this particular Piece of Eden," Monroe said.

"But Owen and Javier already found it," Sean said.

"They interacted with it," Monroe said. "But they didn't witness its final resting place. I don't believe the relic stayed in Mexico." He raised his tablet and the coffee-table hologram came to life again with a black-and-white image of a large old building. "This is the Astor House hotel in New York City, mid-nineteenth century. The Aztec Club held meetings there."

"The Aztec Club?" Javier asked.

"A small military society of veterans who served during the Mexican-American War in the late 1840s," Monroe said. "After Cortés conquered Tenochtitlan, I believe his dagger remained in Mexico City until the American occupation, when it was taken from the Spanish government's treasury. Because, look at this." The screen switched to the images of several men. Sean recognized one of them as Ulysses S. Grant. "Despite its small numbers, the Aztec Club somehow managed to produce six presidential nominees, three of whom were elected, along with several congressmen and other high-ranking officials. Now what are the odds of that? I believe the club established its political power using the Piece of Eden."

"So you're saying these guys were all Assassins?" David said. "Or were they Templars?"

"I'm not saying that at all." Monroe folded his arms around the tablet. "Although some of them might have been either."

"But who are the good guys?" David asked. "The Assassins or the Templars?"

"Neither," Monroe said. "Or both. Depending on how you look at it. Both have good intentions, and both are capable of evil acts."

"I'm still waiting for the part where we come in," Grace said.

"Right," Monroe said. "Now we come to all of you." He switched the display, and six double helixes of DNA stretched across the field in horizontal, parallel spirals. "I've assembled you because you have amazingly high Memory Concordance." Vertical lines appeared, intersecting the DNA strands at matching points. "Your ancestors came into contact in some way with the Piece of Eden, or with one another, during the same event."

Sean hoped that meant what he thought it did.

"What event?" Owen asked.

"The Draft Riots of 1863," Monroe said. "New York City."

"Draft Riots?" Javier asked.

"It was during the Civil War," Grace said. "The government was drafting men to fight the South, but if you were rich you could buy your way out of it."

"That's right," Monroe said. "So the riots broke out across New York. Gangs and mobs in the thousands. It was anarchy."

"And they attacked all the black people in the city," Grace added. "They even burned down an orphanage for black children."

"So are we going back in? Back there?" Sean asked, a little less eager now that he knew more about the situation.

"That's up to you," Monroe said. "But I hope you will. Any one of you might be the key, and I believe it's essential that we locate the Piece of Eden before the Assassins and Templars do."

"Why?" Natalya asked.

That was only the second or third thing Sean had heard her say since meeting her, but when she spoke, he listened. Something about her drew him in. She was beautiful, of course, but there was something beyond that he couldn't identify. But to talk to her he'd have to wheel himself over there, and so far, he hadn't met a girl who found his wheelchair very attractive.

"What will you do with it if you find it?" Natalya asked.

"Hide it again," Monroe said. "Where no memory can uncover it. The important thing is to prevent it from falling into the hands of either the Assassin Brotherhood or the Templar Order."

"How do we know you won't use it?" Javier asked.

Monroe looked around the group at each of them. "You're going to have to trust me, just like I am trusting you. So will you do it?"

"Do what?" Owen asked.

"Go into the Animus," Monroe said. "A shared simulation. Experience the memories of your ancestors, and hopefully find out what happened to the Piece of Eden."

"Hopefully?" Javier said.

"Look." Monroe turned off the display and set the tablet down. "I own this is my fault, and I'm sorry. You're all in danger because of me. I thought I had the Animus secured. Somehow it alerted Abstergo. I was trying to do something right, giving you access to your origins, but that backfired, and now that a new Piece of Eden is in play, the Assassins and Templars won't stop until it's found. But this is your choice." He took a step backward away from them. "I mean that. Your choice."

"What about our parents?" Natalya asked.

"Time in the Animus is mind time," Monroe said. "Dream time. It's subjective, with days of memory passing in a matter of minutes or hours in the real world. You'll be back before morning."

Sean gripped the handrims of his wheelchair. He wasn't about to let another chance at the Animus pass him by. Who knew when another opportunity would come along? "I'll do it," he said.

Everyone turned to look at him.

Sean sat up higher in his chair and met their stares with confidence. "Who's with me?"

"I'll go," David said.

"You'll what?" Grace scowled at her little brother. "What do you think you're doing?"

David shrugged. "I want to help."

"Why?" Grace asked.

"Why wouldn't he?" Sean asked.

"Why wouldn't he?" Grace said. "Didn't you just hear me talking about the Draft Riots? Stop and think about your history classes for a minute. The last time David and I went into the Animus, there were drinking fountains we weren't allowed to use. This is going to be much, much worse."

That was something Sean hadn't even stopped to consider, and he fell into an embarrassed silence.

"Well, I'm going," Javier said.

"I'm in, too," Owen said.

"So am I," Natalya said.

That left Grace and David uncommitted. David had already said he wanted to go, but Sean was pretty sure he wouldn't without his older sister. David looked to her now as she looked around at the group, and finally back at her little brother. "How do you know this will work?" she asked Monroe. "That's all I care about. We're in danger right now. How do you know this will make us safe?"

"It's safer than doing nothing," Monroe said. "If we find the Piece of Eden first, and then I hide it, your genetic memories won't hold the answer anymore. They'll leave you alone."

Sean noticed Grace's rigid posture bend a little as she seemed to give in. "Fine," she said. "I'll go."

"Right on," Monroe said. "The sooner we do this, the better.

The Animus is over there." He pointed across the darkened room to another island of light filled with computers and equipment.

The others all got up from their sofas and walked right toward it. Sean had to back his wheelchair out from between the sofas to maneuver around the furniture and the display table, and got a little stuck for a moment. That hadn't happened to him for a while, and he ground his jaw.

Owen took a couple of steps toward him. "Need a push?"

"I got it," Sean said, sounding sharper than he intended, even though his tone matched the irritation he felt. It had been two years since the accident, and he didn't know when this frustration and anger would go away, or if it ever would. Maybe it would just keep churning inside him until one day he spontaneously combusted from all that pent-up inner friction. He wished he could at least know what to do with other people's attempts at kindness, for their sakes and his. "I'll be over in a minute," Sean said.

Owen nodded. "Okay, then." And he walked over to join the others, though Sean could tell it was an intentionally slow walk, meant to make Sean feel not so far behind, which only caused more frustration.

When Sean finally reached the group, he found them clustered together in front of the Animus, the core of which Monroe had apparently moved up here from his bus. The main terminal sat at the center of a radiating circle of recliner chairs, like the spokes of a wheel with their headrests pointing inward at the hub.

Monroe nodded toward the setup. "Please pick a chair and get comfortable."

"Isn't this just going to repeat the same mistake?" Javier asked. "Won't the Animus let Abstergo know again?"

Sean took another look at him. Maybe Javier was smarter than he'd thought.

"Not this time," Monroe said. "I've got the unit completely isolated and firewalled off in a way I couldn't achieve on the bus. We're safe here."

Sean rolled himself over to one of the recliners and locked the wheels on his chair. Then he heaved himself up and over, lifting out of the chair and into the recliner.

"Whoa," Javier said, standing nearby. "You've got some strength."

"Nah." Sean shrugged. "It's all in the technique."

But he had always been strong. His coaches had remarked on it before the accident. He still had that in his upper body, but his legs had gone to bone and sinew. Sean rotated his hips and then used his arms to heave his legs up one at a time onto the recliner. At that point, he was able to lie back, and he would have been comfortable were it not for the excitement building inside him. He remembered the thrill of his first time in the Animus. His ancestor had been a simple farmer in Ireland, which probably wouldn't have been an exciting simulation for anyone else. But Sean had *walked* his ancestor's barley fields. He had walked them from sunrise to sundown, working his land, and that was enough.

"You've all done this before," Monroe said. "But only a few of you have gone into a shared simulation. Basically, you can't interact as yourselves, or you'll desynchronize. If you go trying to find one another, or you do or say things in front of people your ancestor wouldn't, you'll desynchronize. Got it?"

They all acknowledged they did.

Monroe walked around the circle, helping them each get

hooked up to the Animus in turn. "The Piece of Eden seems to be a dagger of some kind," he said. "We didn't get a good look at it in Mexico, but it seems to have an unusual design. Keep your eyes open."

He reached Sean and handed him a helmet, which Sean pulled over his head, shrouding him in darkness. A few moments later, with everyone situated, Sean heard Monroe move to the Animus controls at the center.

Can you all hear me? Monroe asked through the helmet.

They could.

Right on. Just give me a sec and I'll drop you all into the Memory Corridor. Another moment went by in which Sean tightened his fists in anticipation. *Okay, everyone ready?* Monroe asked.

Ready, several of them said at once, including Sean.

Okay. Memory Corridor in three, two, one—

Piercing light blinded Sean as the visor came to life, immersing him in the void space of the Corridor. As the images around him resolved themselves, the first thing he noted was that he was standing, on his own. And he was tall. Huge, actually.

"You look like a cop," said a man standing next to Sean. He wore a high, fuzzy stovepipe hat, a long dark coat that reached his knees, an embroidered red vest, and plaid pants. Thick sideburns grew down to his jawline, and a huge knife hung at his waist.

Sean looked down at his own dark coat, its brass buttons, and high collar. He wore a flat cap with a short bill and a Metropolitan Police badge on the front. "You're right," he said. "I do look like a cop. I don't even know what you look like. Who—who are you?"

"Owen," the man said, a hoarse edge to his voice, but then he cocked his head to one side. "And I'm . . ." He looked down at his wrist, stared at it a moment, and made a fist. A knife blade shot out from within the sleeve of his coat, and then retracted in a flash. "I'm an Assassin," he said.

Sean took a step away from him. "Good to know."

"I think I'm a Templar," said another man behind him.

Sean turned to face him and the others. The second man who'd spoken was large, but not as large as Sean, and he talked with a slight Irish lilt. He had no hat, and wore a vest over a dingy white shirt, the sleeves rolled up, with a kerchief tied around his neck. A short apron wrapped around his waist, giving him the appearance of a bartender.

"Javier?" Owen asked him.

The bartender nodded. "I always knew my mom had Irish in her."

An older man with white hair and a younger woman in her teens stood near each other behind Javier, both black, both dressed as servants. The girl wore a dark dress with a white, frilly apron that covered her chest and both shoulders. The man wore a black coat and pants, a vest, and a white shirt.

"Please tell me we are not slaves," the girl said.

"You're not," said a petite girl next to them. She wore an elegant red dress with black lace, and had dark, silken hair, dark eyes, and soft features. "New York was a free state even before the Civil War."

"Natalya?" Sean asked the girl.

"Yes," she said.

"I, uh, I think I'm your dad," David said to Grace.

"I think you're right," Grace said. "But I hope you realize that doesn't mean you're in charge."

Okay, Monroe's voice came in. *Memories are almost finished compiling. You can start acclimating to your ancestors' identities. I'll load the full simulation shortly. But there's something else you need to know.*

"What?" Grace asked.

Unlike the rest of you, David is experiencing an extrapolated memory.

"What's that?" David asked.

Well, technically, you don't have any of your ancestor's memories from after the moment his daughter was conceived, because that's when his genes got passed on. So you'll have the memories of your life from before that moment, but not after. But since your ancestor crossed paths with the others here, the Animus is using their memories to create your simulation.

"So what does that mean for him?" Grace asked.

It means he'll have a bit more freedom in the simulation. Since we don't know everything his ancestor was doing in every moment, he won't desynchronize as easily. But it also means he'll need to be at the right place and the right time to cross paths with the rest of you.

"What happens if I'm not in the right place at the right time?" David asked.

It could break the whole simulation.

"Great," David said. "No pressure."

Right. Okay, get ready, everyone. Sean felt the same rushing sensation he'd experienced his first time in the Animus, like a tide or a river pressing against him. He could plant his feet and stand firm against it, or he could just let it carry him downstream. He felt the current taking shape, lodging voices and thoughts against his mind, and he let them sweep over him, bringing with them a new awareness.

He was Tommy Greyling, patrolman with the elite Broadway

Squad out of the Central Office for the last eight months, from the Eighteenth Precinct before that, and before that he'd taken a bullet through his thigh at Bull Run in Virginia, but somehow kept his leg. He'd come home to New York City from that battle only to find himself in a different kind of war, one waged on the streets with brickbats and knives.

"I'm a singer," Natalya said, standing nearby in finery. Her features looked familiar to Tommy. "I'm an opera singer," she said.

Beneath Tommy's admiration of the woman, Sean was aware that it was Natalya who'd spoken, and she had sounded almost frightened. It was obvious she was shy, having said maybe a dozen words since Sean had met her, so maybe it was the idea of being a performer up on a stage that scared her.

We're ready, Monroe said. *I'll initiate the simulation on the count of three. Prepare yourselves. The Draft Riots were hell on Earth.*

CHAPTER EIGHT

Natalya stared into the mirror, alone in a dressing room, but the face staring back was not hers. This young woman, whose ambitious mind and will clamored to rise from Natalya's understudy consciousness to top billing, had black hair that gleamed in the warm gaslight of the room. She had wide eyes, around which heavy makeup had been applied. She wore a scarlet gown Natalya could vaguely recall purchasing in Paris for a sum she was pretty sure would stagger her if adjusted for inflation.

And she was an opera singer. Not just any opera singer. She was Adelina Patti. She had first taken the stage as a prodigy at the age of seven. Now, at twenty, she had already toured the United States, Europe, and Russia. She had sung at the White

House for Abraham Lincoln and his wife, Mary Todd, the previous year by personal invitation.

Someone knocked gently at the door. "Mademoiselle?"

Natalya retreated behind the curtain and let Adelina take the stage. "Yes?"

"It is William," the man said. "I have your fee, mademoiselle. May I enter?"

"You may," Adelina said.

The door opened, and the Niblo's Garden manager entered her dressing room. He was short and somehow round at the middle but nowhere else. He carried a small leather case with him, which he set on the floor at her feet.

"My apologies if this seems vulgar to deal so directly with you," he said. "If your manager had not suddenly taken ill . . ."

"Thank you, sir," Adelina said. "No apologies are necessary. I trust it is paid in full?" She bent and lifted the case by its handles, and found it weighed perhaps eight pounds. At the current market price of gold, it should have weighed ten. "It is *not* paid in full?"

William pulled a handkerchief from his pocket and dabbed at his forehead. "Unfortunately, Miss Patti, it is not. I have brought four thousand in gold, and we will have the remainder, that is, the final thousand for you after the ticket sales for the show."

"I thought my contract made my conditions clear," Adelina said.

"Yes, perfectly clear," he said.

"Five thousand in gold. Payment in advance. In full. Or I will not take the stage."

"Yes, of course." William dabbed his forehead again. "I thought perhaps . . ."

"What? You thought perhaps I would make an exception?"

"That was my hope, yes." William's gaze had fallen to the floor and evidently had become anchored there. Adelina could see he was overwhelmed, and she knew he would not be able to find a way out of this himself.

"All right, here is what you will do, William. You may have noticed I have yet to put on my shoes. I will put them on when the terms of my contract have been met. So you will go down and see what money has been taken in ticket sales, and from that you will draw the remainder of my fee. But I *will* make an exception for you."

William looked up. "Yes?"

"I will accept cash instead of gold."

His shoulders slumped, and he nodded. "Yes, mademoiselle." With a slight bow, he left her room, and she was alone again.

Natalya peered out from behind the curtain of her consciousness, in admiration of Adelina's display of strength and confidence. Natalya had confidence, too, but she rarely showed it. Most people assumed she was shy, but that wasn't what it was at all. She wasn't afraid or anxious of people. She preferred to think of herself as reserved. But there was nothing reserved about Adelina Patti, and even though Natalya knew she would not actually be standing up on a stage singing in front of people, she dreaded the simulated experience, and hoped that perhaps William wouldn't return with the remainder of the fee.

Interesting, Monroe said.

"What is?" Natalya asked.

Adelina Patti was married three times, but had no children of record.

"Well, she's my ancestor, so she must have had a kid at some point."

She did have a few affairs. Maybe she had a secret kid out of one of them.

"Three marriages? Affairs?" Natalya shook her head. "She really did things her own way."

Seems she did.

Several moments later, William knocked at the door, and Natalya bowed out.

"Enter," Adelina said.

William opened the door and walked back into the room, still dabbing at his forehead.

"Do you have it?" Adelina asked.

"I have eight hundred dollars," William said. He pulled a wad of bills from his coat and handed it to Adelina. "I am hoping that will suffice for now. The house is full, and I am sure you do not want to keep your audience waiting."

Adelina smiled and accepted the money, which she placed inside the case with her gold. She then reached for her left shoe and pulled it on, and William let out a deep sigh.

"Thank you, mademoiselle, thank you. I—"

Adelina reached out and handed him the matching right shoe, which he accepted as though it were something both fragile and hot. Then she leaned back in her chair, one foot shod and one still bare. "I will put on that other shoe when you have brought me the remaining two hundred dollars. My audience will wait."

He paled visibly, stammered, and left the room with a hasty bow, still holding her shoe.

Natalya almost giggled within the mind of this young woman. At a time when women had few options, Adelina had used her talent to secure for herself a place of wealth, but perhaps more important than that, of power.

But the time of her performance was approaching, and while Adelina was perfectly calm, Natalya was not.

When William returned, his rapping at the door sounded insistent and desperate.

"Enter," Adelina said very pleasantly.

He burst into the room out of breath. "Here, mademoiselle, here." He handed her a second wad of money, as well as her right shoe. "Two hundred dollars. Payment in full."

She accepted both with a gracious nod. "Thank you, sir." She put the money in the case, as William checked his pocket watch, and then she pulled on her shoe. "I should be glad to perform."

"If you'll allow me to escort you?" William said, extending the crook of his arm.

She took it with her gloved hand. "Of course."

They left the room, which William locked behind them, and then made the crossing of the rearward parts of the theater. It truly was a marvelous venue, perhaps the most modern theater Adelina had seen. Miles of piping for gaslight. A vaulted space crisscrossed with catwalks and an endlessly complicated system of ropes and pulleys for raising and lowering set pieces. And an audience capacity over three thousand.

Natalya's nervousness bounded higher at that thought, even as it exhilarated Adelina.

The night's first opening performances had already taken place, short vignettes meant to delight and heighten anticipation for the main attraction, and the evening's host was already onstage giving her introduction. Adelina stood in the wings, waiting for the moment of her entrance.

Next to her, William leaned in and whispered, "You realize you make more in a week than the president of the United States makes in a year."

Then the stage host named her "the world-renowned and incomparable talent, Miss Adelina Patti," and the audience erupted in applause. The moment of her entrance had come.

"Then, William, next time invite the president to sing." Adelina smiled and stepped out onto the stage.

The applause intensified as soon as she came into the light, and Adelina stopped and offered a low and gracious bow. The host had already retreated from the stage, and she took up her place at its center. The audience before her filled every section of the theater, from the orchestra seats to the highest row in the third tier of gilded balconies above her. She nodded and smiled toward the box seats as the applause continued unabated for several moments. When at last it died down, the conductor flicked his orchestra into action, and as the music rose up Natalya found herself experiencing something she would have never, ever done in real life.

Adelina had come from a family of singers, a home filled with the spirit of entertainment and performance. Natalya had come from a quiet home filled with her grandparents' memories of hardship in Kazakhstan under the rule of the Soviet Union, and their silent determination to keep their heads down and make a better life through hard work. Adelina was a songbird, and Natalya was a plow.

But now Natalya had to sing before an audience of three thousand, something that would have ordinarily been completely impossible for Natalya to think of doing. But she reminded herself that it wasn't actually her, that her consciousness and reservations could remain backstage, letting Adelina shine.

She sang Zerlina's aria from *Don Giovanni*. She sang Elvira from *I Puritani*, and Maria from Donizetti's *La Figlia del Reggimento*. Her voice, clear and rich as honey, filled the theater, and the audience adored her. At first, Natalya watched her as if from afar, keeping a safe distance. But with each song Natalya forced herself to emerge from behind the curtain of her mind a bit more, until the performance was at an end and she felt ready to try something. As Adelina took her final bows, Natalya braced herself and stepped trembling into the light of the stage, pushing Adelina back.

The full size and weight of the audience fell upon her, the glittering cavern of the theater immense and filled with the torrent of their applause. It was too much, and Natalya lost her breath and clasped her stomach. The Animus simulation glitched, dispersing the farthest reaches of the theater in a dark gray fog.

Everything okay? Monroe asked.

"It's fine," Natalya whispered, and she forced herself to remain there, feeling the pressure of the audience's attention, partly out of curiosity and partly to simply challenge herself. She straightened her back to adopt Adelina's posture, and the simulation's integrity gradually returned. She lifted her face toward the lights that lined the upper balconies. She smiled and bowed, and made sure the simulation was fully restored before she let herself fall back and give control to Adelina.

After the performance, William escorted her to an exquisite little sitting room for an intimate reception with some of the theater's more prominent patrons. Again, Natalya watched in awe, moving behind Adelina's mind as the singer glided through the room, enchanting everyone. She sipped chilled champagne and ate oysters, pastries, and other relishes. Orange and vanilla ice cream was provided to stave off the evening's heat and the closeness of the room. But one thing Natalya became gradually aware of was that Adelina felt lonely. Somehow, among all these people, she was alone. Adelina knew very well that none of these theater patrons actually cared about her. She entertained them, and were it not for that, she would warrant only their polite indifference.

Some of the conversations, both direct and overheard, interested Natalya far more than they did Adelina, but Natalya could do nothing to engage with them. All she could do was listen and pay attention as she lived out Adelina's memory of the evening.

"Damn these Copperheads to hell," said a man with white hair and a thick white mustache that curled wide across his cheeks. "And they can take Tweed and Tammany with them."

"Be careful, Cornelius," said one of the men with him.

"Why? Lee's tucked tail and run back to Virginia. Grant's victory at Vicksburg will turn the tide of this war, I'm certain of it. I don't have any fear of these Democrat Southern sympathizers."

"You're too bold, Cornelius," another man said. "The outcome of the war is far from decided. And regardless of the victor, you'll still have business to conduct. Best not make enemies if a bit more prudence can avoid it."

"Bah!" Cornelius said.

Adelina walked on and joined a conversation with a few ladies wearing lavish gowns and lace and jewelry that likely cost even more than hers. After a cordial greeting and a round of compliments on Adelina's performance, the conversation turned back to the roots put down before Adelina's arrival.

"They're still going forward with the draft?" a red-haired woman asked.

"They are," said a silvered dame.

"I fear that's a mistake."

"Draft?" Adelina asked.

"Oh, that's right," the first woman said. "You live in England. President Lincoln is conscripting able-bodied men to fight the Rebels, you see. The city is quite up in arms over it. I thought perhaps it would be called off."

"It would be if Governor Seymour and the mayor had their way," the older woman said. "But Major General Wool is determined to carry it out."

"Do you have sons?" Adelina asked. "Are you worried they'll be called up?"

"Not at all," the woman said, her diamonds flashing. "The Conscription Act allows men to pay a three-hundred-dollar commutation fee to exempt them from service. Even if my sons are drafted, they won't be fighting."

"It really is a small sum to ask," the red-haired woman said.

Even though she was a wealthy woman, Adelina thought the word *small* probably meant something very different to those working in the factories and streets, the laborers living in the squalor of the Five Points and the Bowery, to whom three hundred dollars likely meant a year's wages or more. They couldn't use their wealth to escape the carnage of the battlefield. But Adelina kept this observation to herself.

From there the conversation turned easily to the mundane, and both Adelina and Natalya grew bored. It was quite late when the gathering finally broke apart, and William nervously ushered Adelina into a carriage with the case bearing her fee.

"I really wish you would let me escort you," William said. "Or send someone with you if you find me objectionable."

"It isn't that," Adelina said. William's earlier effrontery regarding her fee no longer irritated her in the least. "I'm simply capable of making my own way."

"I have no doubt of that. But I do wish your manager were with you."

"I do not, and neither should you, unless it is your desire to become quite ill."

William smiled and his nod appeared reluctant. "Very well."

"Good night," Adelina said. "You do have a beautiful theater, and I hope to sing here again soon."

"As do I," William said, and then ordered the driver to take Adelina up to the Fifth Avenue Hotel where she was staying.

The heat of the July night had not yet broken, but at least the New York City air smelled cleaner than the soot-choked miasma that smothered Adelina's home in London. She looked forward to her tour in the refreshing German watering places Mannheim and Frankfurt at the end of the month.

The carriage drove her up Broadway, which still bustled with curious activity despite it being well past midnight. Adelina didn't like the cast of the men still about. They looked like ruffians and experts in mayhem, members of the street gangs that ruled Five Points and the Bowery farther downtown. They rushed to and fro, up and down the street, with purpose and determination, though Adelina didn't know what that purpose might be.

But Natalya knew. The riots were imminent. The gang leaders were probably coordinating and plotting even now. And Adelina had taken a carriage at two in the morning, by herself, carrying four thousand dollars in gold and another thousand in cash. Natalya's first time in the Animus hadn't been dangerous at all. She had experienced her grandmother's arrival in America, the fear and the excitement and the joy of it. But this situation was very different.

She wished she could somehow warn Adelina, but after they had gone perhaps a dozen blocks, and passed Union Square, the carriage came to a halt. Natalya wanted to scream for Adelina to run, but—

"Driver?" Adelina called. "Why have we stopped?"

But the driver didn't answer. Instead, a man's face peered through the carriage window.

"Evening, miss," he said.

"Driver!" Adelina said, but then she realized the cab had stopped here on purpose.

She reached for the door's handle to prevent it turning, but the man wrenched it out of her hands and yanked the door open. His eyes flicked around the carriage's interior and landed on the case. He dove for it, but Adelina grabbed its straps at the same time, and they tugged the case back and forth between them, growling and cursing. The man braced a boot against the outer door frame, but so did Adelina from inside. Natalya couldn't believe her strength.

"Easy now!" the man said. "I just want the bag!"

"Help me!" Adelina cried. "Somebody help me!"

The man leaned in through the doorway to get a better grip, and when he did, Adelina managed to roll a little on the carriage's seat and then kicked him in the face with her free boot. His head snapped back with a grunt, and when he righted it, blood poured from his nostrils down his upper lip and chin. He let go of the straps, and Adelina could see his rage. She braced for his attack as he snarled at her and dove inside the carriage.

Natalya wanted out of the simulation. She hadn't agreed to this. She didn't want to experience this.

"Let me out!" Natalya and Adelina both screamed.

CHAPTER NINE

Grace stood against the wall of a dining room, four men seated at a table before her, a sideboard laden with food to her right. David stood at the other end of the sideboard, looking at her through the ridiculous eyes of an old white-haired man. Ridiculous because to think of him as her father almost made her laugh. He was so trusting and naive, so sincere, but she loved that about him and didn't want to see the world beat or burn it out of him. So she was usually the one who took care of him.

"Eliza, is everything all right?" one of the men at the table asked.

He was very large, perhaps two hundred and fifty or even three hundred pounds, and while it looked as if some of that weight might have once been muscle in his youth, most of it wasn't now. He and the other men at the table were staring at her. They all wore three-piece suits, with delicate, draping pocket watch chains, and jewels that flashed at their cuffs and lapels.

"I'm fine," Grace said.

The men all scowled, and one of them scoffed at her. Grace felt the simulation rejecting her, like getting pushed out of a subway train as the world moves on in a blur. She looked over at David. His wide eyes implored her to do something, say something, but it had to be the *right* thing.

Grace hated this part of the Animus. She hated giving up control of her mind, which had always been the one thing no one else could touch. Her mind was her palace, her temple, and her garden, all at once. But now there was someone else trying to get in, a squatter-mind attempting to scale the walls and take up residence.

"Eliza, what is the matter with you?" the big man asked.

"Nothing," Grace said. She was his servant, and she hated that thought. She was probably expected to call him *sir* and curtsy or whatever.

"It must be the heat, Mr. Tweed," David said, but Grace could tell he wasn't David anymore. The look in his eyes seemed older, with a different kind of worry. "If she needs to lie down, I can finish serving, sir."

The simulation went even blurrier, and Grace could feel its doors shutting in her face, about to leave her behind.

The big man turned his attention back to Grace. "Is that so? Do you need to lie down?"

The invading mind felt desperate, scrambling to get in. If Grace didn't open the gate and allow it through, right now, she'd be out of the simulation, and that would leave David in there alone. Grace couldn't let that happen, so she grit her teeth, hating this and resenting Monroe for making her do it, and she opened the barricades of her mind.

Eliza rushed in, a soft-spoken girl who had lost her mother at the age of eight, whose father had loved her and cared for her as best he could on his own these last nine years in service to Mr. Tweed, and whom she couldn't ever let down.

"I'm so sorry, Mr. Tweed," she said, and curtsied. "I sort of lost myself for a moment. It must be the heat. I'm sorry, sir."

"That's quite all right," Mr. Tweed said, big hands flat at his girth. "Are you well now?"

"Quite well," Eliza said. "It's passed."

"Good," Mr. Tweed said. "I'll have more of the duck."

"Yes, sir." Eliza turned to the sideboard, where the feast had been laid out. In addition to the duck, there were oysters, roast beef tenderloin, ham with champagne sauce, and sweetbreads. She picked up the platter of duck and carried it to Mr. Tweed. After he had served himself, she carried the platter around the table for his guests.

"Boss, your cook is as good as Ranhofer," Mr. Connolly said, a brick of a man with a block-shaped head.

"I would damn well hope so," Mr. Tweed said. "I sent her to Delmonico's for lessons from him. And don't call me Boss."

"I like the term," said Mr. Hall, a twinkle behind his pince-nez spectacles, the twitch of a smile beneath his elegant beard. "Boss Tweed. It suits you."

"Let's see if it sticks," Mr. Sweeny said with a scowl that angled his thick, wide mustache.

"If it sticks, it sticks," Mr. Tweed said. "I take the people of this city as they are, and they can call me whatever the hell they want. But here, it's just Tweed or Bill, understood?" Mr. Tweed sat back in his chair. "Or Grand Sachem," he added, at which a chuckle rounded the table. "It's a pity General Sanford couldn't join us. But I've been assured of his cooperation tomorrow."

"He'll hold back the troops?" Mr. Sweeny asked.

Mr. Tweed nodded.

Eliza and her father attended to the guests for another hour or so, until the food was gone, most of it consumed by Mr. Tweed, and the wine was gone, most of it consumed by the others.

"Gentlemen," Mr. Tweed said, "as splendid as the evening has been, we have some important matters to discuss before we adjourn, and my wife has stated in no uncertain terms she expects me home before dawn. Shall we move to the library?"

The others agreed and rose from their chairs. They moved as one from the dining room out into the main hall, and a moment later, the closing of the library door muted their voices.

"Let's get this wreckage cleaned up," Eliza's father said. "And then we can see what Margaret's cooked up for us in the kitchen."

"I wish Mr. Tweed would hire on more help," Eliza said, stacking the empty silver platters. The brownstone wasn't large, but it was a lot to manage for two servants, a cook, and her scrubber. And Eliza wanted to do something more than clean Mr. Tweed's house. She wanted to make something of herself, the way other black men and women had. Maybe open a shop or a restaurant . . .

"It wouldn't make sense for him to hire on someone else," her father said. "Mr. Tweed is never here. If he didn't use this house to meet with his associates as he does, I doubt he'd keep any of us on. Just be grateful. It could be much worse for us. Lotta folk out there . . ."

He didn't finish, but Eliza knew what he meant. The City of New York and Brooklyn were overflowing with Irish and Germans, and there weren't enough jobs. Blacks were competition, and the city didn't want any more freed slaves coming up from the South looking for work. That's why there'd been talk of the city seceding with the Rebels. That's why the Democrat Copperheads in New York sympathized with the Confederates and wanted the Union to be defeated.

Grace experienced these thoughts with the same anger and powerlessness she had with her great-grandmother's memories of spaces for "whites only." None of it was right, but there wasn't anything Grace could do about it. She looked down at the tray of dishes in her hands, and was struck by the moment's similarity with her last time in the Animus. Her great-grandmother had cleaned houses for rich white ladies, and it seemed to Grace in that moment that the generations of her ancestors held nothing in their hands but stacks of dirty dishes.

She slammed down the tray she was holding a little too hard, and it flipped a serving spoon onto the floor. She left it there, even as she felt the simulation weaken.

"Eliza?" the old man who was her father and David asked. Since David's simulation was extrapolated, he was acting out this moment as Eliza remembered it, and doing a better job than her at staying synchronized. "Is something wrong?"

"It's nothing," Grace said.

"It doesn't seem to be nothing," he said.

Grace forced herself to bend and pick up the spoon, and she felt the simulation strengthen.

"I know you worry for me," Eliza's father said. "But I worry more for you. I need to see you're taken care of when I'm gone—"

Eliza spoke up then. "Please don't talk—"

"I speak the truth." He held up one of his calloused hands. "No sense hiding from it. The truth will always find you out. Your grandmother never saw her freedom, but I made sure any child of mine would be born free. I know you want more than this, and I want more than this for you. One day you will have more, much more. I know you will. But these are very troubled times, and for now, you have work and a kind employer."

Eliza and Grace both watched him for a moment, and both realized he was right. Grace couldn't change this history, as angry as she felt about it, and fighting it would only expel her from the simulation. She'd come here because Monroe said finding this Piece of Eden was the best way to make it safe for her and David. So that's what she would do.

"Yes, Father," Eliza said.

She walked over and helped him gather the silverware.

"You are determined and you are brave," her father said. "You do your grandmother's name proud."

"I hope so," Eliza said.

Grace let Eliza's consciousness out of the corner room and gave the girl free access to the rest of her mind's real estate. Eliza immediately set about clearing the dishes and the table with efficiency and speed alongside her father, though he went a little slower these days, wincing at pains in his joints when he thought she wasn't looking. For now, though, she could make up the difference, and Mr. Tweed had so far seen no reason to let her father go.

They brought all the dishes to the kitchen, where Margaret's scrubber would take care of them, and after that, Eliza's father would polish the silver pieces. Margaret had boiled a lamb shank meant for Mr. Tweed's guests, but Mr. Tweed had declined it to be served, which made for an uncommon and delicious meal for the small staff. They ate together around the kitchen table, but quickly, for the guests would be ready to depart soon. Margaret even put out some mint jelly to eat with the meat.

Just as they were finishing, they heard the library door open, and men's voices bumped one another out into the main hall. Eliza and her father went to see if anything was needed by the guests, who filed out the front door one by one into their carriages and rode off into the warm night. After they had all left, Mr. Tweed summoned Eliza's father alone into the library and shut the door again.

That caused Eliza some unease, and even though she risked getting in trouble for it, she went to stand by the metal grate in the wall near the floor of an adjacent hallway, through which she could hear the conversation taking place.

"Is there any way to stop it?" her father asked.

"I doubt even canceling the draft would prevent it at this point. It is no longer a problem to be solved, but one to be managed."

"How bad will it be?"

"It will be unlike anything seen before in this city," Mr. Tweed said. "Or even this country."

"Worse than the police riots?"

"I believe so, yes. But good will rise out of the ashes. I will be there with the powers of Tammany Hall behind me to rebuild the city in wisdom and strength. But we must act quickly. Are you up to the challenge?"

"I am, Mr. Tweed," her father said.

"I have a letter for you to deliver. I need a messenger who won't arouse interest or suspicion. I also need someone I can trust, and over the years I've come to trust you."

"Where am I to deliver it, sir?"

"There's an establishment in the lower Fourth Ward," Mr. Tweed said. "The Hole-in-the-Wall. Have you heard of it?"

"Yes, sir. It's quite infamous, sir."

"Indeed, it is. There's a bartender there by name of Cudgel Cormac."

"Cudgel? Not his Christian name, I take it."

"No," Mr. Tweed said. "Quite the opposite of a Christian name, actually, with a christening I have no doubt would shock a priest. Deliver this letter to him."

"Yes, sir. When?"

"Tonight."

"Tonight?"

"Yes. Can you do it?"

"Of course, Mr. Tweed."

"Capital man!" Mr. Tweed said. "And now I'll be off and hope Mrs. Tweed isn't too put out. I'd like to have a word with your daughter before I leave."

"Of course, Mr. Tweed."

Eliza didn't know what Mr. Tweed could want with her, but she scrambled as quietly as she could from her eavesdropping spot and rushed to the front hall, walking as if she just happened to be passing through as the library door opened.

"Ah, Eliza," Mr. Tweed said. "I was just telling your father I'd like a word with you."

"Of course, Mr. Tweed," Eliza said.

"At Tammany we've received word there might be trouble on the streets tomorrow. It's why Misters Connolly and Hall and Sweeny were here tonight."

"What kind of trouble?" Eliza asked.

"It's Lincoln's damnable draft," Mr. Tweed said. "The first drawing of names is set for tomorrow. There will be protests, surely. But we fully expect they'll turn violent. It's best you stay off the streets beginning tomorrow morning."

"As you wish, Mr. Tweed. But surely—"

"People of your countenance won't be safe, Eliza." Mr. Tweed looked hard into her eyes. "Anger is a hot coal, and when the people get angry, they need a place to lay it by. There are many who blame those of your race for the current situation. Please, heed me and stay off the streets. You will be safe in this house."

Eliza bowed her head. "I will, Mr. Tweed."

"I'm sorry to be so crude, but there it is." He walked to the front door, and took his hat and cane from the rack near the entry. "You know I bear no ill will to any race or religion. I look at a man, and I see one thing. Do you know what that is?"

"What, sir?"

"A potential voter." Mr. Tweed opened the front door. "If Congress saw fit to give the vote to dogs I'd lead the march against cats myself and chair the committee for flea eradication. Good night."

Eliza had to wonder if Mr. Tweed believed it more likely that dogs would vote than blacks or women. "Good night, sir."

Eliza's father saw Mr. Tweed through the door and down to the street where he helped him squeeze into his carriage. After it had set off down the road, her father returned and handed Eliza the key to the house.

"Lock up behind me."

"Father, don't go."

"Go?" Eliza's father asked, and then looked at her sideways. "Were you listening in, again?"

"I couldn't help it. I worry."

"What about? Me?"

Eliza bowed her head. She had already lost her mother, and that wound could still open fresh and raw at times. She couldn't imagine her life if she lost him, too.

"Eliza," he said. "I survived weeks in the swamps hiding from bounty hunters. I traveled hundreds of miles, and I hid in attics and cellars for days without light or air or end in sight. I've seen horrors that you never will, but for the grace of God Almighty and a Union victory for President Lincoln." He took her by the shoulders and kissed her forehead. "I believe I can safely cross town to deliver a letter, even to a pirate's den like the Hole-in-the-Wall."

"Be careful," she said.

"I will. I shouldn't be more than a couple of hours. Lock the door, but wait up and listen for me when I come back. I don't much like the idea of spending the night outside on the stoop."

"Yes, Father."

He left through the front door and nodded to her from the sidewalk, waiting for Eliza to shut the door and lock it with the key he'd given her. Once she'd done that, she went and finished cleaning up the dining room. She took the tablecloth to the laundry, and then she went to work polishing the silver Margaret's scrubber had already washed, which was something she could do for her father.

Before long she had the house sorted, and would have ordinarily gone up to bed, as Margaret had. But Eliza had to wait up, and couldn't have slept anyway until she knew her father was home. She decided to find a book in the library to read. Mr. Tweed had never specifically forbidden that, so she cautiously walked into the room and looked at the shelves, the scents of tobacco and leather all around her.

The volumes there were remarkably barren of anything interesting, but then, this wasn't Mr. Tweed's primary residence, or even a true residence at all. He had a bedroom furnished upstairs, but had never slept in it that Eliza knew.

She crossed the room to his desk, a vast slab of richly stained and polished wood, which bore a carved square cross at each of the corners. The expanse of the desk held a variety of items, including a sheaf of paper, likely the same paper on which Mr. Tweed had written the letter Eliza's father had gone to deliver. She wondered what could possibly be so important that her father needed to deliver it that night, on the eve of an upheaval. What was worth putting him in danger?

She reached for the topmost sheet of paper, and looked at it closely. Mr. Tweed's heavy hand had left a ghostly trail of his writing behind. But somehow, Eliza didn't need to strain to see it, a peculiar ability she had at times. It was as though the message emitted a subtle radiance that she sensed as much as she saw, and what she read there chilled her.

Master Cormac,

It has come to the attention of the Order that an Assassin has infiltrated the City of New York. His name is Varius, and we know his purpose takes him to the Astor House this night. We do not know what he seeks there, but it must be something of tremendous worth to the Brotherhood for them to risk such an incursion at this volatile time. You must find the Assassin and stop him. Do not hesitate to kill him. I trust your particular discretion in the matter. Bring whatever he carries to my home on 36th Street tomorrow evening. I will come to you there when I can, but I must first be seen by the public meeting my obligations to the mayor and Aldermen.

Nothing can be allowed to disrupt our plans. Tomorrow the city will burn, sweeping away Opdyke and Governor Seymour. The city and the state will then belong to Tammany and the Order, and with New York as our fulcrum we will tip the balance of this war and take back the nation. You have your quarry. Hunt him down.

~ the Grand Master

Eliza stared at the letter, which seemed to burn in her trembling hands. She didn't understand much of what it meant, but she knew it represented something of powerful and merciless intent, and that Mr. Tweed was not what he seemed. This letter went beyond politics and votes to something far larger and more dangerous, and she knew it meant destruction for the city and even beyond if it reached its destination. It was a letter her father must not deliver.

But over Eliza's shoulder, Grace thought she knew what the letter meant. The mention of the Astor House and something of tremendous worth had to mean the Piece of Eden. This was what they had come into the Animus searching for. Grace fought the desynchronizing impulse to take control back from Eliza and do what she had come to do. But Grace didn't have to struggle long, for a moment later, Eliza rose from the desk and rushed out into the main hall.

She doubted she would catch her father in time, but she had to try. She took a scarf from the hat rack to cover her hair, unlocked the door, and stepped out into the night.

CHAPTER TEN

Javier knew it was a different kind of night at the Hole-in-the-Wall, with work to be done before dawn. So far the noses had all come back reporting the city pigs, beaks, and bandogs were none the wiser for the hellfire sure to rain down on them the morrow. The ward bosses all knew something was afoot, but they also knew they were to look the other way. Tweed had made sure of that.

"Cudgel," Gallus Mag whispered right into his ear. "You baptizing that liquor?"

"I am," Cudgel said.

"Why water it down? We running low?"

"No. But we need everyone's wits about them come morning. Won't do us any good if they're all still half-hockey and sleeping it off."

Gallus Mag leaned away, nodding, and then strode off. She was as tall as Cudgel, and wore trousers with suspenders to hold them up, a pistol, and a sock full of wet sand hanging from her belt in case she needed to knock anyone about. But she wouldn't need that weapon tonight.

All day long, coves had come and gone with messages under the white flag of truce. Here and elsewhere in the city, the leaders of the gangs coordinated the next day's mayhem. The Bowery Boys, the Roach Guards, the Daybreak Boys, and the lesser ones, they'd all put aside their enmity for the chance to win a far bigger prize. If successful at their enterprise, they would soon own the whole damn city, to be carved up and portioned out after the kill.

A customer slapped his three cents on the counter and nodded toward the barrel up on the shelf behind the bar. "No glass," he said.

Cudgel nodded and offered him the end of the rubber hose. After the man had taken it between his teeth and given the nod, Cudgel turned the valve on the barrel, dispensing the cheapest blue ruin the Hole-in-the-Wall had to offer. Then he watched as the man sucked and swallowed and sucked until he had to stop to take a breath, and Cudgel cut off the supply. He'd learned to spot the wide-eyed, red-faced look of a man about to gasp, and he could turn the valve at just the right moment to avoid spilling a drop.

The man wiped his mouth with the sleeve of his jacket and teetered. Cudgel didn't know him, and didn't expect he'd be much use the next day, drunk or not.

"Have another?" Cudgel asked. "Got the brass?"

The man shook his head. "That'll fix me."

Cudgel nodded and pulled the hose back, coiling it next to Gallus Mag's jar of pickled human ears. Some she'd ripped off, some she'd sliced off, but most she'd just done with her teeth, and they sat there in that jar on the shelf as a trophy and a warning to anyone thinking of causing mischief in her place. Sadie the Goat had run afoul of Gallus Mag and left the evidence of that brawl behind. Somewhere in that ruddy brew was the ear of a man who'd simply asked Mag her age.

A few more riverfront blokes walked in, and Cudgel gave them a nod to the rear of the place where assignments were being handed out. The key to victory would be simultaneous attacks. With the city's regiments still away in Pennsylvania, the only force remaining was the Metropolitan Police, and their numbers could be quickly overwhelmed if divided by multiplied points of assault.

A brash old black man then walked through the door, wearing a servant's overcoat. Some in the saloon took note of him, and Gallus Mag moved to intervene if necessary. The man, white-haired and a little bent in the back, confidently scanned the room and then walked over to the bar.

Behind the line of Cudgel's mind, Javier recognized him from the Memory Corridor as David's ancestor, and wondered if David also recognized him, but didn't want to risk desynchronization by saying something in the crowded bar.

"I'm looking for Cudgel Cormac," the servant said.

"Who are you?" Cudgel asked.

"My name is Abraham," the man said. "I work for Mr. William Tweed."

Cudgel hadn't seen the Grand Master in person for weeks. It was too risky to the plan. Tweed and Tammany had to be in a position to *end* the riots, not be seen as their agitator, if the scheme were to work.

"I'm Cudgel Cormac," he said.

Abraham pulled a letter out of an inner pocket of his benjamin. "Mr. Tweed asked me to deliver this to you."

Cudgel accepted the letter, and Abraham turned to leave. "Wait," Cudgel said, "until I've read it." There were often orders having to do with the messenger.

Abraham nodded and stood at the bar.

Cudgel broke the envelope's wax seal, imprinted with the Templar cross, and pulled out the letter. As he read it, the pounding of his blood swelled in his ears, a drumbeat calling him to war.

His grandfather, Shay Patrick Cormac, had been a formidable Assassin hunter, and this night Cudgel was called to walk that path and honor that legacy. Varius would submit to the Templar Order or die by Cudgel's hand.

"Will that be all, sir?" Abraham asked.

Cudgel held up the letter. "Mr. Tweed trusts you."

"I try to be worthy of that trust."

"Good," Cudgel said. "In return, I mean to make sure you have safe passage home."

"I can make my own way," Abraham said.

"I'm sure of it," Cudgel said. "But that doesn't change my mind." He cupped a palm to his mouth. "Gallus Mag!"

"What is it?" she called back from across the room.

"Boss wants me," Cudgel said.

She nodded toward the door. "Go on with you, then."

Cudgel removed his apron and came out from around the bar. "Wait here."

Abraham nodded, and Cudgel went down to the saloon's cellar to equip himself. First, he strapped on a few pieces of rigid hide armor, one around his neck, and the others across his back and chest. Then he pulled on his long leather coat, and belted on several knives, knuckledusters, and a pistol. He took his Herschel spyglass, and then he slung his air rifle over his shoulder, along with its bandolier of darts and grenades. The rifle was an ingenious weapon that had come down to Cudgel from his grandfather, given to him by Benjamin Franklin, and he carried it with pride.

Javier appreciated being in a younger body this time. Chimalpopoca had carried the aches of his old age, which had been a strange experience. His attraction to that translator, Marina, had likewise been strange. Cudgel liked women, too, but the only thing that ached for him were the many injuries he'd sustained training and brawling.

Back upstairs, his armed appearance seemed to startle Abraham for a moment as Cudgel stalked past him and said, "Let's go."

He led Abraham from the saloon out into the streets. Gang runners marched and hustled up and down the sidewalks, some of them pushing wheelbarrows full of brickbats and paving stones down the road, arming up for the battle. Cudgel walked Abraham a block west on Dover to Pearl Street, and there he saw Skinny Joe with his wagon and whistled him over.

"I want you to see this man home," Cudgel said.

Skinny Joe stared at Abraham. "Him?"

"He's Boss Tweed's man," Cudgel said. "You got a problem?"

"Sir, I truly can make my own way," Abraham said, but Cudgel ignored him.

Skinny Joe shrugged. "No problem. If he's the Boss's man."

"Good." Cudgel opposed slavery, and had nothing against the black residents of the city himself. They weren't the problem. But he knew it'd be a devil's day for them tomorrow. The Grand Master opposed slavery, as well. He said it was an unsustainable system that stifled progress. But he was willing to use the question of abolition to drive a wedge deep into the country to split it open so it could be put back together in the right way. "Take him wherever he wants to go," Cudgel ordered Skinny Joe. "See he gets there unharmed."

Abraham climbed up into the wagon, and Skinny Joe flicked his horses onward up Pearl Street. After they'd rounded the bend and passed out of sight, Cudgel turned to the rest of his task.

The Astor House was half a mile and a world away from the Hole-in-the-Wall. It was a place where the women sparked with jewels like an ironworks, and the men drank from crystal instead of a rubber hose. Cudgel had once glimpsed the menu for the gentlemen's ordinary, a six-course feast of soup, fish, boiled roast, entree, pastry, and dessert, served nightly in a room lined with marble pillars and white tables. It existed unperturbed by the denizens of the Fourth Ward because Tweed needed the money of the rich just as he needed the muscle of the gangs. Order kept the city in balance.

But sometimes a correction was needed.

From Pearl Street, Cudgel followed Frankfort west, past Tammany Hall, until he reached City Hall Park and the tracks of the Harlem Railroad. Part of the strategy for the next day involved tearing up the railways at strategic points to prevent the rapid transit of patrolmen or weapons. That, and the cutting of the telegraph lines, would give the mob all the advantage it needed to take the island.

Cudgel could see Astor House rising up over the trees like a white fortress near the southern tip of the park, where Park Row met Broadway, the spire of St. Paul's Chapel just south of it. Here, he decided to employ the stealth training he'd received from his grandfather and father, and went up, scaling the nearest wall using cracks and ledges and drainpipes, until he reached the roof. Such running was a traditional Assassin skill, but the Cormacs had long used the Brotherhood's tactics against them.

Cudgel then crossed Spruce and then Beekman, leaping along the rooftops, skirting chimneys and skimming peaks, scattering surprised birds from their roosts, the city below him, the night sky above him. When he reached Ann Street and Broadway, directly across from the chapel and the hotel, he paused and took a sentry position to watch the ground below.

Varius wouldn't use the hotel's front entrance any more than Cudgel would, so he kept his eye on the windows and the roof, but after waiting and watching for an hour, he saw no sign of the Assassin.

Cudgel decided he needed a different, better vantage, so he descended to the street, crossed Broadway, and passed by the four columns at the front of St. Paul's Chapel. He then scaled the church using the quoining at the southwest corner, and climbed the clock tower to its pinnacle, just as an Assassin might do.

At one time, this church spire was the highest point on the island. But now there were other churches visible in the distance, St. Mark's and Trinity, stabbing upward through the flesh of the city like knives.

Cudgel now had a commanding view of Astor House, and more time passed without sign of the Assassin, and though the night deepened, the city stayed awake, quivering in anticipation.

Then Cudgel saw him. He came from the west, over Church Street, and scaled the hotel with ease. He was out of range for the air rifle, so Cudgel simply watched him for several moments, not wanting to move and give away his location, instead smirking and reveling in the advantage he enjoyed. Varius wore the long frock coat of a Bowery Boy, though he'd left the beaver top hat behind. It made sense he'd be a Bowery Boy, as they'd thrown their allegiance behind the Republicans, against Tammany and the Templars.

Javier had thus far let Cudgel lead the charge through his memories, but he recognized the clothing Owen's ancestor had been wearing. A part of Javier wanted to call out, but as with David back at the Hole-in-the-Wall, that carried the risk of desynchronization.

Owen's Assassin appeared to know exactly where he was going, and once he achieved the hotel roof, he skirted along its edge to a particular point, and then climbed over the ledge. He then descended, spiderlike, to a certain darkened window, and climbed through it.

Cudgel wondered what it was the Assassin sought within the hotel. As the Grand Master had said, it had to be something of tremendous worth. It could be an object, or perhaps a piece of information. The first would be easy enough to extract, but the latter would be more enjoyable. First, he'd anoint the bloke with his fists, and failing that, he'd acquaint him with his knives.

But behind the line, Javier already knew what it was that Varius was after, or at least, what he hoped it was.

The dagger. The Piece of Eden.

That's why Javier had been letting Cudgel run the show. As soon as they'd read the letter from the Grand Master, Javier had known this was what Monroe had sent the six of them into the Animus to find.

Cudgel moved, and Javier retreated again as the Templar's mind seized control and descended from the church's tower. He crossed the darkened mouth of the churchyard, with its tombstone teeth, and crouched behind a tree to wait. He had a clear shot at the window, and he readied his rifle with a sleep dart. It was possible the fall could kill the Assassin, but it was a chance Cudgel was willing to take. He had a notion it was an object the Assassin was after, which could be recovered all the more easily from a corpse.

A few stifling moments went by, with nary a wind through the tree branches overhead. A mosquito needled the back of Cudgel's neck, behind his ear, but he never took his eyes from the window.

When at last the Assassin's long frock coat billowed outward from the shadows, Cudgel waited until the man seemed poised to climb back up to the roof, and then he fired. The air rifle popped, the dart hissed, but when it struck the coat, the fabric folded inward like a broken eggshell before whipping back into the hotel.

Cudgel had fallen for a decoy.

He cursed himself as he slung his rifle back over his shoulder, then scrambled up the tree and vaulted over the church's fence into Vesey Street. He landed in a roll and raced up the hotel's face to the window, but hung from the sill before entering. The Assassin was no doubt lying in wait for him.

He let go one of his hands, dangling from the ledge by the other, and pulled a smoke grenade from his belt, which he tossed through the open window. It exploded with a muffled bang, and Cudgel heaved himself up and through the opening.

He landed on thick carpet and dodged away from the window, out of the smoke cloud, but he knew instantly he was alone. Either the Assassin had already fled, or the smoke grenade had driven him from the room. Either way, Cudgel had to find him.

He skulked forward, the only light that which the windows and cambric curtains admitted. The carpet was Turkish, the room well-appointed with armchairs and a table and a desk, but so far no clue as to who used it. There were two doorways, the one to his left standing open, and Cudgel went that way.

He armed himself with two knives, one in each hand, both in plain sight to match the Assassin's weapon of choice, the hidden blade. When he reached the doorway, he stopped to listen, and hearing nothing on the other side, not a breath or a heartbeat, he charged through, only to find another vacant but richly appointed room. Over the mantel of the fireplace hung an emblem, a military cross, with the words CITY OF MEXICO ARMY OF OCCUPATION printed on a circle at its center.

These rooms belonged to the Aztec Club, which the Grand Master had once suspected of being linked to the Brotherhood. But then why would Varius break into the offices of his allies?

Cudgel proceeded through the next doorway straight ahead, blades at the ready, and reached what appeared to be the suite's marbled main entry. Another door stood open to the right, which led into a dining room, and from there Cudgel entered a library, all with no sign of the Assassin. The library's second doorway led him back to the very first room, but he instantly realized its door had been closed when he'd first come through the window.

The Assassin had circled him.

Cudgel raced to the window, looked down into the empty street, and then looked up in time to see the Assassin's coat flap over the ledge to the roof.

He sheathed his knives and climbed out after him, then scaled the hotel wall. Up on the roof, Cudgel ducked and waited. No building stood close enough for a leap, which meant the Assassin was up there, somewhere, hiding among the labyrinth of chimneys and skylights.

"I don't know what's stirring in that idea pot of yours!" Cudgel said, his voice echoing over the roof. "But you're no match for me! My grandfather hunted down Assassins like you! He bested some of the greatest among you!"

A moment of silence followed.

He heard the sharp whistle of a blade flying toward him, and dropped to the ground just before it scalped him. The knife sailed off the roof, down into the street.

"Your grandfather was an Assassin once," came a reply. The voice seemed to be reaching toward Cudgel from somewhere off to the right. "He turned on the Brotherhood and the Creed he'd sworn to uphold! He was nothing but a coward and a traitor!"

"Never a traitor to the truth! He never betrayed the Templar Order!" Cudgel readied his rifle with another sleep dart. "And he taught me how to kill vermin like you."

Cudgel knew the Assassin could make his voice seem as though it came from somewhere else, so he closed his eyes, stilled his breathing, and listened for other signs. When he heard the rustle of fabric to his left, he swiveled his rifle toward the sound, eyes still closed, guided by his ears and an inner sight. He fired.

He opened his eyes when he heard a grunt, and then raced toward the ledge as the Assassin went over.

CHAPTER ELEVEN

Tommy walked up Broadway toward the brownstone where he'd been living since coming home from the war. The house, a newly built and fashionable building off Madison Park, belonged to his wealthy older brother and his wife. They had no children, and plenty of room, and they had generously allowed him to remain there even after the term of his convalescence. But he hoped he wouldn't be pressing their indulgence for much longer. It wasn't that he didn't enjoy their presence. But they didn't have any understanding of what Tommy had been through in the war. At times it seemed there wasn't another soul in the entire city who understood. He felt alone, even in company with others. Especially in company with others, a familiar current of experience that Sean understood very well, even as he enjoyed the use of Tommy's legs.

He was still in his police uniform, having just got off his patrol, and his presence on the street seemed to be having a different than usual effect on the attitudes of his fellow pedestrians. They eyed him sidelong, and though they kept their distance, they were of a confident and hostile character.

He saw Bowery Boys and Roach Guards, both well outside their territories downtown. They stalked up the street alongside one another, ignoring their sworn enemies with grim determination. They carried armloads of clubs and brickbats, axes and lengths of iron bar.

Something was amiss.

"Where you boys going with that?" Tommy asked a nearby bloke who had the Irish look of the Five Points about him.

"I'll answer ya tomorrow." The man wore a smirk that was half-snarl. "That's an oath." And he walked on.

Tommy could have detained the man until he achieved the truth, but it was late, he was off patrol and alone, and the streets were full of the man's allies tonight. So Tommy kept on his own path toward home.

His older brother had done well for himself in manufacturing, and while Tommy had gone off to war, his brother had made money selling the very equipment Tommy and his fellow Union soldiers used in the field. Much of it had been useless on arrival; boots that fell apart in the rain, rations already spoiled in their tins. His brother had claimed ignorance of these defects, as well as a desire to make amends, and Tommy wanted to believe him sincere.

He'd just reached Union Square and passed the high statue of George Washington astride his horse when he heard a woman's scream, calling for help up ahead. Tommy unhooked his locust club from his belt and broke into a run, north through the park, and, deep within the current of that memory, Sean thrilled at the rush of it, the wind through his hair, the pounding of his boots on the gravel path.

When Tommy reached the far side, he saw a carriage pulled over on Broadway. Two ruffians stood outside it, while another's legs protruded from the open door. The driver sat by as if nothing was taking place, which meant he was clearly in on the robbery. Other pedestrians had cleared out.

"Stop!" Tommy bellowed, brandishing his locust club. "Police!"

"Sykes, we got a crusher!" one of the watchers said, and the two outside the carriage turned to face Tommy, one armed with a club of his own, the other with a meat cleaver.

Tommy slowed to a walk some yards away, where he swung his locust club a few times through the air to loosen his arm.

"Christ, he's a giant, ain't he?" the first said to the other. "But they fall the hardest."

"You think you can fell me?" Tommy said. "You're welcome to try, boys. I'm with Broadway Squad."

Upon hearing that, the two balked visibly, shifting from foot to foot. The man within the carriage then withdrew from the vehicle and strode up between his two compatriots, his leaking nose clearly broken. A woman peered out from within the carriage behind them, her hair somewhat disheveled, but seeming otherwise unharmed. Even tossed about by the memory, Sean recognized Natalya's singer ancestor.

"I hear it takes at least five coves to bring down a pig from the Broadway Squad." The leader slipped on a knuckleduster studded with nails. "I bet we can do it with three."

"I wouldn't take that wager, boys," Tommy said, spreading his stance.

The three of them rushed him at once. Tommy ducked the cleaver, and the wide arc of his locust club caught the other two with the same swing, one in the arm, the other in the ribs. They fell back, and Tommy buried his fist in the mouth of the man with the cleaver, breaking teeth. That cove went down in a heap, while the other two came again.

Tommy dodged the knuckleduster, but at the cost of a blow to his shoulder from the club, which only staggered him without doing serious damage. He rallied and returned with a fusillade from his own stick that cracked the man's weapon in half and rendered his arm useless. Then Tommy turned as the other came in, and he smashed the hand wearing the knuckleduster. The nails the bloke had thought so deadly ended up mingled with the bones of his hand. Both men rolled on the ground, cradling their wounds and moaning.

"Look out!" the woman cried.

Tommy spun around just as the one with the ruined mouth was about to hurl the cleaver at him from the ground, but, before the weapon left his hand, the woman leapt from the carriage and bashed his head to the pavement with a very heavy-looking leather case. His body crumpled.

The driver, no doubt stunned by the reversal of his fortunes, whipped his horses into a gallop, barreling away up Broadway.

"What do you have inside that case?" Tommy asked.

"Several pounds of gold," she replied, breathing heavily. She was a beautiful woman, and more petite than Tommy would have thought after rendering a blow like that. "And fortunately, gold is heavy," she said, smiling.

"Truly?" he said. "What are you doing with several pounds of gold? At this time of night? Unaccompanied?"

"Why?" she asked. "Are you about to suggest it was my fault I was attacked?"

"Well, it seems that—"

"It seems that if you are going to blame the victim for the crime, then you might also be a man who would blame this horrendous heat on the thermometer, which is a very curious civic position for a policeman to take."

Tommy opened his mouth, then closed it and fought the smile attempting to break through. "Perhaps you are right."

"Of course I'm right," she said.

"But I think we ought to carry this discussion elsewhere." He tapped one of the groaning ruffians with his boot. "Allow me to escort you home?"

"You're not going to arrest them?"

"A judge won't teach them anything more valuable than the lesson I've just given them. Class is dismissed."

She nodded. "Very well, then I would very much appreciate an escort. You're not injured?"

"Just a bruise or two." He picked up her case of gold. "What is the address?"

"The Fifth Avenue Hotel," she said. "Not far from here, actually."

Tommy extended his hand to gesture her ahead, and they set off up Broadway, walking close to each other, though he towered over her small frame. "You look familiar to me," he said. "But I can't decide how."

"Oh, well, my face appears on posters from time to time."

Her face was certainly pretty enough for a poster, but he

wondered why she would be so advertised. Then he realized. "Oh, that's it," he said. "You're a singer."

"I am."

"What is your name, if I may ask?"

"Adelina Patti. And you are?"

"Tommy Greyling," he said. "At your service."

"Clearly," she said. "But in all things, I wonder?"

The flirtatious way she asked it roused heat in his cheeks. He hefted the leather case. "Miss Patti, do you often carry several pounds of gold about your person?"

"Only when I have been paid for a performance."

"You sang tonight?" he asked. "Where?"

"Niblo's," she said.

That was a theater for the swells, the kind of place Tommy's brother and his wife attended on occasion. The only theater Tommy had been to was the Bowery for a bloody melodrama he hadn't much enjoyed. "The Metropolitan Hotel is right next door to Niblo's. But you chose not to stay there?"

"The Fifth Avenue Hotel is much finer," she said. "Did you know it has a vertical screw railroad?"

"Pardon, miss?"

"An elevator," she said. "Driven by steam. It whisks you from the ground floor to the top. And also, Jenny Lind stayed at the Fifth Avenue."

"Who is Jenny Lind?"

"You do not know your singers, do you? She has an exquisite voice, and is older than me by several years. But you see, I can't have a reputation for staying in lesser hotels than she, or else theater managers might think me a lesser singer. What I do is only half talent. The rest is careful illusion."

Tommy shook his head. "Yours is a foreign world to me, miss."

"As is your world to me. Have you always been a policeman?"

"No, miss." Tommy hesitated to go further. Doing so turned his mind into a dangerous, chaotic place where the present and the past intermingled. Memories of war overwhelmed him, the acrid scent of gunpowder so thick in the air he couldn't see ten yards in any direction, the ghastly howl of the Rebel yell, the feeling of something underfoot he knew, without looking, to be someone's limb torn from their body. But she made him feel as though he would be safe to venture there. "Before this, I was a soldier."

"Were you really?"

"I was."

"And you fought? In the war with the Confederates?" But then she waved her hands before her. "Forgive me. You would probably rather not speak of it."

"No, it's all right," he said. "Though it's true I don't speak of it often. I did fight in the war. I'd be there still if I hadn't been shot—"

She gasped. "You were shot?"

"I was." He tapped his trouser leg directly over the puckered crater of a scar in his thigh. "But the bullet missed the bone, so I got to keep my leg. Many, many other men weren't so fortunate. And I fear many more will be unfortunate, still."

"You're referring to the draft?"

He nodded. "It has set the city in turmoil." But it wasn't just that. Both sides, the Union and the Rebels, looked to any success, no matter how minor, as a sign of hope that victory was nigh, but Tommy feared the conflict would yet go on for years.

Even with the recent victory at Gettysburg, Lee and the army of the South would not stay in Virginia for long.

"I live in London now," Miss Patti said. "It is better for my career, since I tour Europe often. But it distances me from the events going on here."

"Do you enjoy touring?" he asked, glad for a change in the subject of conversation.

"At times, yes," she said. "But it can be lonely. I am surrounded by people so much of the time, and yet I am alone. Isn't that ridiculous?"

"Not to me," Tommy said.

She looked up at him, studying him to the point where he felt another awkward flush in his cheeks. "No, not to you," she said. "You understand, I think, when few people do."

They reached the park at Madison Square, and there was her hotel, five stories tall, skirted with fancy shops long closed for the night. Tommy walked a few paces toward it, but realized Miss Patti had stalled in the sidewalk. He turned back toward her. "Is there something wrong, miss?"

"Would you like to take a walk with me in the park?" she asked, and then laughed, seeming self-conscious. "I know that seems absurd at this hour. But I am wide awake after all the excitement. And I enjoy your company."

Tommy swallowed. He was technically off duty, and though others might see impropriety in her request, he didn't care. Somehow, she set his mind at ease, and made it safe for his thoughts to go places he ordinarily forbade them. "I enjoy your company as well, miss," Tommy said.

"Call me Adelina," she said. "Then will you walk with me?"

"I'd be honored, Miss Adelina."

The currents of this simulation had so far swept Sean to places that thrilled him, and he'd been content to just let it carry him. He liked being Tommy Greyling, walking tall and charging into a brawl. However, he was becoming increasingly aware of a romantic direction for this memory, and aware that it was Natalya on the other side of it. He was attracted to her, and he thought maybe their experience here in the Animus would help her look past the wheelchair once they left the simulation, but thinking about that also made it a bit more of a challenge to relax into the flow of the memory.

They entered the park, and Miss Patti said, "There's a place like this near my home in London. I sometimes walk there late at night."

"Why late at night?" Tommy asked.

"The silence," she said. "No audience. No social gathering. Not even my own voice."

"I'll try not to disturb the silence, then," Tommy said.

"You are not a disturbance."

Yet, for the next few moments, neither of them spoke. They simply strolled along one of the park's paths, the oak and birch and sycamore trees perfectly still, as though the night's warmth had cured and set the air. The stars above them had to contend with the light from the hotel and the streetlamps to be seen. Not far from here stood Tommy's brother's house. At one point, he mentioned that, and then they talked about their families and their childhoods, which were very different from each other. She'd been born in Spain to Italian parents, who had then come to New York when she was a small girl. He'd been born in Brooklyn, his grandparents having come from Germany shortly after their marriage. The two of them strolled for hours, through the night, walking the same paths over and over again.

As the first blush of dawn appeared over the trees and buildings to the east of the park, Miss Patti announced she was feeling tired and sat down on a park bench. She laid her palm over the place next to her. "Come. Sit with me."

Tommy nodded and sat, resting the leather case on the ground. "Forgive me if this is a rude question, but do you always earn that much for a performance?"

"Always," she said. "Without exception."

"How much is in here?"

"Four thousand dollars in gold," she said without hesitation. "Another thousand in cash."

Tommy looked again at the case. "That's . . ." But he could only shake his head. There was far more in that case than Tommy had earned for his entire service to the army, and that seemed somehow right and wrong at the same time. "Good for you," he said.

She frowned, and in the night shadows of the trees, it seemed exaggerated. "I won't apologize for it."

"I'm not asking you to."

"But I can see your disapproval."

"I don't disapprove," he said. "You have a right to charge whatever amount people are willing to pay. If I disapprove of anything, it's the people."

Her expression relaxed. "You haven't heard me sing." She smoothed her dress across her lap. "But I take your point."

"I made no point."

"Yes, you did. I tell myself I am doing something of consequence with my music." She looked down at Tommy's leg. "But a single bullet costs pennies, and is of far greater consequence than all my songs combined."

"It's always cheaper to destroy something."

"What is war like?" she asked. "I feel I ought to know."

Tommy admired her intention and sincerity. There was integrity in her question, even if its naivety left him struggling to find an answer. "I signed on with the Fourteenth Regiment out of Brooklyn. It was the first battle of Bull Run. The Rebels had a spot of high ground called Spring Hill, and we were ordered to take it from them. But they were dug in, and they had more guns. We charged several times, and suffered heavy casualties. Their howitzers tore us to shreds." Tommy had to stop for a moment to keep himself from getting mired in the memory of the carnage. He cleared his throat. "Henry Hill got its name from the family who lived there. A doctor, I guess. He was deceased, but his widow still lived in their house on the hill, right in the middle of the battle. She was in her eighties. An invalid, confined to her bed."

Miss Patti covered her mouth. "She was in the house?"

Tommy nodded. "A captain over one of our batteries, Ricketts, thought we were taking fire from the house, so he turned his guns on it. Blew it to hell with artillery shells. Mrs. Henry was—" He stopped himself, unsure of how much detail to give her.

But Miss Patti laid a small, warm hand over his and squeezed it firmly. "Please, tell me."

"She—she was injured quite severely. I remember one of her feet was almost torn off. She died later that day. There were no Rebels in her house. She was just a lonely old widow. And we killed her." Tommy's voice went hoarse, nearly breaking over the groundswell of his buried remorse. "That's what war is like, Miss Adelina. I can only answer your question with that story, and countless stories like it. War sounds big, but it's writ small, and every life and every death matters."

Only crickets filled the silence that followed.

"Thank you for telling me," she said, her voice almost a whisper. She looked down at the leather case. "What would you do with the money in that case?"

Tommy did not want to answer that. He suspected she was about to give it to him, moved by his story to a concern for her fellow men. But that wasn't why he'd told her, and he didn't want that responsibility, nor her pity. "I'd gamble it away at faro," he said.

"You would not," she said. "Please answer me truthfully."

"Truthfully?" He shifted a little on the bench. "There were men I came home with who're in a far worse state than me. They've lost legs or arms or both. They can't work, and their families are struggling. Some of them are in desperate circumstances. I'd use the money to help them."

She nodded once, emphatically. "I want you to have it. I want you to do just that with it."

"Miss Adelina, I—"

"Please, just Adelina."

"Adelina," he said. "That is very generous of you. But . . ."

"But what?"

He looked into her eyes, and had no doubt of her complete sincerity. None of the objections in his mind seemed worth the injury of failing to honor her intent. "Nothing," he said. "Thank you. It is truly remarkable and good of you."

"It is nothing," she said. "If I could I would—"

A commotion at the southwest corner of the park cut her off. Tommy stood as a boisterous mob of men and women surged north along Broadway, heading uptown. They carried weapons with them—pitchforks, clubs, axes, and knives—and bore signs with the words NO DRAFT painted in crude lettering. The column took a full minute to pass, numbering over a hundred.

"Where are they going?" Adelina whispered.

"Looks like a protest," Tommy said, but he knew the situation was direr than that. All the street activity of the previous night made sense to him now, as did the Five Pointer's oath—*I'll answer ya tomorrow.*

Whatever was happening, it was well planned. Even more alarming, it had managed to bring all the gangs of the Bowery, the Five Points, and the Fourth Ward together under a common banner, with a common enemy.

"There's going to be a riot," Tommy said, and by all signs it would be perhaps the worst the city had seen.

"Won't the army put it down?"

"There is no army," Tommy said. "Every regiment in the city was called to Pennsylvania. The police are all that's left."

"Dear God," Adelina said.

Every patrolman would be needed; Tommy had no doubt of that. But there was something he had to do first. "I need to get you somewhere safe," he said.

CHAPTER TWELVE

Varius sat alone at a table in the Atlantic Gardens beer hall, his drink untouched, the crowd around him unusually subdued. No one paid any mind to the piano player or the dancers, instead given over to serious discussion and planning.

He had tried to keep the Bowery Boys from taking part in the coming riot, but he had failed. His influence over Reddy the Blacksmith, their leader, had its limit, and in the end the gangs of the Bowery had formed an unlikely and uneasy alliance with the men from Five Points and the waterfront pirates, in common cause against the draft.

That development had altered the Brotherhood's agenda, and Varius now waited at the appointed rendezvous for new orders, though he wasn't yet sure in what manner they would arrive, nor how his failure would be dealt with.

Of the many possibilities he considered, none of them involved the Mentor himself, who now sauntered into the beer hall with his silver-tipped cane. Though he was a black man, in a city that hated blacks, the Mentor showed no sign of fear or submission, and Varius pitied anyone who would try to accost him. He wore a blue velvet coat the color of deep ocean, with a matching top hat over his shaved head, a gold Chinese coin hanging from a piercing in his left ear.

When he noticed Varius, he crossed the room and sat at his table.

"Mentor," Varius said quietly.

"Have you ever seen so many people so earnestly engaged in destroying themselves?" the Mentor asked.

"It isn't their fault," Varius said. "The Templars have been working for years through Tammany to bring this about."

"We should have seen it coming." The Mentor glanced around the beer hall. "We should have prevented it. *You* should have done something."

Varius had rebuked himself with those same words, but had never before heard them from another in the Brotherhood, let alone the Mentor. Shame bowed his head low. "I am sorry," he said. "May I ask what brings you from Washington?" For the Mentor to have come meant something far larger and more important than a riot was afoot. Varius wondered if he was to be removed.

The Mentor rose from the table. "Let's discuss this elsewhere."

Varius nodded and followed him from the beer hall out onto Bowery, where they both turned south. Coves streamed through the streets, in and out of their warrens and dens, doing their gang leaders' bidding, stockpiling weapons and delivering messages.

"A riot is messy but efficient," the Mentor said, the tip of his cane clicking against the paving stones. "I'll give them that."

"We have our hidden blades," Varius said. "The Templars have money and the mob."

"They tried something similar in Paris."

"This is different," Varius said. "The people here aren't raging against any nobility. It's one president and one policy they despise. If the city had called off the draft—"

"The Templars would have simply found another match to light the fire. The mob may be a crude weapon, but the Order wields it well."

They reached Number Forty-Two, the Bowery Boy clubhouse, but instead of going inside, Varius led the Mentor down a side alley to a cellar door. He unlocked it, and they descended a flight of flagstone steps to a narrow corridor. At the end of the hallway, they came to another locked door. When Varius inserted a special key and turned it a certain way, instead of unlocking the door, it opened a secret portal in the brick wall nearby. This doorway led them down another tunnel into Varius's lair.

"I don't think I've been here since your father's time," the Mentor said.

"He always spoke well of you," Varius said.

Within the chamber, thick timber posts supported a ceiling arched with ribs of stone, while gaslight sconces flickered around the room, their snakelike pipes exposed along the walls. There was a desk, and a bookshelf, and Varius's armory. The Mentor walked to the desk and leaned against it, half sitting, his arms spread wide with the heels of his palms pressing into the wood.

"New York will burn tomorrow," he said.

Varius stepped toward him. "Mentor, I can stop—"

He held up a hand. "No. You will let it happen. There isn't anything you can do to stop it now. This battle is already lost."

The room grew hotter, and Varius wiped the sweat from his brow. "How may I redeem myself?"

"There is nothing to redeem. This is not about you, Varius, nor your legacy, as noble as it is. We must shift our focus to winning the larger war."

"How?"

"A Piece of Eden."

At the mention of that term, Owen pressed himself against the weight of Varius's mind. Owen and the others had come into the Animus to find the relic, and it seemed his ancestor was about to be given the same task. He wondered if Monroe was listening and watching.

"An artifact?" Varius said. "You have one?"

"We know of one. Here in New York."

"Where is it?"

"The Aztec Club," the Mentor said. "In the Astor House. It is a dagger that once belonged to Hernán Cortés."

"If you knew about it," Varius said, "why have you never told me? Forgive me, but why have we left it there?"

"We have only recently confirmed its existence. The members of the Aztec Club are not aware of what they possess, or we might have discovered it sooner. They treat it superstitiously, as a kind of totem. They do not wield it as it was intended."

"What would you have me do?"

"You must steal it. Tonight. Get it out of the city and take it to General Grant in Mississippi. He is a member of the Aztec Club, so he will recognize it. You must impress upon him its importance, without revealing its true nature."

"Ulysses Grant?"

"Yes. With his capture of Vicksburg, we believe he is the best chance for a Union victory, and the strongest candidate to oppose General Lee. But Lincoln must believe in him. His troops must believe in him. The North must believe in him." The Mentor stepped away from the desk, toward Varius. "If the Confederacy wins, or even forces the negotiation of a treaty, the Templars could take control of the country. Do you understand?"

"I understand."

"Everything we've achieved. Everything my grandmother fought for in New Orleans. It will all be lost."

"I will not fail, Mentor."

The Mentor nodded. "I trust not, Varius. And if any oppose you, bring them peace."

"I will, Mentor."

"You are young, but you have great potential. You are your father's son, and the Brotherhood is with you."

The Mentor left then, returning Varius to the solitude to which he had become accustomed. His father's death had left him the only Assassin operating in New York City, something the Mentor had maintained so as to avoid attracting the attention of the Templars in Tammany Hall, leaving Varius with a legacy to honor. His father had successfully and almost single-handedly held the line and kept the Order at bay in the city.

This riot was Varius's failure, evidence of his shortcomings, burning by its own fuel and stoked by Tammany's political bellows.

Varius crossed the room toward the armory to equip himself. Though newer gauntlet designs had come into use in England, involving darts and rope launchers, Varius preferred the purity of a simple hidden blade, which he could easily conceal within the sleeve of his coat. He belted on a dozen throwing knives and a revolver, and pocketed a pair of knuckledusters. Then he grabbed his set of lock picks, but left his tall beaver hat behind.

Back out on the street, he followed Bayard west into what would normally have been enemy territory. But tonight, with the temporary truce, he took Baxter south, all the way to Paradise Square, the tough and vicious heart of Five Points. Here, the Roach Guards and all their affiliates concentrated their power, and though Varius drew stares and Irish curses passing through, no one challenged him. From there, he followed Worth Street west, across Broadway, and then turned south again onto Church Street.

Then he went up, scaling the walls until he reached the city rooftops, which he traversed soundlessly, leaping and running in agile, fluid movements. He crossed the next nine blocks in free run, until he crossed Barclay and arrived at the Astor House, the chapel of St. Paul's to the south. The church's clock tower rose up high into the heat of the night, and Varius almost wished he had need to climb it for the view. Instead, he focused on the hotel, extending his senses to locate the Aztec Club within it.

His Eagle Vision had never been as strong as he would have wished, but Varius never let that cause him to feel inferior to other Assassins in whom the gift was more powerful. He possessed enough of its sight to search for the Piece of Eden. Such an object would emit an undeniable radiance, if one knew how to look for it.

Varius focused on the building, the contours of its cold and lifeless stone shell encasing brick and mortar, timber and metal. He stared into the building's heart, straining until his eyes watered, reaching for the power of the relic.

Several moments went by. Then he detected it. A faint vibration, as though something was tugging at the fringe of the world's curtains. It was the Piece of Eden, and it rested on the fifth floor.

Varius shimmied down from his lofty perch to the street, crossed it, and then scaled the hotel walls to its rooftop. He then skirted along its ledge, each step bringing him closer to the relic he kept within reach of his senses, until he stood directly over it. From there, he climbed over the ledge and descended along the wall and found the window to the fifth floor open.

The room inside was dark, a thick Turkish rug beneath his feet. A table rested near the fireplace, surrounded by upholstered chairs, and a desk stood nearby. The Piece of Eden wasn't in that room, so Varius moved forward through a door to his left, guided by the compass of his Eagle Vision and the pulsing of the relic's energy.

The next room was larger than the first, with three tables, and chairs lining three of the walls. The fourth wall contained a large fireplace, and above it hung the crest of the Aztec Club. Mementos and souvenirs lined the mantel, and among the watches, pistols, and medals, Varius saw the dagger.

He crossed the room and took it down, feeling its power flow into his fingertips and up his arm. Its design was quite curious. It had no guard, and the blade curved slightly, with a sharp heel near the handle, almost like the prong of a harpoon. Its grip was bound in leather and gold wire, but the shape was flat, as though it was simply an extension of the blade that had been fashioned into a handle. The pommel was perhaps its most distinct feature, forming a kind of triangle, with sharp angles that suggested it was meant to fit together with something else. Varius concluded it wasn't a dagger at all, but a broken-off part of some larger weapon.

He pulled a length of silk out of his coat, wrapped the weapon carefully, and placed it in his pocket. He then turned back toward the room and the window through which he had entered. But as he approached it, he became aware of a sensation to which he'd been previously blind, so consumed was he with the energy of the Piece of Eden.

He had been detected.

But if the observer were someone from the hotel or a common passerby, they would have raised the alarm, crying housebreaker. Instead, his observer had remained silent, watching him.

That could be no ordinary person. Varius had to do something to draw his pursuer out into the open, to find out what he faced, for no chances could be taken with the Piece of Eden. He crept forward to the window, peering out from the shadows, and extended his Eagle Vision.

The person was down below, in the churchyard beneath the chapel of St. Paul's, waiting for him. Varius removed his coat and used his forearm to extend it from the window, as if he were about to exit and climb back up to the roof. The figure in the churchyard shot at him, and a breath later, a dart struck the fabric decoy.

Varius tucked the dart into a pocket, careful of the needle at its point, whipped the coat back inside and threw it on. The figure down there was a Templar, and not just an ordinary Templar, but a Hunter. Someone trained in the ways of the Assassin, an extremely formidable opponent. Varius had heard rumors of one in New York, and under different circumstances, he would have eagerly confronted the Hunter in direct combat. But the Piece of Eden was far too important to risk it falling into Templar hands, should the battle go against him.

He retreated deeper into the Aztec Club rooms, reaching the marble entryway just as he heard the explosion of a smoke grenade. He waited until the Hunter had reached the crest room before he slipped through another door, into the dining room, and then the library. When he heard the Hunter's footsteps on the cold marble floor, Varius opened the library door onto the first room and rushed for the open window through the lingering haze of the grenade.

He hurried out onto the hotel wall and scaled it to the roof. The minute his feet hit the gravel surface, he dove for cover behind the nearest chimney. There were dozens and dozens of them, affording him a maze of brick in which to hide.

A moment later, the Hunter's boots thumped against the roof.

"I don't know what's stirring in that idea pot of yours!" he shouted, and Varius learned his pursuer was a man. "But you're no match for me! My grandfather hunted down your kind! He bested some of the greatest among you!"

That could only mean one thing. This Hunter was a descendant of Shay Patrick Cormac, the great betrayer of the Brotherhood who had murdered the Assassins who'd trusted him, crippling his own mentor. Varius gave into a sudden surge of rage, pulled a throwing knife from his belt, and let it fly, but the Hunter ducked it.

"Your grandfather was an Assassin once!" Varius shouted, casting his voice several yards away to his left, obscured further by its echoes off the chimneys and skylights. "He turned on the Brotherhood and the Creed he'd sworn to uphold! He was nothing but a coward and a traitor!"

"Never a traitor to the truth!" the Hunter shouted. "He never betrayed the Templar Order!"

Varius now understood more fully the opponent he faced, and felt an even greater sense of urgency. It could be this Hunter outmatched him, and if that was the case, escape was the only possible course of action. The Piece of Eden must not fall into Tammany's hands.

He made a silent run for the ledge, but heard the sound of the Hunter's rifle just as he reached it. The dart caught him in the side, and Varius knew he had mere seconds until its toxin took hold. He made a desperate descent—half controlled drop, half free fall—catching ledges with his fingertips on the way down, just enough to slow his plummet.

He hit the ground hard, but rebounded to his feet, nothing broken. He yanked out the dart, which had lodged itself in the leather strap of his knife belt. That meant its needle hadn't fully punctured his skin, and he may not have received a full dosage. He felt something, though. The ground beneath his feet had begun to pitch and yaw, and the buildings threatened to topple. He was vulnerable.

Varius staggered across Broadway, then down Ann Street and into a nearby alley, where he buried himself in its shadows.

From that hiding place, he watched as the Hunter descended to the street and looked in all directions. He walked toward Broadway, and then across it, but he stopped there, appearing unsure of what to do. Varius thought perhaps he might yet evade the Hunter.

People still moved up and down the thoroughfare, preparing for the next day's riot. The Hunter paid them no mind, pulling something from his leather coat, and at the sight of it, Varius closed his eyes in dismay. It was a Herschel spyglass, capable of revealing the heat that living bodies gave off in the darkness.

Varius tried to run, but found his legs had mutinied and no longer responded to his command. He looked down at them, and they seemed to be someone else's limbs, rather than his own. The toxin had finally taken hold of his nerves and muscles.

The Hunter slowly cast the telescope in a circle, but stopped when its lens pointed directly at Varius. He then put the telescope away, and casually loaded his rifle. Varius could do nothing but stare down the barrel as the Hunter took aim and fired.

The dart hit him in the shoulder, stabbing him deeply and fully this time, but he noticed the pressure more than the pain. Within seconds, he felt his mind clouding over, and he lost almost all sense of himself or where he was, but remained aware that he had failed his father and the Brotherhood a second time.

A figure soon stood over him, speaking to him, and beneath the weight of Varius's sagging consciousness, Owen recognized Javier's ancestor. "My grandfather would've killed you," the Hunter said. "I thought I would, too, until just now. I'm Cudgel Cormac, and I think I'd rather you live with the shame."

The cloud over Varius's mind turned to a starless, moonless night, and for Owen, the simulation went black. He floated in a void like the Memory Corridor, but whereas the Memory Corridor had a feeling of potential, this place was filled with total absence and emptiness.

"What's happening?" he asked the void.

Your ancestor is unconscious, came Monroe's voice in his ear. *But he isn't dead, or the simulation would've ended.*

"So what do I do?"

You wait. If you were in the simulation by yourself, I could speed it up past this part, but I have to keep you on track with the others.

"I saw it," Owen said. "I had the Piece of Eden in my hand."

I know.

"But now Javier has it."

Not Javier. His ancestor. It's important you remember that.

"It gets confusing."

It does.

"But either way, now we'll know where it is, right? We should be done with the simulation soon?"

I'm afraid not, Monroe said. *This memory seems far from over.*

CHAPTER THIRTEEN

Abraham would never admit it out loud to anyone else, least of all Eliza, but he was glad for the wagon ride back to Mr. Tweed's house. David was relieved, too. His old bones seemed to come together like the brittle ends of dried-out sticks, which was a very weird and uncomfortable experience for him. But Abraham couldn't stop to listen to his joints complain, or else he might start complaining, too, and that was something he'd sworn never again to do.

"Going to be a mighty conflagration tomorrow," Skinny Joe said over his shoulder. "Mighty conflagration, indeed."

"So I hear," Abraham said.

Okay, Monroe said in David's ear, *you've entered another extrapolated part of the simulation. For the next little while, this blank spot has been filled in with historical data and the memories of other people, combined with the portion of your younger life that got passed on with your genes. Just sit tight, try to do what Abraham would do. Remember, you've got some wiggle room, but if you act too out of character, you can still desynchronize.*

"You're lucky the Boss looks out for you," Skinny Joe said, a subtle threat lurking underneath the surface of his words.

"And why is that?" Abraham asked.

"It'll go hard for Negroes tomorrow."

David wasn't sure how to read that statement. Mr. Tweed had given him the same warning earlier, and even though he wasn't sure if Abraham would say it, David asked, "Does that seem right to you?"

Skinny Joe scowled, and the simulation glitched.

Whoa, came Monroe's voice. *What did I just say? You need to stay in character. You've still got junctions you need to be at with the others, and you can't do that if you piss this guy off enough to do something to you.*

"Seem right?" Skinny Joe said. "You questioning me, boy?"

"I'm just asking if you think it's our fault."

"I don't know if the Negroes themselves are responsible, but, by God, there's a war about them, ain't there? Poor men getting drafted to fight and die to free the very Negroes who'll take their jobs." His voice had risen in pitch with agitation. "Them Negroes is the innocent cause of all these troubles, and come tomorrow, by God, we'll pound 'em."

David knew Abraham would say nothing to that and hold very still, not feeling at all that safe in the wagon in spite of Cudgel's orders. But David felt an intense anger at this idiot's racism, an anger that had been building ever since he entered this simulation, and he couldn't stop himself from speaking.

"Maybe you'll get a pounding of your own—"

The simulation squealed and buckled, and David felt as if he were imploding, collapsing on himself into a singularity of non-existence. The intense pressure bent and twisted his mind, and he screamed but nothing came out. Then everything was black, no simulation, no anything, and he wondered if he'd died—

"Relax," Monroe said. "That did it. You desynchronized."

David's helmet pulled away and he was back in the ware-house, the light overhead burning the backs of his eyes. A sudden vertigo swept over him, worse than any he had felt before. His stomach heaved, and he twisted to his side. Monroe already held a bucket there, and David vomited into it.

Then he did a second time. And a third.

"It's rough," Monroe said, handing him a towel to wipe his mouth. "Desynchronizing messes with your parietal lobes, the part of your brain that keeps you grounded in time and space. It'll pass."

David had never felt this sick in quite this way. It felt like the worst dizziness from the worst roller coaster imaginable. He bent to vomit a fourth time, but only dry heaved, and then he fell back onto the recliner chair, panting, the ceiling and room around him spinning, and he fought a pain as though a vise crunched his skull. The others reclined in their chairs around him, oblivious and, in a really disconcerting way, not quite there.

A new wave of pain overtook him, and he moaned. "I never want to do that again."

"I don't blame you," Monroe said.

"Did I ruin everything?"

"Not yet. But we gotta get you back in there. You've got junctions coming up. As long as you make those, the simulation will hold."

David wasn't ready. But he knew he didn't have time to get ready. At least he had nothing left in his stomach to throw up.

"It will actually feel better back in the simulation," Monroe said. "That's where a part of your brain thinks you are."

"Then let's do this," David whispered, and Monroe helped him get the helmet back on. The darkness inside the visor curbed the sensation of spinning.

"I'll put you back in the Corridor first, and then load the simulation. You sure you're ready?"

"Does it matter?"

"Not really."

"Then do it."

The visor lit up, and a moment later, David was standing in that gray, cloudy space of the Memory Corridor, and back in Abraham's old but now familiar body. Monroe was right; it felt better, like it felt better to get back in warm water when swimming on a cold day. The vertigo stopped, and the pain in his head subsided.

Better? Monroe asked.

"A little."

Good. The simulation is ready when you are. The Animus recalibrated the memory, resetting that racist. Be more careful, okay?

"Okay." David needed no more warnings about desynchronization. One experience with it was all he needed to stay as far away from it as possible.

Here we go. Three, two, one . . .

David was back in the wagon, and Skinny Joe drove on as if nothing had happened. David said nothing more on the ride back to Mr. Tweed's house, using the quiet to get back into his ancestor's mind. He listened to Abraham as though sitting at the older man's knee, and the more he listened, the better he felt, until the vertigo and pain were completely gone, and he was settled even better than he had been before the desynchronization.

They rumbled up Bowery, and the cobblestones set the dirt packed in the corners of the wagon dancing. The commotion Abraham observed on the street suggested that both Mr. Tweed and Skinny Joe were right that there was sure to be a riot the following day. But the word *riot* didn't adequately convey the orderliness of what was happening. A true riot was chaos. These goings-on boasted strategy and planning, and it made Abraham wonder if a war wasn't just a riot with a little foresight.

From Bowery, and later Fourth Avenue, they took Fourteenth Street west, passing under the great statue of George Washington near Union Square, and on the far side of the park, Abraham caught a glimpse through the trees of a distant tussle, a great Goliath of a patrolman taking down a few street thugs.

"The odds won't be with that crusher tomorrow," Skinny Joe said with a huff of malignant laughter. "We'll show 'em, eh?"

Abraham said nothing but wondered who exactly this man thought he was talking to.

They drove on, and when they reached Sixth Avenue, they turned north and traveled another twenty-two blocks. It was quite late when they finally reached Mr. Tweed's house.

"Here you go then," Skinny Joe said. "Safe and sound."

"Thank you," Abraham said, easing himself out of the wagon onto the sidewalk. Though better than walking, the jostling had nevertheless punished his body in its own way, a pain to which David was growing accustomed.

Skinny Joe nodded toward the house. "Stay indoors tomorrow."

"I will," Abraham said, though he wondered why he and Eliza should be safe when the other black men, women, and children in the city clearly would not be.

Skinny Joe carried on with his wagon into the night, about his infernal purposes, and Abraham turned toward the door. He found it locked, but knocked upon it and rang the bell.

Eliza didn't come.

He knocked and rang again.

And again.

He waited.

Still Eliza didn't come.

He assumed she'd fallen asleep, unable to keep her Gethsemane watch. There may have been a window open through which he could have entered, but with the spirit of the city so twisted up about itself with animosity, he dared not risk appearing to anyone as a housebreaker.

Just as Abraham worried about Eliza, David now worried about Grace. He felt uneasy without her around, as if he wasn't quite safe, and he didn't know what to do. He wouldn't risk desynchronization doing something stupid, but he wanted to get inside that house and make sure his sister was still there.

Abraham chose to settle down upon the stoop, just as he had warned Eliza he would. The night was warm and humid, and though he would likely be sore for days, it would be far from the worst night he had ever spent.

Neither would the worst night of his life be among those he'd passed hiding in the swamps these many years gone, bug eaten, shivering and wet, wounds festering in the muck. Nor would it be one of the sweltering nights he'd spent in a coffin with rotting meat, to give off the proper smell, as an abolitionist drove him over the border into Pennsylvania.

Abraham looked up at the night sky, and allowed his mind to drift to that place inside him, far, far downriver, the swampland where the rot of guilt, anger, and hatred choked the roots of the trees, and the brackish water flowed at the speed of pain.

The worst night of his life was the night his first wife had been murdered by another slave, a man newly come to the plantation already addled and missing both ears, whom Abraham had then killed in return.

It was fear that first drove Abraham to run, a terror at what the bosses would do to him when they discovered it, but it was guilt that kept him running. There were many days in which guilt was his only nourishment and had kept his body alive when it should have died.

All these years later, Abraham still knew right where to find that guilt. And the anger. And the hatred. He went there often as he traveled along the Underground Railroad, up through Staten Island, and through his education at the African Methodist Episcopal Zion Church. But it took him until Eliza was born of his second wife to realize he didn't have to stay there. He could leave that dark place downriver and make his home up high, near the clear waters of the wellspring. He could choose where his soul dwelled. The people who ran into trouble, black or white, slave or free, were the ones who went on as though there wasn't a choice to be made. But you can't avoid the swamp by erasing the map.

On nights like this, when it seemed to Abraham that nothing

had changed, and nothing ever would, no matter how many presidents came along with their proclamations, and no matter what those proclamations proclaimed, on nights like this he missed both his wives, and he let himself drift downstream to remind himself of where he'd been, the choice he'd made, and to make that choice again.

Someone shouted.

Abraham opened his eyes to the sight of a passing mob. Not yet dawn, and they were already swarming uptown, ferocious-looking savages. The sight of them worried him, and he wondered how Mr. Tweed could be so certain he and Eliza would be safe in his house. A mob had a mind of its own, and it did not take orders, even from Tammany Hall.

Nowhere in the city would be safe. Abraham knew it, and decided then he had to get Eliza out, at first light, before the riot. That meant there were preparations to be made, and he had to get inside, even at the risk of looking like a burglar.

He labored to his feet and walked around the house, over the hedges and lawn, to the cellar door, his best option for an entry. Margaret often left the delivery men to load down their goods, and then forgot to lock up afterward, and fortunately, she had apparently done so again today.

Abraham was able to enter into the house through the ground. He came up into the kitchen, and then hurried out into the main hall.

"Eliza?" he called.

No response. But she wasn't that heavy of a sleeper.

He checked every room on the first floor, and then the upstairs rooms, and then the attic rooms, and concluded that she wasn't there.

David shared Abraham's panic at the thought of Eliza out in the streets. Abraham had no idea why Eliza might have left the house, but he rushed into the library and wrote a hasty note to his daughter.

My Eliza,

When you read this, I want you to sit down and wait for me inside the house like I asked you to. If we have not reunited by six o'clock this evening, I want you to meet me at the Christopher Street Ferry. The city is not safe, and I must get you out of it. If I do not come at the appointed time, I want you to take the ferry without me. I will join up with you as I am able.

Your loving father, Abraham

Abraham left the note on the table in the front hall where Eliza would be sure to see it, should she return to the house. For now, he believed she had likely tried to follow him, having overheard Mr. Tweed's instructions. That meant she would be heading down toward the Fourth Ward, the thought of which drove Abraham's brittle bones into a run once his feet reached the sidewalk.

David worried, too. He knew the Animus was only a simulation, but if Eliza went through what Abraham feared she might if she got caught in the riot, Grace would have to experience all of it.

Within a few blocks, Abraham had slowed down. The omnibuses and railway on Sixth Avenue weren't running yet, so he had to walk the length of it. Along the way, he passed several mobs going the opposite direction, uptown, and each time he feared they would seize him.

By the time he reached Fourteenth Street and turned east, his legs had begun to scream at him, threatening to give out entirely, and he sat down under the statue of Washington to rest. The sun hadn't roused itself yet, its head still buried under the blanket of the horizon, but it was stirring.

David didn't know if the old man would make it another block, let alone all the way back to the Hole-in-the-Wall. He stopped listening to Abraham's mind, and started doing the talking. And the walking. He got up and took a step down the street, but as he did so the simulation buckled.

Whoa, whoa, whoa, Monroe said. *What's going on, David?*

"Sorry," David said. "I wasn't thinking." He forced himself to return to the statue and sit down, his whole body tense. The simulation smoothed itself out in response.

There you go, that's better, Monroe said. *Everything okay?*

"I'm just worried about Grace," David said.

She's fine, Monroe said. *Her simulation is still running strong. Nothing to worry about.*

David nodded, feeling a bit relieved for her, and until Abraham decided to get up and move, David could sit here and think his own thoughts for a while. "You still there, Monroe?"

Yup.

"This is hard."

How so?

"I can't change what they went through. It happened. It happened already."

It did.

"But now I feel like it's my life, too, so I'm just . . . so *angry.*"

This is new?

"I don't know. I guess my dad and Grace have always kind of shielded me."

And now your shield is gone. Is that it?

"Maybe."

Then maybe it's time you shield yourself.

"Maybe," David said, but then Abraham started talking again, demanding to be heard.

He rose from his rest under the statue and resumed his trek downtown, determined to wear his bones to dust finding Eliza. The pain in Abraham's knees was excruciating, and David knew it, but from a distance, the way his own pain was hard to really remember after the fact, even though it might have been severe.

Abraham limped and hobbled down three blocks of Fourth Avenue, and then managed to board a blessed horsebus going south. It was nearly full, and Abraham took enemy stares from all sides, but managed to keep his head down and safely ride the length of Bowery. He got off at Pearl Street, and as the vehicle pulled away down the road, one of the other passengers, a scrawny boy no more than twelve or thirteen years old, stared right into Abraham's eyes and drew his finger across his neck.

The sight of it shocked Abraham, rooting him to the sidewalk and freezing his blood until long after the horsebus had passed out of view.

Were children to riot, too? What hope was there in a city such as that?

The darkness of the swampland called to him, so Abraham turned toward the pure light of his daughter and pressed ahead, forcing his way down to Dover Street, shoulders first.

The Hole-in-the-Wall was nearly empty inside, but still open. The giantess who managed its crowds had taken Cudgel's place behind the bar, and as Abraham entered, she scowled, the flame of her red hair raging atop her head.

"You again?" She set her fists on the counter and leaned on them. The counter groaned.

"Yes." Abraham walked up to the bar, though this time he carried no letter from Mr. Tweed to protect him. "I beg your pardon, ma'am, but—"

"As you can see, I got no more bartenders for you to take," she said.

"I'm not here about that."

"No more Boss's orders, then?"

"Not directly," Abraham said. "Though I am here about one of his household servants. My daughter, Eliza."

"Oh, her."

"You've seen her?"

"She were in a while ago, wanting to know where *you* had gone." The woman laughed with the sound of a stone rolling downhill. "Now, ain't that ironical?"

"Please, ma'am," Abraham said, not seeing the humor at all. "What did you tell her?"

"No cause to lie to her, so I told her what I knew. You gave Cudgel a message, and then Cudgel took you with him."

"And what did she say to that?"

"Uh, I do believe she thanked me. Then I told her she'd better get herself back to Mr. Tweed's house, same as you oughta do."

Abraham hoped Eliza had done just that. But it was also possible that she'd left the saloon in search of Cudgel, to thus find Abraham, but he had no idea where Cudgel had gone after putting him on Skinny Joe's wagon.

"Do you know where Cudgel is?"

"Surely don't."

"I see," Abraham said. "Thank you. You have been very helpful."

"Helpful, am I?" she said, laughing again. "Not often I hear that, unless I'm helping someone to a drink, or helping them to a pounding."

Abraham noted the jar of ears on the shelf behind the bar. "No doubt helping them see the error of their ways."

"Exactly that," she said. "I'm a preacher, is what I am." She patted the bludgeon hanging from her belt. "And this here is my sermon."

"I'm sure you are very eloquent," Abraham said. "Good night, ma'am."

"Good night," she said. "And God help you tomorrow."

CHAPTER FOURTEEN

Y ou're sure there's going to be a riot?" Adelina asked,
and Natalya thought about how she had not at all liked
the look of those men who'd just marched up the street.

"Those coves may have been carrying protest
signs," Tommy said, "but they were every one of them thugs and
ruffians. Mostly Roach Guards, by the look of them. Trust me,
whatever this pretends to be, it will turn into a riot."

"Will I be safe in the hotel?" Adelina asked.

Tommy rubbed his jaw. "I worry it might be a target if
things go badly."

"So what would you suggest?"

Tommy turned and looked across the square, in the opposite
direction of the hotel. "My brother's house, for now. When we
know more, we can take you somewhere else."

"Very well." Adelina was quite accustomed to visiting strangers' houses in her touring, and she trusted Tommy. If he said this was the best option, she believed him. "Let's go there, for now."

"But I should let you know ahead of time," Tommy said, looking at her earnestly. "My brother and his wife are in Boston."

"I see. But you have a key to let us in?"

"Yes, but . . ."

"But what?"

"We would be alone in the house."

Adelina smiled, finding his integrity quite endearing.

"If that troubles you—" he said.

"It doesn't trouble me," she said.

He nodded. "Then . . . shall we go?"

She nodded back, and they crossed the rest of the way through the park to Fourth Avenue, and then along Twenty-Fourth Street, until they crossed Lexington.

"It's just up here," Tommy said, and ushered her toward a four-story brownstone, with gray stone casings around the windows, and a short flight of steps to the front door. He fumbled a bit with the key in his large hands, clearly nervous.

He was so unlike the men she typically encountered in her travels. To start with, many of the men she knew would not have given her notice if she were to be alone with them. To the contrary, such circumstances had more than once been deliberately orchestrated, since men assumed certain things about actresses and singers. Neither was Tommy wealthy, nor did the self-assurance he carried on the street in his dealings with thugs follow him in his dealings with the opposite sex.

She placed a hand on his arm, hoping to steady him.

A moment later, with a grunt, he got the key to work, and they entered the foyer.

The house was as lovely on the inside as on the outside. At the center of the entry hall, a wooden parquet floor surrounded a tile mosaic, upon which stood a round table graced with a beautiful Chinese vase. Through that hall, they entered into another with a staircase climbing to the second floor. The only light came in through the windows from the streetlamps, the sun not yet high enough to offer anything of value.

"This way," Tommy said, gesturing for her to take the stairs upward. "It's mostly just the kitchen on this floor."

A thick carpet coated the wooden steps so that her climb made no sound at all, except for the rustle of her dress. When they reached the landing, she spied a parlor to the right and a dining room to the left. Without an invitation, she turned toward the parlor and entered through its open, double-glass doors.

Even in the dim light, Adelina could see it was very well appointed. The Turkish carpet beneath their feet was of a luxurious weave and dizzying pattern. Matching sofas eyed each other from opposite sides of the room, while an armchair sat at each of their ends. A Gothic sideboard glowered in a corner, while an enormous painting of a ship tossed by a violent sea hung on the wall above an upright piano. A mirror in a gilt frame graced the opposite wall; above the fireplace, a large marble bust of a woman on the mantel.

"Yes, I think we could pass some time here," Adelina said, moving to recline on one of the sofas. "Don't you agree?"

"If you would like," he said, but rather than sit, he stalked over to one of the windows that looked down on Twenty-Fourth Street and peered between the curtains.

"Will you not sit with me?" she asked.

He turned to look at her, and a moment later he left the window and took one of the armchairs on the opposite side of the room from her, sitting down uneasily, with a stiff back, keeping his arms tucked in.

"Are you still worried for us here?" she asked.

"No, I believe we're safe, for now."

"Then are you not comfortable in this room?" she asked.

"Why do you ask?"

"You occupy that chair as if you're afraid you might soil it."

He looked around. "It's a pleasant-enough parlor."

"Then if not the room, what is it that makes you so uncomfortable? This house?"

The pause that followed told Adelina she had struck a vein, one she could follow deep into the bedrock of his being if she chose.

"It is my brother's house," he said. "It is not my house."

"Does he make you feel unwelcome?"

"No, he is very kind. As is Christine, his wife."

"Then what is it?"

The chair creaked as he shifted. "I suppose feeling welcome and feeling that I belong are different."

"You don't belong?"

He looked around the room again. "Not here, no." Then he looked back at her. "But you do."

She felt in his pronouncement a subtle accusation, even though she didn't believe it had been intended that way. But she wasn't going to apologize to him for who she was and how she chose to make her way in the world. She had nothing to be ashamed of. "I have learned to belong anywhere, Tommy Greyling," she said.

"That would be a splendid skill to have, I think," he said.

"I am fortunate that it comes easily to me." Adelina had certainly felt that she belonged at the reception that followed her performance the previous night. But that did not assuage the loneliness she had felt there. "If not this, what kind of house would you have?" she asked him.

"I actually think I might like to leave the city one day," he said. "I've lived here all my life. When I went away to fight the Rebels, I marched through beautiful country. Farms and fields. Many times I thought to myself I might like to live that way, one day."

"On . . . a farm?"

He nodded. "You seem disappointed."

Adelina hadn't meant to come across that way. It wasn't disappointment she felt, but something more akin to fear. "No, it's just that you're made of better stuff than I am. That sounds both noble and pure."

"But it takes more money than I have or am likely to ever see."

"Perhaps your brother would help you?" Adelina could guess at the cost of the room they now sat in, and, by extension, the rest of the house, and Tommy's brother was clearly wealthy.

"He might." Tommy shook his head. "But I wouldn't ask him."

"Why not?"

"I know where his money comes from. It's another reason I feel uncomfortable in this house."

Somehow, the deeper she mined, the purer his ore seemed, his integrity not just a veneer, but arising from his depths. His mere presence, sitting across from her, huge and stretching the seams of his policeman's uniform, seemed to challenge her. She wanted to know if he truly was as good as he seemed, and she thought for a single, brief moment of asking him where his bedroom was. But she had no intention of taking him there, and such a tease would only serve to make him more uncomfortable. Besides which, she didn't actually want to compromise him, but instead wanted it proven that he couldn't be compromised.

She rose from the sofa. "Shall I sing for you?"

"I, um, that—"

But she gave him no time to find the words he was seeking, crossed to the piano and sat down before it. She had never been a particularly strong musician, but she was competent, and she chose the song she had performed for President Lincoln and his wife. She understood it was then quite popular with the soldiers out in the field, and its lyrics seemed to suit everything she and Tommy had been talking about.

In some ways, Natalya was as terrified of performing in the intimacy of this setting as she had been on that stage before thousands. But she did her best to relax and let Adelina do what she did best. Her fingers stumbled a little in the dim light of the room, but her voice never faltered a note.

Mid pleasures and palaces though we may roam,
Be it ever so humble, there's no place like home;
A charm from the skies seems to hallow us there,
Which seek through the world, is ne'er met with elsewhere.

Home! Home! Sweet, sweet home!
There's no place like home,
There's no place like home.

An exile from home, splendor dazzles in vain,
Oh, give me my lovely thatched cottage again;
The birds singing gaily that come at my call,
Give me them, with peace of mind, dearer than all.

Home! Home! Sweet, sweet home!
There's no place like home,
There's no place like home.

To thee, I'll return, overburdened with care,
The heart's dearest solace will smile on me there.
No more from that cottage again will I roam,
Be it ever so humble, there's no place like home.

She played the last notes on the piano, and looked up. Tommy sat in his chair, his head bowed low enough she couldn't see his face. He remained in that position long enough she began to wonder if she'd put him to sleep. But a moment later, he looked up and thumbed a tear away from his eye.

"You earn every penny," he said, his voice soft.

"Nonsense. I am highly overpaid." She rose from the piano. "But if you repeat that to anyone, I'll deny that I said it."

"Thank you for singing that tune."

"You're welcome." She crossed the room back to her sofa.

"Lots of men I fought alongside, they all loved that one."

She sat down. "I know."

"Many of them . . . have gone home. The first home of the soul."

"I know. I'm sorry."

The sun had risen now outside. Tommy got up from the armchair and resumed his vigil at the window. "They're still marching uptown," he said, craning to look down the street, toward the park. "God, it's a mob."

"Will you be needed?"

"I will be," he said. "But I want to make sure you're safe first."

"Don't worry about me," she said. "I'm sure I'll be fine, here. You must do what you need to."

He let the curtain fall and strode toward the double doors. "I'm going to go out and have a look around. See what I can learn. Are you sure you don't mind if I leave you here?"

"Not at all."

"There's a library upstairs," he said. "I'll return as soon as I can."

With that, he descended the staircase, and she heard him leave through the front door. From the window, she watched him march down the street until he rounded a corner and was gone.

Now that she was alone, Natalya felt free to take center stage. For most of the night, she'd deliberately kept herself far from the action playing out, letting it unfold strictly according to the memory's script. Mostly, she'd wanted to simply watch Adelina being Adelina, a woman very different from her. She was also aware that Tommy was Sean, and Natalya didn't want there to be any confusion over who was attracted to whom once they left the Animus. But she might have been worrying over nothing. That part of the whole simulation situation was just weird.

While Adelina waited for Tommy's return, Natalya decided to have a look around the house, so long as it didn't threaten to desynchronize her. She enjoyed history in school and she also liked design. Even though she had never really cared much for the style of the Victorian era, it was still interesting to be there, almost like walking through a museum.

She left the parlor and went into the dining room, which had a gorgeous, long table with silver candelabra, and a large sideboard or buffet that Natalya thought might be Queen Anne style. The dining room had its own pantry and staircase that went down into the kitchen.

Natalya returned to the main hall and climbed the staircase to the next floor, exploring the library and then the master bedroom, where the vanity contained a slew of beauty products Natalya didn't recognize. Not that she wore much makeup out in the real world. The next floor held a bedroom that she assumed belonged to Tommy, and down the hall from that, an empty room. Well, not empty. It appeared that someone had begun to prepare it to be a nursery. There was a child's crib and one of those old-fashioned strollers covered in lace, both shoved into a corner. Half the room had been wallpapered with roses, but it looked as if the project had been abandoned before its completion, and Natalya wondered at the many stories that room told all at once, most of them sad.

The next floor was mostly attic storage, but there was a small space beneath the eaves that Natalya thought would have made a comfortable bedroom, and a small door that opened onto the roof. The sun was fully up now and already these upper stories were collecting all the rising heat.

Natalya returned to the parlor and sat at the piano. She laid her fingers on the keys and played a discordant series of notes. Natalya's mother played the piano. Her grandparents and her parents had wanted her to play the violin, and she'd taken lessons for several years from an expensive Russian teacher named Mr. Krupin. But he had made it quite clear to Natalya and her family that she had little aptitude for music, so she was eventually allowed to quit. She may have inherited Adelina's memories, but she certainly hadn't inherited her talent.

None of the clocks in the house told the correct time or even ticked—Tommy had evidently been neglecting to wind them— but it seemed that an hour or two had passed since he had gone out.

The street outside was full of sunlight by the time Natalya saw Tommy returning. When she heard the front door open, she rushed backstage and pushed Adelina into the light as heavy footsteps trudged up the staircase.

"The city is in chaos," Tommy said as he came into the parlor.

"Really?" Adelina glanced toward the window and the street that still seemed mostly empty.

"I connected with a patrolman from another precinct. Those mobs we saw last night and early this morning were massing in a vacant lot up by Central Park. From there, around eight o'clock this morning they marched south. At least ten thousand of them."

"Ten—ten thousand?"

Tommy nodded. "They forced all the factories and foundries and millworks to shut down and took the workers with them under threat. They've been cutting telegraph lines and ripping up the railways, to stop communications and movement in the city. They're tipping over horsebuses."

"My God," Adelina whispered.

"This isn't a riot," Tommy said. "It's an insurrection. The main mob is attacking the provost marshal's office where the drafts are taking place. But I don't expect things will stay contained there for long."

"What should we do?"

"It's dangerous to be out and about in the streets. We stay indoors for now."

"Are you needed?"

"I'm staying with you," he said. "I'll see you safely through this."

"I'm sure I'll be fine, you—"

"I'm staying with you," he said, his tone plated in iron. "Until I'm certain you'll be safe."

Adelina nodded, aware that this was not a point on which she could dissuade him. Tommy took up a position by the windows, and in spite of Adelina's attempts to engage him in further conversation, he seemed determined to avoid distraction from his watch. She went up to the library and brought down a book of poems to read, but did so silently.

An hour went by and the day grew hotter. Even had they opened a window, she could see plainly by the tree branches outside that no breeze stirred in them.

Just after another hour had passed, Tommy stood up straighter. "Some of the mob is coming this way. From Third Avenue."

"What are they doing?"

"Looting," he said.

Adelina hurried to the window and looked out. Up the street, several houses down, a tide of men had surged forward, pausing at each residence to hurl brickbats and paving stones. Several women and children had been turned out of their homes into the street, forced to watch as the looters invaded and stole away their lives, tossing furniture and paintings and dishware out through the windows into the street.

"Where are the police?" Adelina asked.

"Putting down larger mobs than this," Tommy said.

"They'll be here soon," Adelina said. "I think we should go. But first, you need to get out of that uniform. If they see you in it, I think they'll forget all about looting."

He reluctantly agreed and went up to a room to change while Adelina kept watch at the window. The mob was only three doors down now. An older woman knelt in the street sobbing, a man with white, wispy hair stood over her, clutching his head where it was bleeding a little from having been struck. Adelina was surprised to see the mob had more women than men, clothed in filthy dresses and skirts, hair wild, unkempt, and stuck to their faces by sweat.

"I'm ready," Tommy said from the parlor doorway.

Adelina turned to look at him.

He wore plaid wool trousers with suspenders, and a white, collared shirt with the sleeves rolled up high. She found she liked this version of Tommy better than the patrolman.

"That'll do," she said.

"We can go out the back way," he said.

They hurried down the staircase to the main entry hall and

had just turned toward the kitchen when a huge paving stone came through the window near the door, sending a shower of broken glass skimming across the floor.

"Go!" Tommy said.

Adelina raced into the kitchen, but didn't see a back door.

"Down the stairs to the cellar," Tommy said behind her.

Adelina spotted the metal, spiral staircase in the corner, and dove down it into darkness, her footsteps clanking and echoing back at her. She reached the bottom, and didn't know where to go, her eyes not having adjusted to the light.

"This way," Tommy whispered, sliding around her. "I think they're in the house, so we must go quietly."

He moved away into the shadows and Adelina heard him fiddling with a lock. Then a wedge of light opened wide, silhouetting him against a view of the house's back lawn. She stepped toward him and together they left the brownstone in the hands of the looters.

CHAPTER FIFTEEN

E liza made her way west from the Hole-in-the-Wall toward the Astor House. That Irish woman, Gallus Mag, had told her that Cudgel had taken her father with him. Eliza didn't know what that man could want with her father. But she knew of no better way to find her father than to find Cudgel, and the message she had read in Mr. Tweed's library mentioned the Astor House as the site of Cudgel's orders. It also meant that her father had delivered the letter she had gone out to stop.

She took Frankfort over to Park Row from Pearl, hoping that Tammany Hall's presence on the corner might lessen some of the danger. The activity in the streets confirmed to her what Mr. Tweed had warned her about. The rioters were planning and massing, mostly ruffians from the slums and docks.

One group took note of her as she passed, staring with open hatred and disgust. "Where you going?" one of them asked as he stepped toward her, nearly into her path.

"I am running an errand for Mr. Tweed. I am his maid." She hoped that would deter him.

It stopped his advance, but he didn't retreat. "That so?"

"It is," she said, chin up, as she walked by him.

"What if you're lying?" he called after her.

She turned around and looked directly into his eyes. "Are you a gambling man?"

His jutting Adam's apple bobbed in his throat.

"It seems not," she said, and continued on her way in the calmest manner she could manage, even though she wanted to run.

After that, she kept mostly to the shadows along the sides of the roads, or blended in with a group of passersby if they didn't seem threatening. She had always been good at hiding, which was why her father had affectionately called her his "little sneak thief" as a girl.

When she reached Park Row and crossed the railway into the park that surrounded City Hall, she found it even easier to hide among the trees. She glided southwest, down past the Croton Fountain to the tip of the park, and she stood there in the shadows studying the Astor House hotel across Broadway from her.

She hadn't been there long when she glimpsed a figure down among the tombstones in the churchyard of the chapel of St. Paul. Shortly after that, she spotted a second figure emerging from a fifth-story window on the south side of the hotel. The one in the churchyard shot something at the one in the window, too quiet to be a gun, and the figure in the window disappeared.

Then the man in the churchyard appeared to fly up the tree and over the fence into the street. In a flash he scaled the bare hotel wall as if someone had hung a ladder for him from the window. Eliza had never seen such a feat.

She crouched down deeper into the shadows and waited to see what would happen next. Several moments went by and then the second figure climbed out the window and up onto the hotel roof, followed by the man from the churchyard. After another few moments, one of the men fell from the roof, but in fits, as he seemed to snatch at the wall and slow his descent. Eliza thought for certain he would break his neck, but he landed hard on the ground and then labored to his feet.

From there, he staggered across Broadway and down nearby Ann Street. Shortly after that, the man from the churchyard climbed down the side of the hotel as easily as he'd surmounted it and stalked in the direction his quarry had fled. Then he paused and pulled a curious telescope from his coat, which he used to survey the streets.

Eliza wanted to duck even lower, but he never pointed the glass directly at her. When it seemed to be pointing in the direction of Ann Street, he put the telescope away, unslung a rifle from his shoulder, loaded it, and fired it with a muffled *pop*. Then he strolled out of view down the street in the direction he'd just shot.

Eliza felt certain one of these men was Cudgel, but she didn't know which one. Mr. Tweed's letter had mentioned another man named Varius. From what she had witnessed, both men seemed equally dangerous, and capable of incredible deeds like climbing walls and surviving what should have been lethal falls.

When the man from the churchyard emerged from Ann Street, Eliza had a choice. She could follow him and try to confront him, hoping he was Cudgel, but it was also possible that Cudgel was the other man down Ann Street, possibly dying or dead at that moment.

Before she could make up her mind, the man from the churchyard scaled the wall of the nearest building to its roof and disappeared, eliminating any chance of her following him. So she took the only option that remained available to her and left the park, hurrying down Broadway to Ann Street.

She didn't see the man right away. She had to walk up and down the street twice before she noticed him in the shadows of an alleyway. At first glance, she thought he was dead, and within the corner of her own mind, Grace recognized Owen's ancestor. But her panic quickly faded as she got near to him and saw the rise and fall of his chest. He was merely unconscious, poisoned in some way.

Eliza tried slapping him awake, but that failed to rouse him. Grace decided to take the risk of desynchronization and banished Eliza to the corner room in her mind. Then she whispered, "Monroe?"

Nothing.

She wondered if he could hear her. "Monroe?" she said more loudly.

Yeah, he said in her ear. *I'm here. Sorry, busy trying to keep tabs on everyone.*

"Is Owen okay?"

He's fine, just in limbo right now.

"So what do I do?"

Same thing he's doing. You wait. As long as Eliza waits anyway.

"But Owen's not Cudgel, is he?"

No, he's not. But Eliza doesn't know that.

"How is David?"

He's fine, too.

"Where is he?"

He's looking for you, actually. I think he might even be heading to the Hole-in-the-Wall. But again, Eliza doesn't know that. If you take off, you'll—

"I know," Grace said. "I'll desynchronize."

Right. So sit tight, and let Eliza run the show as much as you can. Okay? We're getting close. Javier has the Piece of Eden right now. We just have to ride this wave all the way in.

"Okay," Grace said, even though it was hard to let anyone else run the show, apparently even the person whose memory she was experiencing. But she forced herself to let Eliza back out, and gave the girl free access to the real estate of her mind.

Eliza thought about calling for a doctor, but decided against it. That might involve the police or other authorities, who might then interfere with her finding her father. So instead, she settled down in the alley next to him, this stranger, and kept watch over him, making sure he was breathing and that no one found them.

An hour passed this way, and then another, and then the first light of dawn reached down to touch the street with a warmth that promised a sweltering day.

The stranger stirred.

"Hey," Eliza said. "Hey, wake up."

His eyelids fluttered and he groaned.

"Can you hear me?" Eliza asked.

His eyes opened, a little too widely, and she could tell they weren't yet focusing right. He had the look of a drunkard waking from a hard night.

"Who—who're you?" he asked.

"Eliza," she said. "Please tell me you're Cudgel."

He shook his head. "I'd like to kill him, though."

So Cudgel had been the other one, the one Eliza couldn't have followed up to the rooftops, anyway. That meant she also knew who this fellow was.

"You're Varius," she said.

A startled look took over for his bewilderment. "Yes. Who did you say you were?"

"Eliza," she said. "Cudgel took my father somewhere."

"Where is Cudgel?" Varius asked.

Eliza flicked her eyes upward. "Long gone. He climbed up the walls. Like you did."

"You see a lot, Miss Eliza." Varius rubbed his head. "Why would Cudgel want your father?"

"I don't know," she said, not yet trusting this man. "Why would Cudgel want to shoot you?"

He paused. "Let's just say . . . we're very old enemies."

Neither Cudgel nor this man seemed very old. "Do you know how to find him?"

"I'm going to try," Varius said. "Meanwhile, why don't you tell me how you know my name."

Eliza still wasn't willing or ready to trust him and didn't answer.

Varius closed his eyes. "Look, Miss Eliza. We both want the same thing. But Cudgel is a very dangerous man—"

"Aren't you a dangerous man?"

"I am dangerous, too," he said. "That's true. But if you help me, I swear I'll help you, and I won't harm you. You could have harmed me while I was unconscious, but you didn't."

"Only because I didn't know who you were."

"And now you do. So how do you know my name?"

Eliza narrowed her eyes, considering him. She thought back to the contents of the letter, and what they suggested. Mr. Tweed and Cudgel were out to destroy the city and the nation, and this man lying on the ground was their enemy, which might make him her friend. But beyond that, Eliza's vision, the same sight that had allowed her to read the letter in the first place, gave her a glimpse of this man's intent. She knew with certainty he meant her no harm and he would keep his word.

"I read it," she said. "That's how I learned your name."

"Read it where?"

"A letter Mr. Tweed wrote."

"Tweed?" Varius asked, coming suddenly more alert. "Boss Tweed?"

"Yes," Eliza said. "I'm a maid in his house. He sent my father to deliver a message to Cudgel, and then Cudgel took my father somewhere."

"You saw this message?"

"In a manner of speaking. I saw the traces of it left behind on the paper beneath."

Another pause. "Your vision is remarkable."

She made a show of looking him over. "You just going to lie there, or what?"

"I would get up," he said, "but I can't without help. The toxin is still keeping my legs from working."

"Then let me help you." Eliza moved closer so Varius could get an arm over her neck and shoulders. Then, together, they hoisted him to his feet, though he was far from steady.

"What did the rest of the message say?" he asked.

"It called you an Assassin, for one thing," she said. "It said you were after something important in the hotel, and that the riots today are going to tip the balance of the war."

"Let us hope not." Varius leaned on Eliza, and together they limped and shuffled out of the alley into Ann Street and the light of a hot sun. They turned together toward Broadway. "Did the message say anything else?"

"It said Cudgel was to stop you or kill you and bring whatever it was you had to Mr. Tweed's house this evening."

"This evening." Varius nodded. "Then there is still hope."

"Hope for what?"

"To save the country," he said.

They reached Broadway, turned north, and saw the mob.

"Oh no," Eliza said.

"It has begun," Varius said.

Two blocks farther up Park Row, in the small square before the *New York Tribune* building, a mass of rioters surged. There were hundreds, perhaps thousands of them, blocking the streets and the railway. The *Tribune* was for Lincoln, with abolitionist views, which had made it a target for those furious over the draft and emancipation. A man stood up on a wagon before them wearing a light coat and a Panama hat, his fist in the air, bellowing something Eliza couldn't hear from where she stood.

"You shouldn't be seen," Varius said, still unable to stand on his own. "It won't be safe for blacks today."

"Where should we go?"

"Somewhere I can rest. I'm useless to either of us until I get my legs back."

There was an eating house called Windust's nearby, on the corner of Ann Street and Park Row, which was just opening. Eliza helped Varius through the door, and though the maître d' seemed a bit perplexed by their appearance—a black serving woman with a hobbled white man—he nevertheless showed them to a table and offered them menus. They were the only two patrons there at that time, and Eliza helped Varius sit down in his chair before taking one for herself.

"Are you well, sir?" the maître d' asked.

"I will be," Varius said. "After I rest a spell."

"Quite a commotion out there," the maître d' said.

Varius nodded.

"They're protesting the draft, are they not?"

"Among other things," Varius said.

"The Democrats are certainly not fond of the *Tribune*," he said. "Mr. Greeley, the newspaper's editor, dines here frequently. I hope he will be safe from the protestors."

"If he's smart," Varius said, "he'll have cleared out of the city by now."

Varius selected coffee and eggs Benedict from the menu, and insisted upon having some brought for Eliza, too. She wasn't sure what to make of the situation in which she now found herself. Her father had been taken somewhere by a man who could climb sheer walls, and she had just helped a confessed Assassin to his feet and into a restaurant, where they were now about to eat breakfast together.

The food came, and once Eliza had taken a bite of it, she realized she was ravenous, and ate in earnest. She could sense Varius watching her, taking his time with his dish, and she tried not to let it make her feel self-conscious.

"Tell me more about this vision of yours," he said.

"I don't know what else to say about it." Eliza set her fork down and wiped her mouth with her napkin. "At times, I see something, and I know it's important. Other times, I see a man, like you, and I can tell you whether his intentions are good or evil. Sometimes, like with the message, I can see the traces of things left behind as if they're illuminated."

"Does your father have this sight?"

"No. But they say my mother did."

"I'm sorry. How old were you when she died?"

"I was eight years old," she said.

"Did she teach this sight to you?"

"No," Eliza said, wrinkling the space between her eyebrows. "Why are you so interested?"

He didn't answer, and instead took a bite of food, and then a sip of his coffee.

"If you won't answer that, then tell me what Cudgel took from you." Eliza hadn't forgotten that Varius had removed something of great worth from the Astor House.

"That is complicated," Varius said. "Perhaps—"

The door to the restaurant opened and an elderly gentleman walked in. He wore a bleached white duster, like a country preacher, with a floppy hat, farmer's boots, and spectacles upon his nose.

"Mr. Greeley!" the maître d' exclaimed. "Are you quite well, sir?"

"As well as can be expected," Mr. Greeley said.

This, then, was the editor of the *Tribune*. Eliza had to admire his boldness in walking about.

"There's a mob out there, did you know?" Mr. Greeley said. "I do believe they would like to hang me from a tree in the park. But if I can't have my breakfast when I'm hungry, my life isn't worth anything to me."

"You must take care, Mr. Greeley," the maître d' said. "Be cautious."

"Cautious?" Mr. Greeley stomped over to a table without being invited, and took a seat as if it were his custom. "Now is not the time for caution. The fate of the nation hangs in the balance. Caution will see it lost to the Peace Democrats and the Rebels. I would run for president myself, if I thought it was necessary." He then seemed to notice Eliza and Varius for the first time and gave them a nod.

Varius nodded back and turned to Eliza. "My legs are recovered. I'd rather you not be here if the mob comes in looking for him."

Eliza agreed and Varius paid for their meals. Then they slipped out the door into the street. Varius led them across Broadway, seeming fully recovered, then down Vesey Street between the hotel and the chapel of St. Paul's. The heat outside stuck to Eliza's skin within a few paces, humid and relentless. When they reached Church Street they turned uptown.

"Where is Boss Tweed's house?" he asked.

"Thirty-Sixth Street," Eliza said. "Between Fifth and Sixth Avenues."

"That's quite a distance through a city in riot." He narrowed his eyes at Eliza as though pondering something. "We could go up," he said.

"Up? You don't mean climbing the walls, do you?"

"That is exactly what I mean." He smiled. "Trust me. It's in your blood."

CHAPTER SIXTEEN

Abraham came out of the Hole-in-the-Wall unsure of what to do or where to go. His body had arrived at that place of exhaustion where he knew it might give out on him without warning. He had pushed his bones to their breaking point, then gone the entire night without sleep, and he knew the pain was waiting for him a block away, perhaps two, and he would do Eliza no good if he collapsed in the street.

This gap you're in now is pretty wide, Monroe said. *The simulation will be extrapolated for a while, using historical data. It might not feel quite as . . . real.*

"So what should I do?" David asked.

Stay safe, and be ready to get to the next intersection on time. You'll meet up with Sean and Natalya tomorrow afternoon.

"Stay safe where?"

Maybe Abraham knows. Listen to him.

David knew it would be impossible for Abraham to make it all the way back to Mr. Tweed's house until he had rested, and even then, the matter was far from settled. The streets had gone quiet, emptied of the gangs who had taken their protest uptown. Abraham had no way of knowing what kind of dangers or riot lay between him and Eliza, but the image of that boy, the one who'd drawn his finger across his throat, gave his blood cold warning.

With a silent hope that Eliza had heeded Gallus Mag and gone back up to Mr. Tweed's house, Abraham turned down Dover Street, and a block later, he reached the Colored Sailors' Home. Abraham had never visited the place before, but he knew of it, and hoped to find a refuge there.

It was a large brick edifice rising five stories above the street, with a modest sign out front. Abraham knocked on the door, but at that hour he had to try several times and wait before someone answered him.

When the door finally opened, a stocky black man of medium height and middle age greeted him barefoot, in trousers, his shirt hanging loose about him, his eyes more on the street than on Abraham. "Yes? How can I help you?"

"I'm wondering if I might seek refuge with you," Abraham said.

"Oh. Of course." The man rubbed his face and stepped aside to allow Abraham admittance. "Of course, please, come in. All who come in peace are welcome."

Abraham stepped through the door into a foyer flanked by two rooms. A wide hallway reached away into the building, lit partway along by the light falling down a staircase.

Abraham's host shut the door behind them and locked it. "May I ask your name?"

"Abraham."

An Indian woman emerged from one of the rooms off the foyer, dressed in her nightgown, about the same age as the man who had opened the door. "Abraham, welcome," she said.

"I'm William Powell," the man said. "This is my wife, Mercy, and together we run this home."

"I'm grateful for your hospitality, Mr. Powell," Abraham said. "And I'm sorry to intrude at this early hour. I just needed a safe place to rest. I've been on the streets most of the night."

"Of course," Mr. Powell said. "There are beds upstairs."

He and his wife led Abraham down the hallway to the staircase he had glimpsed, and then up it, past a window that looked out onto the street.

"How is it out there?" Mrs. Powell asked.

"Ominous," Abraham said. "The rioters have all begun to move uptown for whatever it is they're planning."

"It'll be a dark day tomorrow," Mr. Powell said. "A day I've warned would come."

"What is it you do here?" Abraham asked.

"We provide a moral home for black sailors on shore," Mrs. Powell said. "A place of safety from the snares and temptations that beset them. We allow no alcohol, and we provide our men with God's word, a library, and the means to better themselves. When needed, we help them find honest work."

They reached the top of the stairs, and Abraham found they were in a long hallway with many empty bedrooms, their doors wide open.

"We also host abolitionist meetings here," Mr. Powell said. "I'm a founding member of the Anti-Slavery Society. We've sheltered and helped many former slaves to escape, along with Albro Lyons, just over on Vandewater Street."

"You do God's work," Abraham said. "I came up through Staten Island."

"God bless you," Mrs. Powell said.

"Good people over there," Mr. Powell said.

"They are." Abraham glanced into one of the nearby rooms, with its simple bed and its Bible upon the table. "You seem to be rather vacant."

Mrs. Powell nodded. "Most of our men left yesterday, as soon as we received warning about the protests. They took the ferries over to Brooklyn and some to New Jersey."

"But not you?" Abraham asked.

"This is my home," Mr. Powell said. "I won't be driven from it."

Abraham admired his courage.

"This room is cleaned and ready for you." Mrs. Powell swept a hand toward one of the open doors. "Please, rest. You're welcome to stay here until the trouble has passed."

"I won't impose on you for long," Abraham said. "I need to find my daughter. I plan to leave with her this evening for Hoboken."

"Then take what rest you can," Mr. Powell said.

These were good people. Almost too good, in a way. Maybe this was what Monroe had meant about it seeming not quite real.

They left him in the room, but he didn't shut the door, and he lay down upon the bed above the covers, without even removing his shoes. The mattress, though thin and old, received him with as much tenderness and care as it could, and his body thanked it. The pain in his knees and back lessened, and he sighed and closed his eyes.

The simulation went black, images fleeting into and out of view, like holding a flashlight in a darkened room, seeing only what its beam could illuminate at one time. The streets of the city, the moon above a swamp, Gallus Mag laughing with Skinny Joe. It almost felt as if David was desynchronizing.

"What's happening?" he asked aloud. "Monroe?"

He's dreaming, Monroe said. *Nothing to worry about.*

"Dreaming? But it's so dark."

The Animus is extrapolating them to fill the gap, Monroe said. *Just sit tight and relax.*

David was having trouble relaxing. Eliza was out there in the city somewhere, which meant Grace was out there, too. She was the one David really worried about. She was the one who always made sure nothing bad happened to him, who took the heat and never once made him feel like he owed her for it.

But the simulation had done something to that relationship. His experience of Abraham's concern for Eliza had changed David's concern for his sister. He wasn't just looking to her to take care of him anymore. He was looking to take care of her.

"When do I meet up with Grace?" David asked.

You have an intersection with her after you meet Sean and Natalya.

"What kind of intersection?"

There was a pause. *Not sure,* he said, but it seemed as though he was holding something back.

The dream state went on for some time, but eventually Abraham woke up, and David settled down to listen to his mind as the old man rose from the bed. His knees and back ached, but with the memory of pain, rather than present injury. He checked his watch, and found he had slept through the morning and it was now after one o'clock in the afternoon.

Out in the hallway, Abraham heard voices and followed them down to the library. There he found Mrs. Powell reading to three children, two girls and a boy. The boy looked to be about twelve. One of the girls seemed near Eliza's age, the other much younger, with shriveled legs, sitting on her mother's lap.

Mrs. Powell looked up at Abraham standing in the doorway. "Please, come in."

"I don't want to intrude," Abraham said.

"Nonsense, come, sit. Did you have a good rest?"

"I did," he said. "Where is Mr. Powell?"

"He went out against my wishes to find out what's been happening."

"But you've had no disturbances?"

"Not at all," she said, her voice cheerful, her eyes on her children.

"You don't have to pretend, Mother," the oldest daughter said.

Abraham cleared his throat. "Thank you again for your hospitality. I think I'll be making my way home now."

"Oh, please, Abraham," Mrs. Powell said. "At least wait until William is home. So we know how the city fairs."

Abraham considered that suggestion, and concluded it was probably wise. If Mr. Powell could provide him with some intelligence about the rioters and their activities, Abraham could plan the safest route uptown.

"Very well," he said, and took one of the armchairs in the room. The sailors' library was nothing like Mr. Tweed's. The choices here weren't as numerous, the volumes much handled. But something about this place felt honest and full, whereas Mr. Tweed's library, for all its shelves, felt barren. This room was used for what it was intended. Abraham could feel the learned conversation in the air, as if the battered wooden shelves and floor had soaked it up.

Mrs. Powell went back to reading a fairy tale from Hans Christian Andersen, about a princess who could apparently feel a pea through any number of mattresses and bolsters. The younger Powell children giggled at the story, while the older daughter paced around the room, peering out the windows.

"I wish Billy were here," she said with a sigh.

"Who is Billy?" Abraham asked.

"Our oldest son," Mrs. Powell said. "He was just made a surgeon-in-chief for the army. He wanted to help with the war effort."

"You must be proud," Abraham said.

"I am," she said. "Though I wish he received the same pay and respect as a white surgeon."

"*I* wish he were *here*," the oldest daughter said again.

A door opened on the floor below them, and then a moment later, footsteps came up the stairs. Then Mr. Powell walked into the library with his mouth open, as if he was about to say something, but he shut it as soon as he seemed to notice his children. "Mercy, could I speak with you out in private?"

"Of course," Mrs. Powell said. "Mary, would you take Sarah?"

The oldest daughter went over and took her younger, invalid sister in her arms, while Mrs. Powell rose from her chair.

"Abraham," Mr. Powell said, "might I have a word with you as well?"

"Of course." Abraham had been hoping for as much.

The three of them moved into the hallway and down to its far end, where they would be out of the children's earshot.

"It's dire out there," he said. "Twenty black families in Baxter and Leonard streets were driven from their burning homes. The rioters destroyed Crook and Duff's restaurant. They just now burned down the State Armory on Twenty-First. They've assaulted the *Tribune* building. They're everywhere in the city, looting shops and homes, and setting them alight, seizing any black man they can get their hands on and beating him. Some unto death, I hear. The police are powerless to stop them. The patrolmen are outnumbered many hundreds to a man, and where they've managed to drive back the mob, it either returns stronger or simply moves elsewhere."

"Heaven help us," Mrs. Powell said.

"The *Tribune* building isn't far from here," Abraham said.

Mr. Powell nodded. "I pulled down the sign on our building, but we're well enough known even without it. I'm afraid it would be very dangerous for you to venture out right now."

Abraham had to agree, but it filled him with despair. He hoped above all that Eliza was safely within the walls of Mr. Tweed's house, but he couldn't be certain of that. If only he knew her whereabouts, he would be content to remain where he was.

"But my daughter—" he began.

"I'm sure she would want you to keep safe," Mrs. Powell said. "Just as you want her to keep safe."

That made sense to Abraham's head but not to his old heart.

"You are free to stay with us," Mr. Powell said. "Until this evil business is done with."

"But who can stop it?" Mrs. Powell asked.

"At this point," Mr. Powell said, "only the army can restore order. This isn't a riot, it's a rebellion, and I fear the city could be lost."

They returned to the library and Mrs. Powell resumed reading, though her voice sounded absent.

Shortly after two o'clock, Mary, the oldest daughter, who still stood at the window, called to her father. "They're coming!"

Abraham rushed to the window with Mr. Powell and saw she was right. A large group, perhaps twenty or thirty strong, marched down the street, chanting and brandishing their crude weapons. They appeared to be heading directly for the Sailors' Home.

"Quickly now," Mr. Powell said, his voice calm, but urgent. "I want you all to go up to the roof and then over onto the neighbors'. Try not to be seen." He took his youngest daughter, Sarah, from his wife's arms. "Let's go now, and be silent."

Abraham followed the family up the stairs to the third floor, and then up to the next, and the next, until they reached a narrower staircase to the attic, which opened onto the roof through a low door. Abraham saw there was a removable wooden bridge spanning the alley between the Sailors' Home and the building next door, out of view of the street. Mr. Powell had obviously prepared for this. He shuttled his family across the bridge until they were all on the other side, handing Sarah to his wife, and then he sent Abraham across.

"Pull the bridge away, if you would," Mr. Powell told him from the opposite roof.

The sounds of the rioters echoed up to them, full of venomous speech and threats such that Abraham had not heard since the plantation, words that set his body trembling against his will.

"You're not coming with us?" he asked Mr. Powell.

"I will not be driven from my home," Mr. Powell said. "Now that my family is safe, I will face this mob, should they dare to enter it."

Mrs. Powell raised her voice to a hiss. "William, please—"

"Mercy," Mr. Powell said, "I will not surrender to King Mob. I will not yield to their hatred. I cannot. It is not in my nature."

Again, Abraham found himself admiring this man. "Would you like me to stay with you?" he asked, willing but terrified, knowing he would be nearly useless in a physical confrontation.

"I ask no one to stay with me," Mr. Powell said. "Now, if you would be so kind as to pull the bridge away."

Abraham looked down at the wooden gangplank, then bent and took the end with both hands. The Powell boy came to help him, and together they pulled the bridge across the gap onto their own roof. Abraham looked again at Mr. Powell, standing resolute.

"Thank you, son," he said. "I love you all. Stay here, stay quiet. You will be safe."

"I love you, William," Mrs. Powell said, and her children echoed her sentiment.

Mr. Powell turned away and left the roof through the attic door, leaving the rest of them alone and separated from him.

The family then gradually settled, to wait and to hope. Mary had tears in her eyes, as did Mrs. Powell. The boy sat stoically, and Sarah curled in her mother's arms as if they were her own city and so long as she could stay there, the world was at peace, even as New York burned around her.

The scent of smoke spiced the air, and as Abraham gazed uptown, he saw a procession of black columns rising up into the sky, some near, some far, some large and some small, all of them ominous.

The mob's screeches and whooping intensified, but so far remained out in the street, not in the house. Perhaps they feared a force of hardened sailors would greet them should they charge through the door. But time passed without any intrusion, and the sky clouded over, which did not break the heat, but stopped the sun from beating Abraham about his shoulders.

"Perhaps they'll just leave," Mary said.

"Let us pray they do," Mrs. Powell said. "Right now, together. Come, children, hold hands."

Her children gathered around her, and as she began her prayer, Abraham bowed his head. With eyes closed, he imagined he saw Eliza trapped in Mr. Tweed's house, a mob outside, the house an inferno behind her. She was calling to him, but he couldn't hear her voice over the flames. He could only see the terror in her face, her mouth open in a silent scream.

Okay, David, said Monroe. *Time to get moving to the next intersection.*

David stepped away from the group. "You couldn't have mentioned that *before* I climbed up onto this roof?"

Sorry. But you need to hurry.

David knew Abraham would feel guilty abandoning Mrs. Powell and her children on the roof. Their prayer ended, he turned back to speak with her, but found her looking at him, smiling, as if she already knew.

"Go," she said. "Go to your daughter."

"But—"

"All will be well," she said. "We have prayed, and I feel certain God has heard us. He will protect us, for it is his work we do here."

Abraham wished he had her faith, but after the life he had led, he had far too many questions for God, for which a good long conversation with him was needed. But he kept his doubts to himself, and bade farewell to Mrs. Powell and her children.

"When this is over," she said. "Come back to see us. Our sailors can always benefit from the wisdom of good men."

"I will come back to see you," Abraham said.

He found a tree at the back of the building and descended to the street, his muscles already fatigued before he'd touched ground. The tree deposited him in an alley off Water Street. He followed it uptown, away from the mob outside the Sailors' Home on Dover.

You're on track, Monroe said. *Just keep moving north.*

"That's where I'll meet Sean and Natalya?"

Monroe paused again. *That's right.*

"I'm coming, Eliza," Abraham whispered to himself.

"I'm coming, Grace," David said.

CHAPTER SEVENTEEN

Tommy led Adelina west over fences and through the back lawns of the neighborhood. They encountered others along the way, people who'd likewise fled from their homes out the back ways. But Tommy could see in their eyes they didn't know what to do, or where to go. The mob seemed as though it was everywhere at once.

"Go to the police precinct," he whispered to each of them as they passed. "You'll be safe at the police precinct."

He and Adelina eventually emerged through an alleyway onto Fourth Avenue. They cut up to Twenty-Sixth and then over to Madison Square, thus far avoiding any further mobs.

"Do you smell that?" Adelina said. "It's smoke."

Tommy spun around, searching the sky above the buildings that surrounded them, and spotted the column just to the southeast. "I think that's the State Armory," he said. "My God, they've fired it."

"Armory?" Adelina said. "Does that mean the mob is now carrying guns?"

"I pray not," Tommy said. As it was, he had no idea how the police would be able to suppress this uprising. There were perhaps fifteen hundred patrolmen available to the city, if all reported to their precincts, but right then, there were far fewer than that on duty. Against a mob of ten thousand, and still growing. If the rioters were equipped with carbines and rifles, it would be impossible to beat them back.

They crossed Madison Place into the park, passing the bench where they had spent time talking the previous night.

"Oh!" Tommy said. "Oh, damn me for a fool!"

"What is it?" Adelina asked.

"Your gold," he said. "I left your gold at my brother's house."

"Well," Adelina said, "strictly speaking, that was your gold you left, not mine. And loathe as I am to think of it filling the pockets of thieves and ruffians, I don't think it's worth going back for."

He hadn't thought to go back for it, but that didn't stop him from slapping the side of his head.

"Stop that," Adelina said. "There are far more important things in this world than gold. I'd much rather spend our time worrying about what we're going to do now. Do you still think my hotel will be unsafe?"

Tommy looked back over his shoulder. The main body of the mob was moving downtown by way of the wide avenues, but smaller groups of rioters had splintered off down the side streets. His instinct told him they would spread their havoc from the

East River to the Hudson, every block, every street. They would eventually reach the hotel.

"I don't think it's safe," he said.

"Then where should we go?" she asked. "A police precinct?"

"That mob could easily overrun a precinct, if they determine to. I had to tell those people something."

"Then where?"

"The Seventy-First Infantry has their arsenal up on Thirty-Fifth and Seventh Avenue. The mob might take on the police, but I doubt they'll take on the army."

"I thought you said the army was out of the city."

"The arsenal will be garrisoned," Tommy said. That was the only place he could think of within the city that would be safe enough. The only other option would be to get Adelina *out* of the city, assuming the riots didn't spread to nearby towns. "Do you have friends or family in Brooklyn? Or New Jersey?"

"I have an aunt in Hoboken," she said.

"Hoboken, good," Tommy said. "The Christopher Street Ferry will get you there, if that becomes necessary."

Tommy knew there was a provost marshal's office on Broadway at Twenty-Ninth Street, so he led Adelina west along Twenty-Sixth to cut around it, waiting to turn uptown until they'd reached Seventh Avenue. They had almost ten blocks to walk, which would not have been far under normal circumstances. They had only made it three when a roving band of rioters came around the corner. Tommy hurried Adelina down a nearby alleyway, behind a broken wagon missing its rear axle. He had left his locust club behind, afraid it might give him away as a patrolman, so he wasn't equipped for a brawl.

"Thank you," Adelina whispered after the mob had passed.

He looked at her. "For what?"

"For all of this. For taking care of me. You don't really know me. You don't even know if I deserve this."

"You deserve it," he said. "Everyone deserves it."

She sighed. "You're a good man, Tommy Greyling. You may be the best man I've ever met."

"Adelina—" She silenced him with a lingering kiss on his cheek, and he felt his skin grow hot where her breath had blessed him and her lips had graced him. He stammered. "That's not . . . You don't . . ."

"*Shh,*" she said. "Let's just keep moving."

So they left the alleyway and continued up the street. Tommy was still flustered by what had just occurred, but he knew Adelina was not the kind of woman to make much of such things. She had likely kissed many men on the cheeks, so even though such a thing was singular to him, it likely meant little to her.

The roiling current of Tommy's mind tossed Sean in confusion as well. He knew it was Adelina who had kissed him, yet he also knew Natalya had experienced it, and he wondered what that might mean outside the simulation.

But they continued onward. Smoke plumes marked distant fires, the rioters seemingly bent on destruction. Tommy and Adelina successfully avoided several more mobs, hiding and waiting them out on the journey to the arsenal, which they reached after one o'clock. It was a fortress of a building, three stories of white stone with octagonal towers at three of its corners, and a massive square bell tower at the fourth. Soldiers stood out front, armed with rifles and bayonets.

The sight of their uniforms threatened to drag Tommy back to the battlefield still raging in the distant recesses of his memory. His hands began to sweat, his breathing quickened, and his pace slowed.

"What is it?" Adelina asked him.

"Nothing," he muttered, but the smoke in the air suddenly looked and smelled of gunpowder, and his leg throbbed.

"Tommy," Adelina said, taking his arm. "Tommy, what's wrong?"

He felt her hand on him, but it wasn't enough to pull him back, and over her voice he heard the echoes of gunfire and horses.

"Tommy, look at me," Adelina said, shaking him.

He glanced down at her, into her eyes. She reached up and laid her hand aside his cheek, the same cheek she had earlier kissed, and a shudder rippled his back, silencing the roar and soothing the pain in his wound.

"There you are," Adelina said. "You went so pale."

"I'm sorry," he said. "I—"

"Don't apologize," she said. "You have nothing to be ashamed of. Are you well?"

"I think so."

"Good." She took his hand and squeezed it. Then she nodded toward the armory. "Is this still our plan?"

"Yes," he said. He hadn't had an episode like that in quite some time, and it had caught him unawares. But now he was prepared.

They marched toward the arsenal's main entrance, but before they'd reached it they were greeted by an older soldier, a gray codger with a jutting chin.

"What can I do for you?" he asked. "You here to volunteer, young fellow?"

"Volunteer?" Adelina asked.

"They put out a call," the man said. "All able-bodied veterans to report here. We've mustered quite a force."

"That's not why we've come," Tommy said. "I'm wondering if you would take this woman into the arsenal and keep her safe until the trouble has passed."

"Wait, you're not coming with me?" Adelina said.

"I'll wait until I know you're safe and settled," Tommy said.

The old man looked to his compatriots, who shrugged. "Not sure about this, as we've not been given orders relative to civilians."

"So there's nothing forbidding it," Tommy said.

"Not strictly speaking, no." He narrowed his eyes and sucked on a cheek. "This way, then," he said, and led them through the arsenal's main door.

They entered into a bare and cavernous foyer, and from there the old veteran took them to an anteroom lined with benches, where he instructed them to have a seat and wait.

"I'll find out the particulars."

"Much obliged to you, officer," Adelina said with a gracious smile.

The man tipped his cap. "Thank you, miss, but I was never an officer." And he walked away from them, smiling.

After he'd left, Adelina whispered, "I knew he wasn't an officer," and gave Tommy a wink.

Then they waited for well over an hour. Soldiers came and went through the room, along with volunteers answering the call of recruitment. It became obvious to Tommy they had mustered a modest force of veterans who had seen battle. If fully armed, they would constitute a considerable foe to the rioters, but seemed in no hurry to go out and meet the mob.

When the old soldier finally returned, he did so shaking his head. "I'm afraid I'll have to ask you to leave," the old man said. "We've been ordered to send civilians to the Metropolitan Police precincts."

"But the precincts aren't safe." Tommy tried to sound calm and reasonable, even though this smacked of bureaucratic idiocy. "Most are manned by only a handful of patrolmen. They'll be overrun."

"I'm sorry," the man said. "No civilians are to be admitted into the arsenal at this present time, by order of General Sanford."

As absurd as the situation was, Tommy knew it would do no good to argue further, so he rose from the bench and Adelina did the same. They followed the old man back out into the street, the skyline blackened deeper than when they'd gone in. Tommy turned to the old man.

"Look at that." He pointed at the smoke rising thickly in the distance. "With the troops you've mustered, why aren't you out there taking on the mob?"

The old man snapped his crooked back straight. "We're waiting on General Sanford's orders."

"That gall you?" Tommy asked, needling him. "It would gall *me* to be held back."

The old man swallowed his words and said nothing.

Tommy shook his head and pulled Adelina away some yards, back down Seventh Avenue. "This reeks of politics," he said.

"What do you mean?" Adelina asked.

"Sanford's a Democrat, and he reports to Governor Seymour, who is also a Democrat."

"So?"

"There's a good chance the Democrats see this riot working in their favor against Lincoln and the war. If they can stop the draft, they have a better chance of forcing Lincoln to make peace."

"You're saying they want this?"

"I'm saying Sanford has put down riots in this city before, so why not now? He has no reason to hold his troops back, and yet he's in there with his volunteers doing nothing." But now they were back on the street, and he still had to get Adelina to safety. "I think we should proceed to the ferry at Christopher Street," he said. "That will take you to Hoboken."

"Very well," she said. "But I feel you still mean to leave me."

"I have a duty to this city," Tommy said. "Once you are safe, I mean to wage war on these rioters, and I don't plan to make any arrests or take any prisoners."

Adelina said nothing to that, and together they moved south in the same way they'd made their way uptown, staying inconspicuous and out of sight. As they approached Thirtieth Street, they saw looters and houses aflame ahead, and dodged eastward a block to avoid them, toward one of the largest smoke columns. As they moved down Sixth Avenue and reached Twenty-Ninth Street, they saw the smoke rising from the charred and smoldering remains of the provost marshal's office. Fortunately, the mob had moved on from it, their work accomplished, so Tommy guided Adelina toward the ruined building.

Smoke burned Tommy's eyes, the air filled with fluttering scraps of ash. Adelina coughed and covered her mouth with her sleeve as they passed the building, now a jumble of splintered and blackened bones, the ground around them littered with scraps of wood and iron, bricks and paving stones.

When they reached Broadway, they turned downtown, heading toward the Fifth Avenue Hotel. Tommy didn't know what they would find there, but he planned to move back over to Sixth Avenue when he felt it was safe and follow that down to Christopher Street.

"Tommy, look," Adelina said.

Up ahead, through the smoke, Tommy glimpsed a group of four thugs viciously kicking and beating a figure on the ground, an old black man by the look of it.

"Stay back," he whispered.

"What are you going to do?"

"Crack some heads," he said. He skulked back to the wreck of the provost marshal's office and snatched up a crowbar and an iron pipe, a weapon for each hand. Then he sneaked forward, advancing on the ruffians as quietly as he could.

"Filthy nigger!" one of the men shouted, planting a boot in his victim's stomach. "I'll kill every goddamn nigger in this city!"

"Kick his eyes out!" another of them shouted.

When Tommy was as close to them as he thought he could approach without alerting them, he broke into a full, silent charge. The thugs looked up at him, but not in time. Tommy threw all his weight behind the iron in his hands and barreled through the rioters. The crowbar caught one of the ruffians by the jaw. The pipe knocked the skull of another. Tommy's momentum carried him a dozen feet before he skidded to a stop and spun around to rush the remaining two.

They stood in shock, staring at their fallen comrades, who would be of no use to them now, but had their guards up before Tommy reached them. One had pulled a knife and the other held a brickbat.

Tommy laid into the one with the brickbat first, disarming him, and immediately swiveled to take on the other. But the knife stabbed Tommy in his side before he made it around. Pain blazed from the wound, but Tommy suppressed and ignored it, and hooked his opponent's neck with the crowbar, yanking him forward as he hit his face with the pipe.

The brickbat hit Tommy in the shoulder, throwing him forward. But the ruffian had missed his one shot at Tommy's head, which meant Tommy had no trouble turning around and felling the fool with a succession of blows that broke the man's forearm and shoulder.

All four thugs down, Tommy dropped his weapons, which clanged to the ground, and did a quick probe of his knife wound. It was bleeding heavily, but not at a life-threatening pace. The blade had pierced the muscle at Tommy's waist, but not his abdominal cavity.

The victim groaned on the ground, and Tommy knelt down to inspect him. The poor man was conscious, but nearly ruined. A broken jaw, broken cheeks and eye sockets, bleeding from one of his ears. Tommy was certain the man had multiple broken ribs, and possibly more internal damage to his organs.

"Is he alive?" Adelina asked, running up.

"Barely," Tommy said.

The man whispered something, but Tommy couldn't hear what he'd said.

He leaned closer. "What's that, friend?"

"Tweed," the man said, gasping. "I work . . . for Tweed."

"Tweed?" Tommy said. "William Tweed?"

The man nodded a fraction of an inch. "Thirty-Sixth Street," he said. "Fifth and Sixth."

"Fifth and Sixth Avenues?" Adelina asked.

"I think so," Tommy said. "I think it's an address."

"We should take him there," Adelina said.

"He needs a hospital," Tommy said. "Soon."

"No." Adelina shook her head. "I think we should listen to him. I think he knows what he needs."

Tommy looked again at the old man and thought maybe she was right. With his injuries, at his age, he wasn't likely to survive the night, no matter what the doctors at the hospital were able to do for him.

"All right," Tommy said, and then he spoke to the old man again. "What's your name, friend?"

"Abraham," the man whispered.

"Abraham, I'm going to sit you up." Tommy wedged his hands under the man's shoulders. "It's probably going to hurt. Are you ready?"

Abraham nodded again.

Tommy raised him as gently as he could, and Abraham whimpered all the way into a sitting position.

"Hold him up," Tommy said to Adelina.

She knelt down and put her arms around Abraham in an embrace, keeping him steady, while Tommy turned around and presented his back.

"Now," he said. "Adelina, gently raise his arms, one at a time, and lay them on my shoulders."

Abraham groaned behind him, and then one of the old

man's hands came over Tommy's head, past his ear. Tommy reached up and took hold of it so it wouldn't fall, noticing that Abraham's knuckles were bleeding and bruised. He had put up a fight.

Abraham groaned again, and Adelina placed his other arm on Tommy's opposite shoulder. Tommy took hold of it as well, and then he gently pulled both of Abraham's arms forward until he had his elbows, folding Abraham's arms around his neck.

"Don't be afraid to choke me," Tommy said. "Hold on tight." Then he shook his head and said to Adelina, "Christ, this is going to hurt him if his ribs are broken."

But when he heaved upward, rising to his feet with Abraham hanging on his back, Tommy felt a sharp pain in his knife wound, as if he was getting stabbed again. He grunted and flinched, and Adelina noticed.

"What's wrong?" she asked. "You—my God, you're hurt!"

"I'll be fine," he said through gritted teeth. He still had to carry the man on his back seven blocks.

"But you're bleeding!"

"I'll be fine," Tommy said. "Trust me. I am acquainted with injuries."

He bent at the waist to a severe angle, hoping to take the pressure off Abraham's arms and ease the old man's pain. Then he set off, back up Broadway, then over to Sixth Avenue, then uptown, struggling with every step. Tommy knew he was strong, but he also knew he had his limits. Two brawls in two days, a sleepless night, and a knife wound.

He would soon find out if those were his limits.

CHAPTER EIGHTEEN

Cudgel watched the city burn from the top of the Fifth Avenue Church's bell tower. After defeating the Assassin, he had brought the stolen relic here to wait until sunset, when he was to deliver the dagger to the Grand Master. Cudgel had planned to involve himself fully in the day's excitement, but after acquiring his prize, he dared not the slightest risk losing it.

So from his vantage two hundred feet above the streets, he had witnessed the mob unfold a red tapestry of fire, blood, and fear over the city.

Through it all, Javier had felt utterly helpless. He wanted to do something to stop it, but he didn't dare leave the church tower, remembering Monroe's warnings about desynchronization. Now that Cudgel had the Piece of Eden in his possession,

Javier wouldn't risk blowing the whole reason they'd come into the simulation. So instead he had to watch, and he had to experience Cudgel's satisfaction at the chaos and destruction he had partly caused.

Much of it had been strategized and executed according to design. Both provost marshal's offices, the one on Broadway and the other on Third, had been put to flame before they could carry out the draft. That was the entire pretense for the protest, after all, which became the riot Cudgel expected even more quickly than he'd thought it would.

Other stages did not go as planned. The attempt to seize the Second Avenue Armory had failed, perhaps because Cudgel hadn't been there to lead the assault. Instead, he'd watched the building burn from a distance, destroying thousands of rifles, carbines, and other guns, aware that it was probably the mindless rioters who'd set it afire, taking with it their only chance at true victory. Without guns, the mob would not succeed in taking control of the city, no matter how long Sanford kept the army out of it.

But the mob didn't need to take the city.

Cudgel looked down at the dagger in his hand. If the weapon was what he believed it to be, a Precursor relic, then the Grand Master would no longer need the mob.

Though the mob had done its work well. As evening approached, fire and smoke rose up from all quarters of the city. None of it bothered Cudgel. It was necessary work that had to be done. The city had become too unwieldy, and there were larger issues at play in the war. A few lives lost and a few buildings burned could not compare to the peace and prosperity of the nation.

Away from that battlefield, Javier didn't know what to make of Cudgel's absolute certainty. He was in the Templar's mind, so he couldn't help but at least partly see things Cudgel's way, while at the same time he deplored what the Templars were doing.

Then evening came, and it was time for Cudgel to take the dagger to the Grand Master. He wrapped the relic up and slipped it into a pocket of his coat, and was about to descend to the street when he noticed a new fire to the north. He'd thought the rioters had moved downtown, so he pulled out his Herschel spyglass and used it as a telescope to see what the mob had done.

It was the Colored Orphan Asylum. The mob had set fire to it.

Cudgel put the spyglass away, his mouth dry, his stomach sick. While he believed in the cause of the Order, and would follow any command given to him, the idea of murdering children gave him pause, and in that moment, Javier felt his mind and Cudgel's to be at peace, rather than at war.

Cudgel descended the bell tower rapidly, sliding and dropping from ledge to ledge, until he reached the street. After struggling to move north a block and a half, he scaled a building to escape the throng in the streets, and then made his way over the rooftops.

The orphanage had never been a target. Cudgel's personal objections aside, it didn't make sense as one. The Grand Master had made it clear: The riots would only succeed if held forth as a popular uprising, and fail if judged as evil and barbarous. Some degree of looting was acceptable and expected, but the burning of an orphanage had gone too far. Cudgel had to do something, and it had to be done quickly.

He descended to the street again when he reached the Croton Reservoir, but climbed its walls and raced along its wide, brick embankment, the man-made lake on his left, the ghostly ruins of the Crystal Palace just to the west.

The column of smoke ahead of him grew bloated on the fire's feasting, and by the time Cudgel reached the orphanage, the building was completely engulfed in flame and lost. A dozen firemen stood by, helpless, held back from their duty by the mob shouting curses.

"Burn their filthy nest!"

"Murder every last monkey!"

The scene horrified Javier, and angered Cudgel, and they both hoped the children had escaped.

Looters churned in the street, their arms full of bedding and furniture and other goods they'd managed to haul out before the fire took charge. Cudgel moved north along Fifth Avenue through the throng, searching for the children, and turned onto Forty-Fourth Street just as the orphans emerged from an alleyway, having apparently exited the burning building through a back way.

As the children filed out, Cudgel counted some three hundred or more of them, and they had walked right into the waiting hands of the thick mob. Before the rioters could turn their aggressions on the orphans, Cudgel had to create a diversion to give them time to escape, something to draw the mob's fury, and the only thing he knew to be more maddening to the mob than blacks would be a sympathetic white.

"If there's a man among you," he cried, "with a heart within him, come and help these poor children!"

The response came as swiftly as Cudgel had expected it to. The mob seized hold of him, swearing and cursing him for an abolitionist and a Lincolnite, and he allowed them to pull him away, keeping hold of his rifle, even as the officers of the orphanage moved the children west, away from danger.

Cudgel withstood a few painful kicks and blows, waiting until the children were well underway before he went to work on his captors. Some were half-hockey, and none were seasoned brawlers. With a few throat punches and hard elbows to kidneys, Cudgel slipped away and up the wall of the nearest building.

From there, he raced along with the children, keeping watch from on high as they marched west, mostly likely toward the Twentieth Precinct police station house. When a group of twenty or more orphans got separated from the main body, Cudgel descended to the street once again.

"Come along," he said to them, approaching with his arms spread wide. "I won't hurt you. Come this way."

They looked up at him, cheeks smudged with tears and soot. Some were perhaps ten or eleven years old. They held hands with the smaller ones, some as young as three or four.

"All will be well," he said. "I'll protect you. But we need to hurry."

He pushed them forward, ushering them down Seventh Avenue two blocks, through a crowd that sneered and eyed them like feral cats. The street was a tinderbox, and it would only take one spark for all those children to die. Farther down the road, Cudgel spotted a few horsebuses from the Forty-Second Street line parked against the curb. Most of the city's drivers hadn't dared to run that day, out of fear for their animals and their vehicles, but Cudgel knew one of the men up ahead, a Tammany informant.

"Paddy McCaffrey!" Cudgel shouted.

The driver looked up.

"Boss wants these children unharmed!" Cudgel said, leading the children to the bus.

"That a fact?" Paddy asked.

"It is a fact," Cudgel said. "Get them on these buses and take them to the Twentieth Precinct. Now."

Paddy's face blanched. "This mob'll skin me alive if I do that!"

"Oh, yeah?" Cudgel stepped closer to him and poisoned his voice with menace. "And I'll open you up right here in the street if you don't. Understand? Now, hurry."

Paddy scowled but nodded, and Cudgel helped usher the children up into the bus, and when they filled that one, he put them on the next, until they were all aboard. The mob took note as Paddy spurred his team forward through it, and some of the men shouted, shaking their fists.

"Let me through!" Paddy bellowed.

"Come on, boys!" A red-faced barber stepped toward the bus brandishing an axe. "Let's break this stage open and wring some necks!"

Cudgel pulled a slender blade from his belt and moved to intercept the man. Just as the barber raised his weapon over his head to strike, Cudgel knifed his liver, a quick thrust, and the axe tumbled to the ground. The mob around them barely noticed until the barber collapsed, but Cudgel had already stepped away, and the horsebuses had trundled on.

The violence of that memory didn't trouble Javier, and he wondered if it should have. He had begun to ally himself too closely with Cudgel, who stayed with the vehicles for several more blocks until he was sure they were out of the worst of the riot, and then he broke away, turning toward the Grand Master's house. He kept his perception honed as he moved down Broadway with the relic, as if feeling ahead with the point of a sword.

He doubted the Assassin would be of any further hindrance. It had proved an easy thing to defeat him, but Cudgel wondered now if he shouldn't have just killed him. The decision to let the Assassin live had been strategic, and undoubtedly arrogant. Cudgel wanted the Brotherhood to know there was another Hunter in New York, a Cormac. But it may have been better to take no chances with a relic at hand.

When he reached Thirty-Sixth Street, he turned east, the setting sun at his back barely visible through a thick curtain of charcoal clouds. The day's heat hadn't surrendered yet, but the air wasn't quite as lifeless. The sky threatened rain, which would aid the city and the police in controlling the fires, another unfortunate turn in their plans.

Cudgel approached the Grand Master's brownstone, and, from a distance, he felt something amiss. He drew near enough to see the front door stood open, apparently kicked in, and immediately climbed up to the roof of a neighboring house. From there, he found an attic window into the Grand Master's residence, broke it open, and slipped inside.

Dust and shadow stifled the air within. Cudgel crept forward through the attic, head ducked, careful of the creak in the wooden floorboards. He found the attic door and opened it a crack, finding the hallway empty, but heard voices coming up from somewhere in the house below. A woman crying.

As far as Cudgel knew, the Grand Master didn't live here, but maintained the house for meetings. The only people present should have been the servants, and for a moment, Cudgel wondered if some of the mob had done the unthinkable and invaded the Grand Master's property.

He crept along the hallway to the staircase and peered downward through the square spiral of the banister. The voices seemed to be coming from the first floor, so Cudgel descended two flights of stairs and waited in the shadows of the second floor.

"I'm so sorry," a woman was saying as another woman cried.

"He wanted to be brought here," said a man's voice. "He wanted to see you."

Cudgel didn't recognize either of them, but they didn't sound like rioters, here to loot the house.

The sobbing woman broke into a scream that rent the air all through the house and chilled Cudgel to the deepest reaches of his chest. It even sent him back up the staircase a step, and nearly distracted him from the shadow moving toward him.

He ducked just as a throwing knife buried itself in the wall where his head had been. Then the Assassin charged. His shoulder caught Cudgel in the side and sent him falling down the stairs, but Cudgel caught the banister and flipped himself over it, landing easily on the ground floor a dozen feet below.

Three others appeared in the doorway of the library, no doubt drawn by the commotion: Eliza, the Grand Master's servant, another woman in a fine dress, and a huge bloke who carried himself like a copper. Javier knew them to be Grace, Natalya, and David.

But Cudgel didn't. He also didn't know where the Grand Master was, but this house had been compromised, and he had to get the relic to safety above all else.

He bolted for the open front door, the sound of throwing knives striking the floor behind him. One pierced his upper arm, near his shoulder, as he fled outside. He grimaced as he pulled it out and dropped the blade in his run down the street. He wasn't sure if he could climb with the injury, but he made the attempt, and, in spite of the pain, he reached the rooftops, aglow with nearby fires and adrift with smoke and ash.

He didn't wait to see if he was being pursued. Until he knew more, and with his damaged arm, this was not a combat situation. He thought his best chance to evade the Assassin and his allies would be the chaos of the mob up near the burning orphanage, so he raced northward.

At Thirty-Ninth Street, he did manage a backward glance, and saw the shadow of the Assassin flying toward him, gaining ground and closing the distance. It was possible Cudgel wouldn't outrun him before he reached the mob.

He dropped to street level at Fortieth and dove into the ruins of the Crystal Palace. A fire had destroyed it almost five years earlier, but with the sun now below the horizon, the heavy cloud cover had brought on an early darkness, and the Palace offered Cudgel ample places to hide.

He scudded forward, dodging through the decaying metal skeleton, its skin of glass still clinging to its bones in places, reflecting broken images back at him. The glittering structure had stood over a hundred feet, and some of its ribs still reached for that height. Cudgel passed under several towering statues of Greek and Roman warriors, and nymphs and queens that remained in the wreck, charred, broken, and forgotten.

Once he had gone deep enough into the ruins, he turned to look back, scanning his surroundings for any movement. He saw no sign of the Assassin, but that meant nothing.

Cudgel took up a protected position behind a pile of twisted metal beams and unshouldered his rifle. He had no time for smoke grenades, and went for the sleep darts he had used earlier, then loaded the weapon and waited, cursing himself for letting the Assassin live.

The roar of the city's devastation was somewhat muted here, and Cudgel closed his eyes, listening again for the sound of the Assassin. A flapping sound to his right set his rifle into motion, but he realized before he pulled the trigger it was a bat.

As he was bringing the barrel back into a forward position, he detected a slight rustle behind him, and before he could react, felt a gloved hand grab his chin, yanking his head back, and then a pressure at his throat from the Assassin's hidden blade.

But Cudgel's hide armor did its job, giving him just the fraction of a moment he needed to deflect the blow, and then the fight went hand to hand.

Cudgel dropped the rifle and instantly had two knives out, slashing and stabbing in a desperate assault, but the Assassin pivoted to defense and blocked his attacks. The pain in Cudgel's shoulder blazed, and he knew the disadvantage would prove lethal in sustained direct combat. He rolled away and sprinted off into the ruins, but he heard the Assassin chasing after him.

He decided to attempt a feinted stumble, gripping his knuckle-duster, and went down into a crouch. The Assassin caught up to him quickly, and as soon as he came within reach, Cudgel spun around, bringing an uppercut almost from the ground. His knuckleduster caught the Assassin in the jaw, hopefully breaking it or shattering his teeth.

The blow launched the Assassin backward into the air, but Cudgel didn't wait for him to land before running again. He'd bounded several yards when a second throwing knife caught him hard in the back, and he stumbled forward, sliding into the ground of charcoal and glass.

The blade was too high for him to pull out, lodged between his ribs, and his breathing already hurt, so the knife had likely punctured the top of his lung. He could no longer fight, or run.

Cudgel went for the one remaining weapon he had available. He didn't know what power the relic had, and he hadn't even thought to try it until now, leaving that to the Grand Master. But in his desperation, he reached for it and brought it out from his pocket as the Assassin drew near.

The relic felt warm in his hand. He gripped the dagger tightly, and forced himself to his feet, stiff and wincing the whole way.

"Do you even know what you hold?" the Assassin asked him.

"It's a Precursor relic," Cudgel said. "Do you think I'm an idiot?"

"I think you're a mindless tool," the Assassin said. "But you must be a useful one."

"I would rather be a useful tool for peace than an agent of chaos."

The Assassin threw his arms wide. "Look around you! You think this isn't chaos?"

"This is the refiner's fire," Cudgel said, reaffirming his grip on the dagger. "This is necessary to rid the city of those who would hold back its progress." He coughed, and blood came up into his mouth. "These riots will be over in a matter of days, and at the end they will have cleared away all our opposition. The Order will bring about the fullness of its purpose for this nation at last. You are the fool for resisting it. For not seeing it." As Cudgel spoke, he felt a pulsing sensation, a kind of energy radiating up his arm from his hand. From the relic.

The Assassin had stalled in his approach. He appeared confused, as if he might actually be listening to Cudgel. Whatever power the dagger possessed, it seemed to have exerted its influence.

But Javier knew what was happening. He had experienced it before, in the memories of Chimalpopoca. This was what the Piece of Eden did.

Cudgel seized the moment of distraction and pulled out one of his knives. Then he flipped its blade between his fingers and hurled it at the Assassin.

The knife plunged deep into his stomach. The Assassin frowned at it, as if stunned, and Javier wondered if it was Owen or the Assassin looking out. Then his knees buckled and he went down on his back.

Cudgel let out a sigh, but the pain in his lung made him regret it. He didn't know if the knife in his back would prove fatal, but he had to somehow get the relic to the Grand Master before he died.

He was a Cormac, and he would serve the Order until the end.

CHAPTER NINETEEN

liza stood on the ledge, six stories above the alleyway, her chest heaving with her frantic breathing, her heartbeat a distant locomotive in her ears. Grace had retreated to the farthest corner of the farthest room within the palace of her mind. She had never done well with heights, and this memory, simulated or not, terrified her.

Varius stood on the opposite side of the alley, having just leapt across the divide. "You can do it," he said. "You've jumped wider gaps already today."

"But never from so high!" Eliza replied. She may have successfully made other jumps, but she hadn't worried those falls would kill her.

"Eliza, listen to me. You're afraid, and you believe your fear is telling you that you can't do it. But that is a lie. Your fear tells you nothing. You tell yourself you can't do it, to escape your fear."

"How is that supposed to help me?" Eliza said, grateful the day was at least free of wind, or else she would never have gone near the edge.

"Embrace your fear," Varius said. "Draw it into your arms and dance with it—"

"Dance with it?" She found it hard to lift her eyes from the chasm. "What do you mean, dance with it?"

"Fear is the cold flame. It can fuel you. You can use it to achieve feats you haven't imagined possible, if you ignore the lies you tell yourself and embrace your fear."

"How?"

"Let it burn through you. Feel it in every part of you, every muscle, every sinew, every bone. Extend that awareness to the world around you. The same vision that allowed you to read that message will tell you if you can make this jump."

Eliza closed her eyes.

"Feel it," Varius said. "And jump."

Eliza did what he asked. She focused on the icy fire raging through her body, from the center of her chest to the extremities of her arms and legs. She felt the power and strength it gave her, which she had never noticed before. She ignored the lie telling her she couldn't do it, and when she opened her eyes, and looked at the gap, she knew she could, with absolute certainty.

And she did, sailing easily across the chasm.

"There, you see?" Varius said. "You were born to this."

"You keep saying that. What does that even mean?"

Varius looked hard at her. "I've been considering you since we met this morning. Testing you. And now I know you were born to be an Assassin."

"Oh, really?" Eliza resisted the urge to laugh. "Speaking of which, what did Mr. Tweed mean by calling you that, exactly? Do you kill people?"

"I bring them peace."

Now Eliza did laugh.

"You find that amusing?"

"I mean no disrespect, but bring them peace?"

"It is the truth. My purposes are solemn and sanctified."

"Sanctified? By what sort of priest?"

"By no priest," he said. "By the free will of mankind."

"And how do you know I was born to this?"

"Your sight, for example. It is called Eagle Vision, and it is often inherited. I received mine from my father. We're a Brotherhood, and we have a Creed we live by. We stand against tyranny and those that would enslave and oppress others."

"And you stand against Mr. Tweed?"

"Boss Tweed is what we call a Templar. His Order seeks peace by force, at the expense of free will. Our two factions are at war, and have been for all of history. They now seek to take control of this nation."

"And you think I'm an Assassin? Like you?"

"No, I think you have Assassin blood in you. To be an Assassin, you would have to first be trained and then swear loyalty to the Brotherhood and the Creed."

He seemed to be suggesting that was a possibility for her. But Eliza shook her head. "I'm just a maid. I'm not—"

"The Brotherhood does not judge your occupation, your status in society, or the color of your skin. All people are equal under the Creed. But we can save this discussion for another time. For now, there are more pressing matters."

Eliza didn't know what to make of what he was telling her. The sensible part of her rejected it. Even if it were all true, and she could see that Varius was being sincere, she thought it would be wrong to want any part of it. And yet, she did. This Assassin was suggesting a life beyond that of a servant. A life fighting for freedom. A life that made a difference.

"But you're doing extraordinarily well," Varius said.

A warm glow of elation and pride replaced the cold flame of her fear. "Thank you," she said.

"And trousers suit you," he added with a wink.

Eliza had balked at first to wearing men's clothing, but she was hardly the first woman to don a pair of pants. She'd even heard of some women disguising themselves as men to go off and fight the Rebels. Now that she'd been wearing them for much of the day, she had to admit they were practical, even if they made the heat of the day more unbearable.

"The afternoon has almost passed," Eliza said. "I think we should start heading toward Mr. Tweed's house, if we want to get there ahead of Cudgel."

Grace was relieved and glad at that, since she still had no idea where David was, even though Monroe had said he was safe.

"You're right," Varius said, but a grin spread across his face with a mischievous cant to it. "Shall we race there?"

"Race there?"

"Free run, as I've been training you all morning."

Eliza didn't know if she was ready for that. "But I—"

"But nothing!" Varius said as he tore away. "We race!"

By the time Eliza recovered herself and started running after him, he had already left the building they'd been standing atop behind, and he kept his lead for some distance, leaping from roof to roof, scrambling over peaks, chimneys, and gables.

Along with her pants, Varius had bought her a pair of gloves, and she was glad for them, as the free-running he'd taught her used her hands as much as her feet, and the stone and wood of the rooftops would have torn her skin away.

They'd spent most of the day among the rough pinnacles and valleys of the Five Points and the Bowery, which were surprisingly quiet, given the rioting elsewhere, and her focus had been on not falling and breaking her neck. Now that they raced northward, she noticed the smoke rising uptown, and realized the extent to which the mob had harmed the city.

"Keep with me!" Varius shouted. He dropped down to the level of the street, and then raced up to the wall of a chapel, the Church of the Ascension, and climbed.

Eliza followed him, but she was getting tired. The muscles in her arms quivered, and a fear of falling took hold once she'd reached a lofty height. But rather than listen to the lie, she focused on the fear, embracing the cold flame coursing through her arms, and found her strength not only restored, but magnified.

She reached the top of the square bell tower, with its parapets and four smaller steeples at the corners, and went to stand beside Varius.

"Look out there," he said. "With practice, some Assassins can extend their vision and awareness across an entire city."

Eliza's gaze swept the length of the island, but all she could see was smoke. "This city's on fire," she said. "We should do something."

"No," he said. "The riots will run their course, no matter what we do. I have a more important task."

"Does it involve this dagger? The one Cudgel stole from you?"

"It does," he said. "Even if we lose New York, that relic can win the war."

Eliza didn't understand that.

"Let's move," he said before she could ask.

They climbed back down the bell tower and the church, and resumed their journey uptown, no longer racing, but moving in step with each other. It seemed to Eliza that her whole body was changing. As she attempted and succeeded at the challenges Varius gave her, she felt as though she was tapping into something deep within her, a wellspring of familiar waters. Perhaps it *was* in her blood.

Grace had to admit, she felt it, too.

They reached Mr. Tweed's house well before evening, and as they climbed the steps and approached the front door, and Eliza inserted the key into the lock, she hoped with every moment that her father would be inside.

But when she turned the key and went in, she found the house empty.

"Father?" she called. "Papa?" But she went unanswered.

Eliza turned around and locked the door behind them as a precaution against the looters.

"There's a note," Varius said, pointing toward the table along the west wall.

Eliza rushed over, snatched it up, and read.

Varius walked toward her. "What does it say?"

"It's from my father," she said. "He was here. He asks me to wait, and he'll come back. If he doesn't, I'm to go to the Christopher Street Ferry at six o'clock."

"You should go," Varius said. "Before Cudgel arrives."

"But what if my father comes back? I want to be here."

"It is your choice," Varius said. "But he's given you a plan, and it would be best to keep to it, for your safety. But when the riot is over . . . if you come back to the city . . ."

"Yes?"

"You have a path open before you. If you want to take it."

"You mean being an Assassin."

"Are you opposed to such an idea?" Varius asked.

"I'm not opposed to it," Eliza said. "But I'm not in favor of it, either."

"Consider it," he said. "My task will take me out of the city for a time, but I will return soon, and I will find you if you wish. We can continue your training."

"I will think about it," Eliza said. "Where are you going?"

"I must take the dagger to General Grant."

"Ulysses Grant? Why?"

"It will help him win the war."

"But how—?"

The front door crashed open behind them, and Eliza turned as a hulking brute lumbered in. Though Grace recognized him as Sean, Eliza didn't know him, and her first thought was of a looter. But then she noticed the stranger's side was covered in blood, and he had someone's arms draped around his neck.

Eliza stepped toward him. "What is the meaning of—?"

"Miss," the man said, wheezing. "I have Abraham with me."

"What?" Eliza said. She stepped around him, and a terrible sob burst from her when she saw that it was her father, but he was barely recognizable. Both his eyes were swollen shut, and his face was a pulpy mess of bruises. Grace had to remind herself it wasn't David, it was their ancestor, but she still felt all of Eliza's pain.

"Where can I set him?" the man asked.

"In the library," Eliza said. "This way."

She pointed the way and then followed after the man, her hand upon her father's back, which felt cold to her touch in spite of the heat outside. Varius helped the stranger to lay her father upon one of the library's leather sofas. Once free of the weight, the stranger stumbled, teetering like a tree about to fall, but a woman rushed up to his side to support him.

Eliza nodded toward them but turned her attention back to her father. She didn't know where to start helping him. He needed a hospital.

Varius knelt down beside the sofa. "Let me examine him," he said. "I have some experience with these things." He touched and pressed, gently but with apparent determination and purpose, moving from her father's eyelids and face down to his torso, and then along the length of his arms and legs, bending his joints and feeling for breaks. When he was finished, he sat back, looking at her father with the back of his hand against his mouth. "Eliza . . ."

"Tell me," she said.

"He's alive, but barely. I believe his skull is fractured. The bones of his face are shattered. He has at least four broken ribs, one of which may have punctured his lung, because he seems to be bleeding internally."

Eliza sobbed again, and gasped, and covered her mouth as tears fell from her eyes. "Oh, Papa," she said. "Papa!"

Grace nearly lost it within her own mind. If David had experienced all of that, if Monroe had let her little brother go through that pain, she was going to unleash a holy fury on him.

Varius turned to the two strangers. "What happened? Who did this?"

"Thugs," the man said. "Rioters. I stopped them when I saw them, but they were already going at him."

"Thank you," Eliza said, feeling as though her chest had become an eggshell. "Thank you for saving him."

"You're injured, too," Varius said, pointing at the man's side.

"I'll be fine," the stranger said, though a moment later he lowered himself into one of the library's armchairs.

"What is your name?" Eliza asked him.

"Tommy Greyling," he said. "This is Adelina Patti."

The woman nodded her head toward Eliza, and Eliza noted the tears in her eyes, too. Then she turned back to her father and knelt down as close to his face as she could. She stroked his forehead, afraid to touch any other part of him. If his chest was moving, she couldn't see it, so she laid her head upon his breast to listen.

She heard his heart beat once, weakly. Then it went quiet. Then it beat again. Then it went quiet, as if each beat required almost everything he had left to give.

"I wanted to take him to a hospital," Tommy said. "But he asked to be brought here."

"Papa," Eliza whispered, her tears falling down upon her father's blood-soaked shirt. "Don't leave me. I can't lose you, too."

Varius suddenly looked up at the ceiling, and then left the room without a word.

"Where is he going?" Tommy asked.

But Eliza ignored him. "Please," she whimpered. "Papa, please." And then the eggshell of her chest caved in, and she sobbed openly against her father's chest, squeezing her eyes shut so tight she saw stars. A few moments passed this way, and then she felt a change in him, something passing up his body, and she pressed her ear against his heart, listening.

A beat.

Then quiet.

It stayed quiet, and she pressed her ear more tightly.

Another beat, as faintly as the flutter of a leaf in a breeze.

Then his heart went quiet again, for too long, and he expelled a long, raspy sigh, but took nothing back in. He became stillness and silence.

He was gone.

Eliza couldn't breathe. Her chest had seized up and she clutched at it, gasping, and when she finally took some air in, she wailed. There were no words behind it, no thoughts, only pain, rage, grief, loneliness, fear, and Grace felt it all with her.

Something thudded outside the library in the hall, and then Eliza heard the heavy impact of boots on the floor. Varius wasn't in the room, and she knew Cudgel was due to arrive at any moment.

She got up and hurried to the doorway, flanked by Tommy and Adelina, and from there, she saw Cudgel standing in the hall, looking surprised. Varius raced down the stairs behind him, but before anyone else could react, Cudgel ran for the front door.

Varius threw several flashing knives at him at blinding speed, five or six in the space of a moment. One of them struck Cudgel just before he made it outside. Varius charged after him, and Eliza did, too.

"Wait," Adelina said. "Don't—"

But the woman fell silent when Eliza turned around and they met each other's eyes. "That is the man responsible for my father's death," Eliza said, and then she charged out into the street.

She couldn't see Cudgel or Varius, but she knew if they had vanished from the streets they would take to the roofs, and she followed them up. Once she reached the rooftops, she glimpsed Varius in the distance, free-running north, and she flew after him.

Before she had gone far, she realized just how much Varius had been holding back while teaching her that day. She could not yet keep up with him, but she pressed forward, the smoke from the fires closing in around her, burning her lungs and her eyes. She crossed one block, and then another, and another, descending to the streets when she knew she couldn't make the leap. In her pursuit, she had no fear to embrace. It was fury that drove her.

When she reached the ruins of the Crystal Palace, she heard noises coming from within and realized that was where Cudgel and Varius had gone. She entered that place of metal and glass, keeping to the shadows, becoming invisible.

She heard her father's voice in her ears. *My little sneak thief.*

The deeper she went, the clearer the noises became: grunts, footsteps, the sound of a fist cracking against bone. She passed under statues lurking in the ruins like ghosts and through metal tangles twisted by fire and their own weight, following the sounds of combat.

Then she heard Varius speaking. "Do you even know what you hold?" he asked.

Eliza moved toward the sound, and her foot bumped up against something. She looked down. It was Cudgel's rifle.

"It's a Precursor relic," another voice said, which must have been Cudgel's. "Do you think I'm a fool?"

Eliza picked up the rifle. She'd held a gun once before, but it had been a long time ago, and a carbine with a much shorter barrel. But she tucked the rifle under her arm, her finger on the trigger, and slipped forward through the wreckage.

"Look around you!" Varius said. "You think this isn't chaos?"

"This is the refiner's fire," Cudgel said. "This is necessary to rid the city of those who would hold back its progress." He hacked a wet-sounding cough, and then both men came into Eliza's view.

Grace recognized them as Owen and Javier, friends facing off against each other once again. Javier held the Piece of Eden in his hand, and Owen stood only a few feet away from him.

"These riots will be over in a matter of days," Cudgel said, "and at the end they will have cleared away all our opposition. The Order will bring about the fullness of its purpose for this nation at last. You are the fool for resisting it. For not seeing it."

Eliza didn't know why Varius was just standing there. The Assassin looked confused, dumbfounded. And then suddenly, Cudgel flipped a knife in his hand and hurled it, and the blade struck Varius square in the stomach. After a stunned, silent moment, his body folded to the ground. But Eliza kept still, concealed in the shadows, and took aim with the rifle.

Cudgel sighed, making a gurgling sound, and when he turned away, Eliza saw a knife protruding from his back.

She had little confidence in her aim, so there was only a moment in which she could shoot him before he was too far away. She raised the barrel and sighted along it, right at his back, and calmed her breathing. She pulled the trigger, and felt the rifle butt slam into her shoulder at the same time she heard its muffled bang.

It wasn't a bullet that struck Cudgel, but some kind of dart. He staggered forward without turning around, and stumbled into a shuffling run. Eliza pursued him, but kept her distance as he gradually slowed and his legs wobbled, and before he had made it out of the Crystal Palace ruins, he collapsed.

Eliza quickened her pace to approach him, but carefully. He turned his head toward her, a trickle of blood leaking from his mouth. Grace knew it was Javier, but she had to stay back and let this moment unfold for Eliza. This was her revenge.

"You're Tweed's servant," Cudgel said. "Abraham's daughter?"

Eliza could see he was paralyzed by his own toxin, just as Varius had been, and she moved to stand over him. This was all his fault. His and the Grand Master's. Her beautiful father was gone. Her loving, constant, peaceful father, taken from her by the devil in human form.

"You killed him," she said.

"Who?"

"Abraham!" she shouted.

He tried to shake his head, but it looked more like a shudder. "No, I . . . Skinny Joe . . ."

"He's dead," Eliza said. "They beat him. A harmless, kind old man, and they—"

"I didn't beat your father," Cudgel said.

"Perhaps not," Eliza said. "But you fed the dogs who did, and then you set them loose."

He said nothing in reply to that.

Eliza noticed the dagger in his hand. She reached for it, and she could see the terror in his eyes, but he could do nothing as she took it from him. It was a curious thing, and it was hard to imagine it being worth the price that had been paid for it. But its edge was very sharp.

"You did something with this," she said. "This dagger. You stopped Varius with it. Confused him somehow. That's what Varius meant when he said General Grant could use it to win the war, isn't it?"

Cudgel said nothing, but he didn't need to. The tears glossing his eyes said everything Eliza wanted to hear from him.

"There is a path open to me," she said. "I wasn't sure if I would take it. But now I am." She laid the blade against his throat, and his eyes blinked and opened wide. "I will become an Assassin," she said. "And you and I will meet again." His eyes closed and he lost consciousness. She rose and left him to dream of his failure.

Varius was unconscious when she returned to him, but with the help of Adelina and Tommy Greyling, Eliza managed to get him to a hospital, and an hour later, she stood at the Christopher Street Ferry with the two of them. They seemed to be quite attached to each other, though Tommy appeared to have different ideas about the ferry than Adelina.

"Come with me," she said.

"I'm not going to do that," he said. "I'm not going to leave the city in the hands of the mob."

"But you are injured," Eliza said, offering support to Adelina.

"I'll pay a visit to the infirmary," Tommy said. "They'll stitch me up right, and then I'll be back at the front line." He looked down at Adelina. "Go to your aunt's. Stay there until the riots have passed."

"But I need to see you again," she said. "When—"

"I'll see you again," he said. "The very next time you sing in New York, I promise I'll be in the audience cheering you."

"That's not what I mean," Adelina said.

"I know it's not," he said. "But that's the only way it can be. I may only be a patrolman who wants a farm, but I know that much."

Adelina looked down. "Don't say that."

"Say what?" Tommy asked.

"Don't talk about yourself that way. You are . . ." But she didn't finish what she was about to say. Instead, she shook her head at the ground, almost as if she were angry, and when she looked up, she was crying. "I think I love you, Tommy Greyling."

"And I think I love you, Miss Adelina." He smiled. "But the ferry is about to leave, and you must go now. I need to make sure you're safe."

"I'm safe," she said. "I've always been safe with you." She wrapped her arms around him then, and after a moment, he did the same, nearly enveloping her, and they embraced for some time. Then she pulled away, wiping her eyes, and walked down the pier toward the boat without looking back.

Tommy watched her go and said to Eliza, "Make sure she gets to her aunt's, if you can."

"I will," Eliza said.

"And what will you do?" he asked.

"I have a task to complete," she said, the dagger tucked away in the pocket of the trousers she still wore. If she was going away to war, she needed to look the part. "After that, I think I'll come back to New York. I still have unfinished business here with Cudgel and Mr. Tweed."

Tommy nodded, looking a bit perplexed, and Eliza bade him good-bye. Then she boarded the ferryboat, which was filled to capacity with black men, women, and children. They huddled together, some of them nursing injuries, driven from their homes by hatred and violence, pain the look in every eye, and "why?" the unspoken question on every lip. The answer was that the city and the country were not free. Not yet.

The boat's steam engine chugged them along, out into the Hudson River toward New Jersey, and as the distance from the island grew, it seemed the whole city glowed red beneath a mountain of coal.

"It looks like it might rain," a young mother said, eyeing the clouds as her infant daughter slept in her lap. "That'd be a mercy."

"You pray for mercy, then," Eliza said. But to herself she whispered, "But I will fight for freedom."

CHAPTER TWENTY

O wen's simulation went black, but not the black when Varius was unconscious. A black that meant the simulation was over, and suddenly he was standing in the gray of the Memory Corridor, and he was there as himself.

You doing okay, Owen? Monroe asked.

"Did I die?" Owen asked. "I felt . . ." He had felt the knife enter his stomach, and he had felt his heart pumping out his blood, and he had felt his body going cold and numb, starting at his feet and moving upward.

No, you didn't die. Close, but Eliza saved you. Did it hurt?

"Not bad, actually." It wasn't the pain he remembered, but the fear. Varius's fear.

That's because the brain isn't built to store physical pain memory. In fact, it's supposed to mostly forget it, or else we wouldn't be able to function.

"I'm glad for David, then." The mob had really worked him over, a level of violence and hatred Owen still couldn't understand. "He's okay?"

I wouldn't say that. He might not remember the physical pain, but he remembers the emotional pain. That, our brains hold on to.

"Can I talk to him?" Owen had examined David, or David's ancestor, and he felt sick thinking about what that poor kid had gone through.

Soon, Monroe said. *You need to stay in the Memory Corridor a bit longer.*

"Why?"

Think of it like deep-sea diving. You can't come up too quickly or you get the bends. In this case, it's the brain bends. Little bubbles of your ancestor's consciousness that can cause all kinds of problems. Right now, you need to concentrate on leaving all those memories behind. You need to get your ancestor out of your head.

That would be hard. He'd been living in Varius's mind and memories for two days. Owen felt as if he knew Varius as well as he knew himself. It almost seemed as though they could be the same person. But he knew they weren't, and he also knew it hadn't actually been two days.

"What time is it?" Owen asked.

Almost four thirty in the morning. You guys have been in the Animus for a couple of hours.

"A couple of hours?" Owen shook his head. That seemed impossible.

It could have gone even faster, if it was just you. I had to slow things down a bit to keep you all integrated in the simulation. That way . . . Hang on. Javier's coming in.

Owen looked around, filled with a sudden avalanche of anger and hatred at the mention of Javier's name. But that didn't make sense. He wasn't angry at Javier; he was angry at Cudgel. But Javier was Cudgel, in a way.

Before he could sort it all out, Javier appeared next to him, and Owen almost took a swing at him before he caught himself. Instead, they just stared at each other.

"I want to kill you right now," Javier said.

"You almost did kill me," Owen said.

"I know," Javier said. "This is messed up."

Relax, you guys, Monroe said. *You're out of the simulation. You're Owen and Javier, not your ancestors.*

"You're talking like it's a switch," Javier said. "Like we can just flip it on and off."

I know it's easier said than done, Monroe said. *Just focus on your lives. Focus on your friends, your family, your home, your neighborhood. Focus on your memories, all the things that make you who you are. Remember, you're lying in a warehouse with a visor strapped to your head. Some of you are drooling.*

"Thanks for that," Javier said.

Hey, just trying to keep you grounded.

As time in the Memory Corridor passed, Owen noticed a lessening in the pressure of Varius's consciousness against his. As if he had more room to stretch and breathe inside his own mind. He thought about his grandpa's shop and his grandma's immaculate garden. He thought about his mom's polo shirts from work, and he thought about his room. He thought about his father.

Owen's whole reason for going into the Animus had been to get Monroe to help him find out what had really happened the night of the bank robbery. But the Animus had done something to that motivation. Where Varius feared he wouldn't live up to his father's legacy, Owen's grandparents and his mother feared that Owen would.

Owen didn't know what that meant, or how he felt about it. But he knew he looked up to his father, just as Varius looked up to his, and the experience of the Animus had made that even stronger.

"I don't even know what to think right now," Javier said to Owen. "She could have cut my throat."

"What?" Owen said. "Who?"

"Grace," Javier said. "No, not Grace. Eliza. She had the Piece of Eden."

Owen grinned, because he knew that would have given Varius a lot of satisfaction.

"You think that's funny?" Javier said.

"No," Owen said. "It's not that."

"Then why're you smiling?"

"It's nothing . . . My ancestor . . ."

"Your ancestor what?"

"Come on, man," Owen said. "You threw a knife at me. Are you really going to get all mad about this?"

Javier frowned, but said nothing more.

Let's bring you out now, Monroe said. *If you're ready.*

"I'm ready," Owen said.

"Me too," Javier said.

The Memory Corridor vanished, replaced by the black shield of the helmet's visor. Owen pulled it off, blinking against the lights of Monroe's warehouse hideout. He sat up with the stiffness of a long nap and looked over at Javier, who was getting out of his chair. Sean, Natalya, and Grace still seemed to be in the Animus. Monroe sat at a computer terminal in the middle of them, watching multiple computer monitors that seemed to be feeding him images and information from the simulations. Javier stepped over to him to look at the screens.

"What are they doing?" he asked.

"Heading to the ferry," Monroe said.

"Where's David?" Owen asked.

Monroe looked up, and nodded toward the circle of couches over in the next island of light, across the room. "He's there."

Owen turned and saw David on one of the sofas, hunched down low enough to bend at the neck. So Owen left Javier and Monroe and went to sit by him. David was staring straight ahead, along his chest where his glasses rested, his face empty of emotion. But his eyes were red, as if he'd been crying.

"That was brutal," Owen said.

David didn't respond.

"I'm sorry, man. I wish that didn't happen."

Still, David said nothing. He hadn't even acknowledged Owen was there, and after several minutes of awkward silence passed, Owen was about to get up and go back to the others.

"But it did happen." David put his glasses back on. "That is exactly what happened."

"I know. I'm sorry. Did it hurt?"

"Of course it hurt," David said, burying his shoulders in the cushions as he pushed himself upright. "What do you think?"

"Sorry, man." Owen held up his hands. "I was just asking."

David looked over at the Animus station. "But that wasn't even the worst part."

"What do you mean?"

"I mean, when they were beating me, and kicking me, I felt it, kind of. But the thing I kept thinking about was my daughter. That's so weird to say. My daughter. I didn't know where she was or if she was hurt or anything, and I knew I was going to die and I couldn't do anything more to help her . . . That was the worst part."

"Wow." Owen's eyebrows lifted. "That's like . . . But at least you don't have to worry about her anymore, right? I mean, she became an Assassin."

"Yeah, Monroe told me. That might make you feel better, but that would make Abraham feel worse."

"Really? Why?"

"That's not where he'd want her soul to live."

"What?"

David just shook his head. "Never mind. It's too complicated."

Owen sat back and looked at the kid in front of him, and he realized something had changed, and it wasn't that David was just upset. The Animus had changed him. David had gone into the simulation seeming pretty young, and maybe even naive, but it was as though he'd grown years in the last couple of hours.

"Guys." Javier waved them over. "Sean and Natalya are coming out."

"What about my sister?" David asked.

"Not yet," Monroe said.

Owen got up and walked over, but David stayed on the couch. By the time Owen reached the Animus station, Natalya had her helmet off, her hair matted against her head, and was rubbing her eyes. Sean was looking at her, and it was pretty obvious to Owen that he liked her. He just wasn't sure whether their simulation had anything to do with that. They had been together when they brought David to the Grand Master's townhouse.

"How're you guys doing?" Javier asked.

"I'm fine," Natalya said. "I think."

"Me too," Sean said, examining his side. Then he went to stand up, but his legs crumpled and he fell hard, banging into the machinery and wires on his way down, and ended up sprawled out on the ground.

Owen bent to help him. "You okay, man?"

"Yeah," Sean said, really quietly, his face red. "I'm fine."

"You need help?" Owen asked.

"No, I got it," Sean said. He stretched for his wheelchair, snagged the footplate with the tips of his fingers, and pulled it closer until he was able to pull himself up into it. "I forgot," he said with a downcast smile.

"I imagine that would be easy to do," Javier said. "After the Animus."

"Especially when you think about who your ancestor was," Monroe said.

"Yeah." Sean nodded, but his shoulders slumped a little. "You're right."

"When does Grace come out?" Owen asked. He wanted to talk to her. With the time they'd spent together in the simulation, he felt somewhat close to her, even though they hardly knew each other.

"She's on her own now," Monroe said. "We ran out the Concordance for this particular memory, which is why you're all out here. But her ancestor has the Piece of Eden, and Grace is following it to the end." He spun around in his office chair to face them. "While we wait, I want to talk to all of you."

Owen and the others took up places around the recliners, some sitting, some standing.

"David, would you come over here?" Monroe called, and as David walked over, Monroe tucked his hair behind his ears, leaned back in his seat, and folded his arms. "There is something I need for all of you to know, and I mean know it like you know gravity."

"What's that?" Javier asked.

"You. Are. You," he said. "That's your center. That's the truth you fall back on, the truth you can't escape."

"Who else would we be?" Sean asked.

"Use of the Animus can have side effects," Monroe said. "They're called Bleeding Effects."

"Bleeding?" David said. "What do you mean, bleeding? Like out our ears or something?"

"No," Monroe said. "Not *blood* blood. Transfer. Certain aspects of the Animus bleed over into the real world. Into you. Well, they're already in you, in your DNA. It's more like the Animus switches your DNA from genotype to phenotype."

"What does that mean?" David asked.

Javier answered him. "Your genotype is all the code you're carrying around, right? All of it, even the stuff we don't see, the recessive stuff. Your phenotype is what we see. It's the reason Sean has blue eyes and Natalya is short."

"That's right," Monroe said. "We all have genes that are turned off. The Animus can turn them on."

"Like what?" Owen asked.

"Well." Monroe linked his hands behind his head. "If your Assassin ancestors developed Eagle Vision, you might find that you have Eagle Vision now."

"What's Eagle Vision?" David asked.

"It's like heightened awareness," Owen said, and then he looked at Grace, still lying there with a visored helmet over her head. "She has it."

"But there are other Bleeding Effects, too," Monroe said. "Mental effects. Behavioral effects. You might find you have new abilities you didn't have before, if your ancestor had those abilities. You might get confused sometimes about what's real. What's your memory and what's your ancestor's. You might have flashbacks."

"You're telling us this now?" Javier said, adjusting his stance.

"Would it have changed your decision?" Monroe said.

It wouldn't have changed Owen's choice, and looking around the room, he didn't think anyone else would go back and do it differently, either.

"So like I said"—Monroe looked at each of them—"You. Are. You. You aren't your ancestor, and who they were doesn't mean anything about who you are. If they were an Assassin, so what? If they were a Templar, who cares? You take your own path, by your own choices. You're not a hostage to your DNA. Okay?"

They all nodded, some with less enthusiasm than others. Owen didn't quite accept what Monroe was saying. In the Animus, it had meant something important to Varius to do what his father had done and to follow in that legacy. It brought Varius pride and a sense of purpose. Would Monroe take that from him?

Monroe glanced back at his computer terminal, scanning the monitors. "I think the memory is ending," he said, pulling on a headset with a microphone. "I'm going to load the Memory

Corridor. Why don't you all go over to the couches? This will take a few minutes."

They did what he asked, and ambled over to sit down together. Owen and Javier ended up on opposite ends of the same sofa. Natalya took one of the armchairs, and Sean wheeled his chair up next to her. David had the other couch to himself. No one spoke for a few minutes, until Natalya sighed.

"I've got to get home," she said. "My parents are going to freak out."

"Mine, too," Sean said. "They worry about me a lot more since the accident."

"When did it happen?" Javier asked.

Owen had wondered about that, too.

"A couple years ago," Sean said. "Drunk driver."

Owen turned to David. "What about your parents?"

"My dad will be pretty upset if he finds out. But the first thing he'll ask is if Grace was with me. Then he'll blame it all on her. My mom will just go along with whatever he says."

"What if Grace wasn't with you?" Owen asked.

David shrugged. "I never really get in trouble."

"Well," Javier said, "my mom will freak out. My dad will be disappointed in me."

"Which would you rather have?" Sean asked.

Owen wished he still had his dad to disappoint.

Javier shook his head. "I don't know. They're both bad."

"My mom and my grandparents will just think I ran away," Owen said. "I think they've been expecting me to for a while."

"Hey, guys," Monroe called. "Grace is out."

They rose from their seats, David more quickly than the rest, and hurried over to the Animus station. Monroe was just helping Grace get her helmet off when David walked up and threw his arms around her. It looked as if he was crying a little, and Owen caught a glimpse of the younger boy he'd seen before the experience in the Animus. Grace closed her eyes and hugged him back.

"Hush, I'm okay," she said to him. "It's okay."

David held on for another moment, and then he nodded against her and stepped back, wiping his cheeks with the heel of his hand.

"What did you see?" Monroe asked her.

"I saw the Civil War," she said, her eyes wide and seeming to contain the reflections of things beyond what was in the room. "I even fought in it."

"And did you see what happened to the Piece of Eden?" Monroe asked.

Grace nodded and swallowed. "I carried it all the way to Vicksburg, on the Mississippi River. I found General Grant, and I gave it to him. He recognized it from the Aztec Club. By that time, I had figured out how to use it. It helped me through some tough spots while I was bringing it to him, actually. So I was able to show him how it worked. Well, not completely. But enough that I think he got that it was more than a souvenir from Mexico."

"So what happened after that?" David asked.

Grace shrugged. "I don't know. The memory ended once I handed it over."

"What happened after that," Monroe said, "is that Lincoln made Grant the general of all the Union Armies, and Grant won the war, and eventually he was elected president for two terms. I think it's safe to say he kept the Piece of Eden with him during that time, and maybe until his death."

"Where did he die?" Natalya asked.

"After he learned he had throat cancer," Monroe said, "he moved from New York City to a cottage on Mount McGregor to write his memoirs. That's where he died. The cottage is still there, kind of a museum."

"So is that where the dagger is?" Javier asked. "Seriously? You couldn't have just guessed that?"

"Perhaps we could have," Monroe said. "But the dagger could also have been *any* number of places, and now we have a pretty good idea where to look. I can't thank you all enough for what you've done to help me. You trusted me, and that means a lot. I won't let you down. I promise when this is all over, you'll be safe."

"So we can go?" Natalya asked.

"Yes," Monroe said. "Yes, definitely. I'll drive you all in the bus." He bent over, threw a couple of levers, and lifted what looked like a heavy cpu out of the Animus.

"What's that?" Javier asked.

"The Animus core," Monroe said. "I try not to let it out of my sight. Come on, let's go."

So that was the end of it. They all moved as a group from the room, out into the hallway, and then back to the main warehouse where Monroe had parked his bus and his motorcycle. Owen and Javier helped Sean down the stairs in his wheelchair, and then they all headed toward the bus.

Aside from Javier, Owen wondered if he would see any of them again. They really were strangers. He didn't even know what schools they went to. And yet, they didn't feel like strangers, which was probably one of those Bleeding Effects Monroe had talked about.

"All right," Monroe said, his keys jangling as he opened the side door and set the Animus core inside. "I think we'll drop off Natalya first—"

The windows overhead exploded inward, raining glass, and figures dressed in black swarmed in, dropping down on them from above on razor-thin lines of rope.

"Templar agents!" Monroe shouted. "Run!"

CHAPTER TWENTY-ONE

avier ducked toward the bus as the agents reached the floor of the warehouse. The others had all scattered haphazardly, but Javier noticed Owen running toward Monroe's motorcycle. Suddenly, the bus engine rumbled, Monroe behind the wheel. Javier stepped away from the vehicle as it lurched forward, moving toward the warehouse's roller door.

"Javier!" Owen shouted, climbing onto the bike. "Get on!"

The Abstergo agents had fanned out through the room. There were a dozen of them at least. They already had Sean, who couldn't escape from them. And just then, one of them fired a Taser at David, and Grace screamed. As her brother fell twitching to the ground, she threw herself at the agent, but Javier didn't see what happened to her.

He sensed someone coming up on him and spun around as an agent fired a Taser at him. But he whipped to the side and dodged the probes, a reflexive move that surprised him. When the agent threw the Taser gun to the side and came at him, Javier went hand to hand, blocking and punching, holding his own. But the agent wore some kind of black paramilitary armor that prevented Javier from doing much damage.

A deafening cymbal crash echoed through the warehouse as Monroe plowed his bus through the roller door, ripping it down and creating an opening.

"Javier, now!" Owen shouted, holding out a helmet.

Javier laid a final elbow jab in the agent's throat and raced over to the motorcycle. "You have the key?" he asked as he got behind Owen and put his helmet on.

Owen didn't answer, but the engine started, and the bike launched forward.

Abstergo agents raced to stop them from both sides, firing Tasers at them and missing. A few of them even put themselves in the bike's path, but Owen veered around them, and a moment later they shot out of the warehouse into the street. Away to the right, they saw Monroe's bus speeding off.

"Go the other way," Javier said. He figured it was better to separate, and it was also likely the agents would have an easier time of it running down an old vintage bus, and he wanted to be far away when Monroe got caught.

Owen gunned it, and the bike ripped along the waterfront, speeding past other warehouses and buildings, the sun about to come up.

"Are they following us?" Owen shouted.

Javier looked back and saw a couple of black sedans racing after them. "Two cars," Javier shouted. "We gotta lose them."

Owen nodded and throttled the bike. They sped up, but Javier didn't think speed alone would let them escape. He scanned the road ahead, squinting in the blinding wind, and spotted a narrow alleyway.

"There!" he said, pointing. "They won't fit!"

Owen slowed just enough that he could make the turn, and dove into the alley. The corridor was almost too narrow for them. The bike's handlebars nearly scraped the walls, which would have crashed them. Owen drove them as fast as they could go without wrecking. When they came out the other side, there weren't any black cars in sight, just delivery vans and other vehicles parked among the warehouses.

"Which way now?" Owen asked.

They couldn't go home, or they'd just bring the agents with them. They didn't really have any place they could go. "Just get out of the city," Javier said. "Maybe we can hide in the hills."

Owen steered the bike out of the waterfront docks and got them on the freeway, taking the northbound on-ramp, and, before long, they'd put the agents far behind them. They didn't say anything more until they'd driven beyond the city center and through a band of suburban neighborhoods. Then the pavement ended and they hit the bumpy, rutted dirt roads that led them up into the hills.

"These helmets have some pretty serious tech," Owen said. "But I don't know how to work it."

"Just find a place with some trees," Javier said.

The sun had crested the tallest of the rounded peaks before they finally pulled off the road and parked in the shade of a large sycamore, near a thick stand of sumac. Someone had rolled some stones together for a fire pit, and the blackened rocks surrounded a pile of ashes and scorched beer cans.

Javier pulled his helmet off, and so did Owen.

"What now?" Owen asked.

Javier had no idea. Going into the simulation was supposed to make them safe from this kind of thing. Monroe had told them his Animus was off-line and untraceable. But somehow, Abstergo—or the Templars—had found them, and a little piece of Cudgel in Javier was glad about that. But even though Javier had basically *been* a Templar, the larger part of him had still wanted to run at the sight of the agents.

"Do you think they got everyone?" Owen asked.

"It looked like it," Javier said. "I think we were the only ones who escaped. Except for Monroe. I can't believe he just took off."

"I think he was trying to make a way for us to escape," Owen said. "At least, I hope he was."

"They probably caught him, too, in that stupid bus."

Owen kicked at a rock. It bounced off the sycamore and landed in the bushes. "This is insane!" he shouted. "What did we go through all that for?"

Javier thought about what it was he had just gone through. He remembered the sharp pressure of the knives stabbing him. Cudgel's fear and grief of knowing he had failed and that he was about to die. He remembered the seconds that had passed as he lost consciousness, tasting blood, and the pain of the blade in his back with each breath.

"Hey," Owen said. "Are we good now?"

Javier looked at him. He mostly saw Owen, and very little of the Assassin. Still, he wasn't sure if they were good, but he wanted them to be. "Yeah. I think so."

"I saw you fighting that agent." Owen shook his head. "That was incredible."

"I don't know how I did that. I didn't even think about it. I just went for it."

"That must be a Bleeding Effect. Your ancestor could fight, and now you can, too."

"I guess so."

Owen turned and glanced back down in the direction of the city. "Seriously, what are we going to do?"

"They'll be looking for us," Javier said. "I think we have to stay up here for a while."

"But don't you think we should help the others?"

"How?" Javier asked. "I mean, sure, I'd love to help the others. But it's just the two of us, and we don't even know where they took them."

"So, what, we just sit here?"

"For now," Javier said. But it felt like stalling, because eventually they'd have to return to the city. He sure as hell didn't know how to live off the land, and he knew Owen didn't, either. They'd be thirsty and hungry before long. But they'd go back to the city and then what? Those agents weren't playing around. At least they were using Tasers and not guns. That meant they wanted everyone alive, probably to find out what they knew about the Piece of Eden.

Javier grabbed a big log and dragged it over closer to the fire pit, and then he brushed his hands off and sat down. Not that he planned to light a fire. It just seemed like the thing to do. It reminded him of the cookouts his family used to have on the beach, grilling shrimp and chicken on skewers right over the flames, wrapping blankets around themselves after the sun went down. They hadn't done that for a while. The last time had been a kind of welcome home after his brother got out of prison, so it was different, and no one had really been into it.

Owen sat down next to Javier on the log. "So we just sit here," he said.

"Yup."

For the next hour that's what they did, talking mostly about the simulation as the day got warm and dry. They stayed away from the fact that they, or their ancestors, had been trying to kill each other, and focused on the other aspects of the experience. The city, their weapons, their ancestor's abilities. But eventually they wore that topic down until there wasn't much of it left, and then Owen took the conversation where Javier didn't want it to go.

"So what happened to you?"

"What do you mean?"

"I'm not talking about the Animus," Owen said. "Before that. Why'd you start ignoring me?"

Javier really didn't want to talk about that. But he knew Owen wouldn't give it up. Owen never gave anything up, and they were stuck together on a log in the mountains. Javier figured he might as well get it over with.

"I've just been dealing with a lot of my own stuff," he said.

"Like what?" Owen asked.

"Just stuff, man. I don't know."

"Well, why didn't you tell me?"

Javier didn't want to answer that, either, but Owen asked again, so Javier decided to keep going and be upfront with him.

"Look. What you went through with your dad and everything, I know how bad that was, and I get why you're mad. But you were so focused on it *all* the time, and—"

"And what?" Owen said, sounding angry.

Javier sighed. "Just let me finish—"

"What do you expect?" Owen said, his voice getting loud. "They sent my dad to prison and he died there."

"Yeah, they did," Javier said. "But they sent my brother to prison, too."

"That's because he beat the crap out of someone!"

When Owen said that, Javier had to get up and walk away a few steps, turning his back. Anger pulled his hands into fists and tightened the muscles around his neck and shoulders, and who knew what the hell he would do to Owen with these Bleeding Effects. After a few minutes of deep breathing to calm himself down, he turned back around.

"I just had a lot of my own crap without having to deal with your crap, too. That's all it was. It wasn't personal."

"Seems personal to me."

"Well, there's nothing I can do about that. You take it however you want, but that's what happened."

Owen was quiet for a few minutes, staring into the cold fire pit. "So what's this crap you had going on?"

"I don't want to talk about it."

"Is everything okay?"

"It's fine."

"Is it your mom? Or more stuff with your brother?"

Javier looked up at the sky as a bird flew out of a tree. It was big, a falcon or a hawk, he could never tell the difference.

"It isn't anything like that," he said. "I came out to my family a year ago."

"Oh." Owen sat back on the log. "I didn't know you were . . ."

"Yeah," Javier said. It hadn't been easy. His family was all Catholic or Baptist, and even though he knew his parents wouldn't kick him out of the house or anything, he had worried about their acceptance of him when he told the truth about who he was.

"How did your parents react?" Owen asked.

"My mom was really great about it. My dad took a few days to come around, but he's cool now."

"What about your brother?"

"That's why he went to prison," Javier said. "Some redneck called me a faggot, and Mani just went off on him." At the time, Javier had watched his brother beating on that guy, feeling a weird mix of gratitude, fear, and pride. "I don't even think the guy thought I was gay. I think he was just using the word to insult me."

"Does anyone else know? No one at school's said—"

"Nobody knows except my family. And now you."

"Wow." Owen nodded. "It's really not a big deal. I'm sure you could tell—"

"Look, I appreciate what you're saying, but right now I'm just trying to fit in, okay? It'll happen in its time. When I'm ready."

"Okay," Owen said, and after a pause, he added, "Thanks for telling me."

"Like you gave me a choice." Javier meant it half-jokingly, but he was actually kind of relieved that someone else finally knew, and he was also glad it was Owen, because with Owen, he knew it wouldn't change anything between them.

A few more hours passed. Javier spent them listening for approaching vehicles and worrying about the others and what Abstergo had done with them. He was also starting to get hungry and legitimately concerned about what he and Owen were going to do.

Around midday, a stranger came walking out of the trees, startling them. He had a shaved head, dark complexion, and wore sunglasses, with black pants that almost looked like military fatigues, and a hooded leather jacket over a white T-shirt.

"How're you fellas doing?" he asked.

Javier glanced at the bike. "Should we make a run for it?" he whispered to Owen.

"That guy looks familiar," Owen said, seeming a lot less concerned than Javier felt.

The stranger pushed his sunglasses up on top of his head, still strolling toward them. "I'm Griffin," he said, his voice deep and drawn out, a bit like a slowed down audio track of someone talking. "And from the looks of it, Monroe has gotten you guys into a hell of a lot of trouble with the Templars."

So this guy clearly knew who they were and what was going on, but the way he said the name Templars led Javier to believe he wasn't with them. Javier and Owen looked at each other, and in that moment of hesitation and confusion, Griffin drew closer.

"Don't worry," he said. "I'm not here to take you in or take you out."

"Then what are you doing here?" Owen asked.

"I just want to talk."

"About what?" Javier readied himself to run, but worried that Owen wouldn't, and he wasn't going to leave him behind.

Griffin reached the fire pit and stopped, glancing back and forth between them. "I want to talk about you, and your futures."

"How do I know you?" Owen asked.

"I took down a Templar agent for you the other night," he said. "I wanted to stop you from going with Monroe, but you outran me." He glanced over at the motorcycle. "On that, if I'm not mistaken."

"You're the Assassin," Owen said.

Griffin nodded and walked over to the bike. Then he reached under one of the motorcycle's angled panels and yanked out a bundle of wires.

"Hey!" Javier shouted.

"This is an Abstergo bike," Griffin said. "And you don't really know how it works. I just took out a tracking device that's been broadcasting your location for the past few hours. It's a pretty high-frequency signal, so someone would have to get pretty close to pick it up. But *I* found you."

Javier had no way of knowing if that was actually true or not. Maybe it was Cudgel's mind still influencing him, or maybe it was just common sense, but he had no desire to engage with an Assassin. Owen, however, no longer seemed troubled at all. Perhaps his Assassin ancestor was influencing him. A Bleeding Effect of some kind.

"You said you wanted to talk to us." Javier decided he might have to run without Owen. "So what do you have to say?"

Griffin leaned against the bike and folded his arms. "Abstergo has your four friends in their custody."

"What about Monroe?" Owen asked.

"He got away. I'm not sure where he is."

"And?" Javier asked. "Or did you just come here to state the obvious?"

"I need to know what your friends are going to tell Abstergo," Griffin said. "I need to know why Monroe had you all together. I assume you went into the Animus searching for a Piece of Eden. Am I right?"

"Why would you assume that?" Javier asked.

"Abstergo's been after Monroe for a long time," Griffin said. "For him to risk coming out of hiding, he would need to have something he thought would change the game, and the only thing big enough to do that is a Piece of Eden."

Owen looked at Javier, and then he said, "Can I talk to Javier alone for a minute?"

"Sure," Griffin said. "But make it quick. We're running out of time."

Griffin pulled his sunglasses back down and walked away a short distance, far enough Javier didn't think he could overhear them, but close enough that the Assassin clearly wanted to keep his eyes on them while they talked.

"I think we should tell him," Owen said.

"Are you crazy?"

"Maybe he can help us find Monroe and rescue the others."

"Or maybe he's lying and he's just using us to get the Piece of Eden."

"But I've been in the memories of an Assassin."

"So?" Javier said. "That doesn't make you an Assassin. Or are you already forgetting what Monroe said?"

"It's not that," Owen said. "I'm not confused. I trust them."

"All of them? Without question?"

"I trust the Creed," Owen said.

Javier just stared at him. That confirmed it, this was definitely a Bleeding Effect, because the Owen he knew wouldn't blindly trust some guy who'd just walked up asking what they knew about a powerful weapon that could win wars and turn generals into presidents. Owen's time in the Animus had changed him. But there also wasn't anything Javier could do to stop Owen if he decided to side with Griffin.

"Well, what's *your* plan?" Owen asked. "Just sit up here in the hills forever?"

Javier swatted at a fly that had buzzed into his face. "Whatever."

"Whatever? What does that mean?"

"That means . . . do what you're going to do."

Owen stood there a moment, and then he nodded once, firmly. "I'm going to tell him. If he turns on us, it's on me." Then he called to Griffin, and when the Assassin sauntered back over, he said. "Yes, we went into the Animus searching for a Piece of Eden."

Javier shook his head and took a step backward away from them. He wasn't going to be a part of this.

"Where?" Griffin asked.

"New York City," Owen said. "1863."

"Which Piece of Eden?"

"It was a dagger," Owen said. "From the Aztec Club. But Cortés brought it over to Mexico from Spain."

"Cortés?" Griffin's demeanor shifted, hardening up. "Do you know where he got it?"

"The king gave it to him," Owen said. "But I think the king got it from the pope."

"Did the Animus show you where the Piece of Eden is now?"

"Maybe," Owen said. "We think it might be somewhere around the house where Ulysses Grant died. He had it last."

"Thank you," Griffin said. "This is exactly what I needed."

But now that he had what he needed, Javier wondered what that meant for him and Owen. "What happens now?" he asked.

"Now?" Griffin took a seat on the log. "Now I'd like to ask you two to come with me."

CHAPTER TWENTY-TWO

When the Abstergo agents came in through the roof of the warehouse, Tommy Greyling would have fought them, and fought them hard. When they grabbed Natalya, he would have broken any hand that touched her. But Sean could only sit in his wheelchair and watch as two agents seized him from behind. He tried to scramble out of his chair, even if it meant crawling. But they pinned him to his seat.

He was powerless.

David tried to run, but they Tased him, and at that point, Grace lost it. She ran screaming at the agent who'd done it, pummeling him with her fists, but two other agents tackled her and restrained her.

Monroe's bus rammed the warehouse door, ripping it down,

and he sped off, followed by Owen and Javier on Monroe's motorcycle. Sean didn't blame them for escaping, but it angered him, as if they were abandoning the rest of them.

A couple of black cars pulled up to the front of the warehouse, and after a few of the agents had piled in, they tore away after Owen and Javier. Then a big white armored van drove right into the warehouse, and agents opened up the back doors. First, they put Natalya in, and then Grace and David.

"Where are you taking us?" Sean asked as they wheeled him over.

The agents said nothing. They wore full bodysuits of armor, and sleek helmets, so he couldn't see any of their faces.

Several of them lifted him up in his wheelchair, and he swayed helplessly as they loaded him into the van with the others. The interior smelled of machine oil and vinyl. Agents strapped Natalya, Grace, and David onto a bench along one side of the vehicle, and they rolled Sean to the other side and strapped his chair to the sidewall.

"Where are you taking us?" Sean asked again.

The agents ignored him and filed out of the van, after which they shut the double doors and latched them, trapping them in a cell filled with yellow, artificial light.

"This is Monroe's fault," Grace said, looking over at her brother. David seemed dazed, with blank and glassy eyes, still suffering from the effects of the Tasing.

"Is he okay?" Sean asked.

"That agent said he will be," Grace said. "He said it takes about an hour for the effects to wear off."

"Blaming Monroe doesn't do us much good," Natalya said. "Does it?"

"I don't care!" Grace shouted. "We wouldn't be here if it wasn't for him!"

The van's engine barked and rumbled, and with a jolt that tipped the other three sideways in unison, they were moving. The compartment had no windows, so they had no indication where they were going.

"We can't tell them anything," Sean said.

"What do you mean?" Grace asked.

"They know we were looking for a Piece of Eden," he said. "We can't tell them where it is."

"You keep to yourself whatever you want," Grace said. "We're on our own here. Monroe took off, and so did Owen and Javier. My main priority is to get me and my brother home safely, and I'll say what I need to say to make that happen. I don't care if my ancestor hated Templars or not."

"After what you saw in the simulation?" Natalya asked.

"Especially after what I saw in the simulation," Grace said. "My brother should not have had to go through that, and that's on Monroe, too."

She put her arm around her brother, but David still said nothing, looking up at his sister as she spoke, his mouth hanging a little slack.

Sean could see it wouldn't do any good to keep arguing with her, so he decided to let it go until they reached their destination. When he knew more about what was going on, maybe he'd have a better idea of what to do about it.

They drove for a while, jostled and bumped, listening to the whine of the tires, and Sean lost track of the time. It felt like an hour or more had passed before the van seemed to slow. But it didn't stop, which meant they had probably left the freeway.

They also seemed to be mounting an incline, because Sean felt a slight tug of gravity against his chair.

David roused himself along the way, fully alert and back to himself by the time the van finally came to a stop. The engines went quiet and the vehicle settled into place.

Then Sean heard the latches at the back, and he and the others turned to look as the rear doors squealed open. The agents in riot gear were gone. Instead, a woman in a white lab coat stood below them outside, holding a clipboard. Two burly guys flanked her, wearing gray uniforms that had a martial appearance, or at least that of security, with the Abstergo logo on their chests and upper arms in reflective silver. All three individuals had name badges clipped to their clothing, the men at their breast pockets and the woman at the lapel of her coat.

The woman looked athletic in the way she held herself, her brown hair in a pixie cut, her front teeth prominent when she smiled.

"Ladies and gentlemen," she said with a refined-sounding, slightly French accent. "I am deeply sorry for any distress we've caused you." She touched her chest. "My name is Dr. Victoria Bibeau. I'm with the Lineage Research and Acquisition division of Abstergo Industries, and I'd like to welcome you—"

"Welcome?" Sean said. "Did you just say *welcome*? Really?"

Victoria's smiled dimmed a few watts. "I did, and I realize how odd that word must sound after the manner in which we brought you here. But if you'll allow us to explain, I think you'll understand it was purely in the interest of your safety."

"You Tased my brother!" Grace said. "How safe is that?"

"Not safe enough, trust me." Victoria turned to the men at her side and gave them each a nod, after which they stepped up into the van. "That should not have happened and I apologize. I'd like to invite you all into our facility. We'll get you checked out and make sure everyone is unharmed, and then we'll work on getting you home, okay?"

The two guards unstrapped the four others and ushered them out of the van. Then they lifted and lowered Sean in his wheelchair.

Sean looked around and found that the van had parked in the middle of a wide circular drive of freshly paved asphalt, surrounded by tall pine trees that gave the breeze a spicy, almost citrus smell. Several large buildings rose up multiple stories among the trees, composed almost entirely of glass, connected to one another by enclosed and elevated glass walkways. The entrance to one of the buildings lay on the other side of the drive from them, while the road that had brought them there wound off into the forest.

Sean hadn't known what kind of place to expect following an Abstergo abduction. Some kind of prison or dungeon. But this looked like the exact opposite of that.

"If you would follow me, please," Victoria said, and walked backward toward the entrance slowly, facing them and smiling.

The implacable guards made no threatening move or gesture, but their presence was enough to set the group in motion. Natalya, Grace, and David all followed Victoria, and Sean rolled along behind them, the guards following close behind.

They reached the entrance and Victoria swiped her badge to open the doors. They glided apart without any sound, and almost without being seen, the glass was so clear. Inside, they came through another set of doors into a lobby where the Abstergo logo frosted an enormous pane of glass behind a reception desk. The man seated there, wearing a headset and a skinny tie, nodded to Victoria as she led Sean and the others by.

They came around the glass, and the building opened up before them high and vast, rising three stories to a ceiling of glass that appeared to be retractable. Each floor wrapped around a main atrium, open and transparent, the outer walls on all sides also made of glass, allowing a view of the forest in every direction. Abstergo employees walked along or rode the escalators, some casually, some seeming to be in a hurry, just as Sean would expect to find in any corporate office.

"We call this facility the Aerie," Victoria said. "For obvious reasons. This building is one of five that comprise the complex. Perhaps I can give you a tour after we've gotten you squared away."

Again, Sean had not expected this, and felt disarmed by it. If Abstergo had truly abducted them, this was the nicest kidnapping he had ever heard about.

Victoria led them across the atrium's floor to a far corner, and there she let them into a lounge area scattered with angular modern chairs and coffee tables, all of it a little cold and sharp around the edges.

"Please," Victoria said. "Help yourself to the food and beverage counter."

Sean looked where she pointed, and saw an array of fruit, pastries, coffee, and a cooler stocked with water, juice, soda, and some of that irritating, mildly flavored water that Sean thought was still basically just water.

He wheeled himself over and grabbed a bagel and a soda. Grace picked out a banana and poured herself a cup of coffee, while David took a blueberry muffin and an irritating water. Natalya held back.

"You sure you don't want anything?" Victoria asked her.

"I'm fine," Natalya said. "What exactly are you a doctor of?"

"I'm a psychiatrist," Victoria said.

"You're a shrink?" Sean wasn't sure how he felt about that.

"I am." Victoria smiled. "But my role here goes well beyond that. Please, let's all take a seat." She chose a chair at the head of an arrangement of furniture, and the others all sat down facing her, while Sean wheeled himself into the group.

"To begin with," Victoria said, "let me again apologize for how that operation was carried out. David, are you okay? How are you feeling?"

He had just taken a huge bite of a muffin, so instead of answering, he gave her a thumbs-up and the smile of a chipmunk with packed cheeks.

"Good," Victoria said. "That's a relief. Now." She looked down at her clipboard. "We have Grace and David, Natalya, and Sean, correct?"

They all nodded, eating their food.

"Then we are missing Owen and Javier?" Victoria asked.

They nodded again.

"Do you know where they might have gone?"

Sean swallowed his bite of bagel. "No idea. We really don't know one another that well. We only met for the first time last night."

"I see," she said. "And Monroe? Do you know where he might be?"

Sean shook his head, even though he was pretty sure Monroe had gone searching for the Piece of Eden. He noticed that Grace and David were looking at each other, maybe about to say something, but Sean willed them to keep silent. They did, for now.

"Well, let us hope we find them all soon," Victoria said. "Now then. Let me lay out the situation for you as we understand it, and then if you can, we hope you'll fill in the gaps for us, all right? To begin with, we know Monroe brought you all together to use a stolen Animus with modified specifications. We know you came into contact with an object. A Piece of Eden. Do you understand what that is?"

Sean tried to keep his face blank, but he must have done a bad job of it.

"I can see by the looks on your faces you know exactly what I'm talking about." Victoria glanced down at her clipboard again. "You went into the stolen Animus searching for the Piece of Eden. Did you find it?"

No one answered her.

She waited a moment, and then she sighed and set her clipboard down next to her chair. "Are any of you aware that Monroe used to work for Abstergo?" she asked.

Sean hadn't known that, but it didn't surprise him. It had to be something like that for Monroe to have an Animus.

"He is not who you think he is," Victoria said. "He was a very high-level researcher, until he suffered a personal tragedy. After that, he became erratic. His judgment became impaired. I tried to support and help him through it—we all did—but in the end, he stole some very valuable Abstergo property and he left."

"You mean the Animus?" Grace asked, laying her empty banana peel on the coffee table.

"Among other things," Victoria said. "We've been searching for him because the equipment he took can be very dangerous if not used properly."

"What about calling the police?" David asked.

"We work with local law enforcement," Victoria said. "But legally, we have some latitude in using our own security team."

"Legal to Tase people?" Grace asked.

"Our team did not know what they would find in that warehouse," Victoria said. "We received the signal that the Animus was in use. We didn't know who was using it, and we didn't know how they might be connected to Monroe. That's why our people went in with nonlethal contingencies in place. The plan was to simply take everyone into custody. While the transport brought you here, we examined Monroe's warehouse and gained a better understanding of the nature of the situation."

"And we're gaining a better understanding still," said a man in a slate-colored suit as he walked into the room. He was very tall, with pale blond hair swept back from his forehead, and eyes the color of vibrant moss. "Pardon the interruption," he said.

"Not at all, sir." Victoria rose from her seat. "Please, join us."

The tall man walked over to them and took a chair next to Victoria, his movements quick, fluid, and efficient. "My name is Isaiah," he said, "and I am in charge of the Aerie. We've been analyzing Monroe's data, and I believe we can dispense with some unnecessary secrecy. You know about the Assassins and Templars. You know that the Templars control Abstergo Industries, and by now, you've probably guessed that I am a Templar. You are right. I am. So is Dr. Bibeau, here."

Victoria nodded and smiled.

Sean was a bit surprised he would just come out and admit it that way, even if he had seen Monroe's data. That wasn't what he would expect from the secret organization behind a global conspiracy.

"The Templars look different than we once did," Isaiah

said. "Corporations have replaced kingdoms, and CEOs have taken the place of politicians. Our organization adapts and becomes what is necessary to be most effective, and we believe the pursuit of technology promises the greatest advancements for the human race, which is where Abstergo comes in. There isn't anything sinister about us. Contrary to what Monroe may have led you to believe."

"Tell that to Boss Tweed," David said.

"Good point." Isaiah chuckled, the kind of easy laugh Sean's mom might call infectious. "Yes, there are certainly notorious figures in our history, as you will find in any group that has been around long enough. But if I might present you with a counter-perspective, did you know that Boss Tweed used his influence to build orphanages, schools, and hospitals? Under his control, the city of New York spent more on charity in three years than had been spent in the previous fifteen combined. He helped found the New York Public Library, and secured the land for the Metropolitan Museum of Art. Did you know he paved the way for the construction of the Brooklyn Bridge?"

No one answered him, but Sean hadn't known any of that, and he assumed by their silence the others hadn't, either.

"It is harder to dismiss Tweed now, isn't it?" Isaiah said. "As a man, he made terrible, unforgivable mistakes. But as a Templar, he brought enlightenment and undeniable progress to his city. Who knows what he might have achieved if the Assassin Eliza hadn't brought him down on corruption charges?"

As Isaiah spoke, Sean was finding it increasingly difficult to reconcile Monroe's image of the Templars with what Sean was experiencing for himself.

"You can judge us by our worst examples," Isaiah said. "Or you can think about the hundreds and even thousands of Templars you've never heard of who nevertheless dedicated their lives to the betterment of our world." His green eyes looked at each of them, and when they reached Sean, it felt as if his gaze gently took root. "Did Monroe tell you all how important you are?"

"What do you mean?" Sean asked.

"I've looked through his DNA analysis of all of you, and it is extraordinary. I believe the six of you together represent something we call an Ascendance Event. According to my theory, the phenomenon has only been documented a handful of times in all recorded history, and is not well understood, governed by sympathetic genetic forces we're still decoding. That was actually what Monroe was working on here at Abstergo, with his modified Animus. He was researching these Ascendance Events, looking for the next occurrence. Which is where you enter the picture. There is a confluence, a convergence, a synergy in your coming together. Individually and collectively, your potential is beyond our ability to quantify. I find it breathtaking."

Sean thought back to the image Monroe had showed them of the places where their DNA lined up. Their Memory Concordance. "Are you talking about the Piece of Eden?" he asked.

"Pieces of Eden," Isaiah said. "Multiple."

David pushed his glasses up. "I don't understand."

Isaiah turned to Victoria. "This is Dr. Bibeau's area of specialty. I'll let her explain it."

Victoria nodded and cleared her throat. "My research has led me to believe the Piece of Eden you went searching for is one of three. They were originally part of a whole, a Trident of Eden. Each dagger is actually one of the Trident's three prongs, and each has a different power, or effect on those people exposed to it. According to legend, one prong instills faith, one instills fear, and one instills devotion. Are you with me?"

The four of them nodded.

"Good," Victoria said. "Now, you've heard of Alexander the Great, right? Well, we know he possessed a Staff of Eden, a symbol of his rule when seated upon his throne. But on the battlefield, he needed a weapon."

"The Trident of Eden?" Grace said.

"Exactly," Victoria said. "His armies were undefeated. With the Trident to fight, and the Staff to reign, Alexander created an unparalleled empire and became perhaps the most powerful ruler the world has ever seen."

"Rather inspiring, isn't it?" Isaiah said.

Sean agreed with him on that, and he also noted how passionate and animated Victoria became as she went on.

"When Alexander died," she said, "I believe the Trident was broken into thirds and divided among the dynasties that succeeded him. One prong went to one of Alexander's generals, Seleucus, who founded the Seleucid Empire, which lay to the east and took in parts of Asia. Another prong went to the general Ptolemy, who founded a kingdom in Egypt. And the third prong went to Alexander's people, the Macedonians. The Macedonian prong and the Ptolemaic prong ended up in the hands of the Roman Caesars. The prong you found is one of those. My guess would be it's the faith prong. It stayed in Rome and eventually ended up in the Vatican. From there, Pope Callixtus III, a Spaniard, gave it to Alfonso V, king of Aragon, I assume to repay the king for his support. The prong stayed in the Spanish monarchy until Charles V gave it to Cortés. Are you still with me?"

"Barely," David said.

Victoria rubbed her hands together. "I'm still piecing together what might have happened to the other two, but we believe you found the faith prong in New York City."

"Or at the very least, we know your ancestors interacted with it," Isaiah said. "However, the incredible thing is that it seems some of your ancestors also interacted with the other two pieces."

"Seriously?" Grace said.

"Utterly," Isaiah said. "Please understand, the combined powers of the Trident of Eden can turn a man into a king, and a king into a god, and you are all connected to it. As I told you, this is an Ascendance Event. You are all rising up as one from the wellspring of your ancestors. It's as if your lineage and DNA have been moving toward this moment for generations. That is why we need your help. This is something only you can do."

"And how do you expect us to help?" Natalya asked, one of the few times she'd spoken since they'd arrived at the Aerie. Sean couldn't forget the image of the agents grabbing her in the warehouse, and still felt shame at his inability to protect her as Tommy would have.

"Dr. Bibeau," Isaiah said, "did you explain the . . . the situation? With Monroe?"

Victoria nodded.

Isaiah glanced toward the building's wall of windows and out into the forest beyond. "Monroe's story is truly a tragic one," he said. "I still greatly admire his brilliance, and the man he once was." Then he brought his gaze back into the room. "But if you were successful in your search for one of the prongs of the Trident of Eden, and Monroe takes control of it . . . he could do a great deal of damage."

"So what's Monroe's story?" Sean asked.

Isaiah sighed. "His father was a terrible man. Monroe spent his childhood in unimaginable circumstances, much of which he has deeply repressed. This condition would render him or any person an unsuitable candidate for the Animus."

"Why is that?" Natalya asked.

Victoria spoke up. "The psyche of an abused individual is too unstable, too fractured. I tried unsuccessfully to help Monroe through therapy, but he wanted to use the Animus to go back into his father's memories, to exorcise his own demons."

"But I forbade it," Isaiah said. "For his own safety and sanity. That is why he left Abstergo and stole the project he had been working on."

Sean looked at Grace, and she looked back at him. There had to be more to the story. It wasn't that Sean didn't trust Monroe. But there had always been something a bit off about him and his modified Animus, and Sean could tell that he and Grace were having the same doubts. Sean still believed Monroe had good intentions, but he wondered whether they should tell Isaiah what they had learned, which was what Grace had wanted from the beginning.

"Don't do it," Natalya said to them.

"Maybe we shouldn't," David said.

But Sean's mind had changed since coming here. The situation was not as Monroe had described it at all. These people weren't evil or trying to conquer the world, and that seemed obvious to Sean now in looking around this place and listening to Isaiah and Victoria. Abstergo wanted to help and improve mankind through innovation and progress, and Sean also appreciated that they seemed to believe he and the others could play an important part in that.

"Maybe you shouldn't what?" Isaiah asked.

Sean took a deep breath. "We did find the Piece of Eden. And Grace saw where it ended up."

Grace nodded along with him. "I did," she said.

And then she told Isaiah where.

CHAPTER TWENTY-THREE

Owen knew Javier didn't agree with his decision to trust Griffin, but he also knew this was the only way. And contrary to what Javier assumed, Owen was actually aware of the pull of Varius's mind inside his, perhaps leading him to trust Griffin more quickly than he should have. But that didn't change the fact that Owen and Javier had very few options available to them. The Templars had captured the other four, and Monroe was missing. They couldn't go home, and they were basically on the run.

But there was another, more personal reason. The Abstergo agent from the night before had indicated that he knew something about Owen's father. The only way Owen figured he could find out more about that would be to become a part of the game.

Griffin looked up from the log where he was sitting. "What do you say?"

"You want us to go with you?" Javier laughed. "I say, no freaking way."

"What do you mean by go with you?" Owen asked.

Griffin leaned forward, his elbows on his knees. "I'm assuming Monroe found Assassin ancestry in one of you? Or Templar? Maybe both?"

Owen nodded.

"So what?" Javier asked.

"So," Griffin said, "that means you may have Eagle Vision ability. You know what Eagle Vision is, right?"

Owen nodded again. This time, so did Javier.

"Good," Griffin said. "So look at me."

"We are looking at you," Javier said.

Griffin shook his head and held up his empty hands. "No, I mean really look at me. Eagle Vision can help you discern whether another person is a threat or an enemy. So discern me. What do you see?"

Owen hadn't tried to use his Eagle Vision since leaving the Animus simulation. But he remembered how Varius had done it when he located the dagger in the Aztec Club, and now Owen tried to do the same. He extended his awareness, opening his mind, studying Griffin's face, his features, the way he held himself, the tension in the smallest muscles in his body that could not lie. Owen's Eagle Vision told him that Griffin wasn't a threat. At least, not at the moment.

"Go on," Owen said.

"I'm assuming you actually saw the Piece of Eden in the Animus?"

"We both did," Owen said, at which Javier's eyes opened a bit in surprise and anger.

"Then that makes you the best candidates for the search," Griffin said. "I've never seen the thing. You actually know what you're looking for, and you may have the perception to find it. So I need your help."

"Why should we help you?" Javier said. "I'm not sure anyone should have that thing, even Monroe. But he's probably already halfway there."

"I get it," Griffin said. "Who knows what Monroe has been telling you about the Brotherhood. But hear me out for a minute." He held out the flat of his hand, and with the other he ticked off fingers, one by one. "Alexander the Great. Julius Caesar. Attila the Hun. Genghis Khan. The Russian tsars. Do you know what they all had in common?"

Javier rolled his eyes. "Pieces of Eden?"

"That's right," Griffin said. "Anytime a Piece of Eden appears, someone uses it to seize power, and the free will of the people suffers. It's unavoidable. That's why I don't want to use it. I want to keep someone else from using it. How do you know Monroe won't turn around and become a dictator?"

"He won't," Owen said.

"How are you so sure of that?" Griffin asked.

Owen wasn't sure. The truth was that he did have doubts about Monroe. But he wanted to trust him, just like he wanted to trust Griffin. Because he felt as though he needed them both.

"Do you know anything about my father?" Owen asked.

"Your father?" Javier stepped toward Owen and tugged on his arm. "What are you talking about?"

"I only know some of what happened to your father," Griffin said.

"So he wasn't an Assassin?"

"No."

"But that Abstergo agent you took out said—"

"Your father was involved," Griffin said. "I don't know how. But I can help you with those questions."

"How?" Owen asked. "Monroe said my DNA won't work. I need my dad's DNA from after he got arrested."

"I can get into places Monroe can't," Griffin said. "The police may have your father's DNA on record. From his arrest. They may even still have a sample locked up in evidence. You help me find what I want, and I'll help you find what you want."

This was what Owen had gone to Monroe about in the first place, which had proven to be a dead end. But Griffin was offering Owen a chance to maybe, finally get some answers. To Owen, that wasn't even a choice.

"I'm in," he said.

"Owen," Javier said. "Don't—"

"I'm in," Owen said again, more forcefully. Now that he knew what Javier had been going through, he felt guilty that he hadn't been there for his friend. But that didn't change the fact that this was still something Owen had to do. "He's not our enemy. Come with us."

"What about my mom, man?"

"That's easy," Griffin said. "You call her and tell her you're safe, you just needed to get away for a while. She'll probably call the police and tell them you've run away, but that's not a problem. We can avoid the police."

"It's not like we can go home," Owen said. "Either we go with Griffin, or we hang out up here in the hills. She'll worry about you either way."

Javier looked around at the trees. He swatted at that stupid fly again. "I don't like this."

"I know," Owen said. "But you don't even have to trust Griffin or Monroe. I'm asking you to trust me. You don't need Eagle Vision for that. We'll be in this together."

Javier hung his hands on his hips and studied the dirt for a full minute. Then he looked up. "Okay. I trust you. Let's do this."

"Okay," Owen said.

"Good," Griffin said. "We've already wasted too much time. Both of you get on that bike and meet me at the bottom of the road."

"What?" Owen said.

But Griffin had already set off, free-running through the trees, and a few seconds later he was gone.

"Well, this is off to a great start," Javier said.

Owen strode toward the motorcycle. "Come on."

He climbed on the vehicle, and Javier got on behind him. The engine gave a slight quiver as it stirred up, like the beating wings of an enormous beetle. They pulled their helmets on, and then Owen sped them back down the packed dirt road they'd climbed a few hours ago, churning a wake of dust behind them.

When they reached the bottom of the hills, they found a vehicle waiting where the paved road began, a nondescript white sedan that drew little attention to itself.

The driver's window rolled down and Griffin leaned out. "Follow me."

Then the car peeled away, faster than Owen would have expected, and he throttled the bike after it. They flew down the country roads, past orchards and groves, the trees creating a strobe of shade and sunlight across the visor of Owen's helmet. Then they hit the freeway, and Griffin led them back into the city, eventually pulling into a gated lot of storage units. Owen wondered what they were doing there as they eased down one of the rows, and Griffin came to a stop.

Griffin climbed out of the car and walked over to one of the storage units. He looked up and down the row, and then unlocked the roller door and raised it. After he drove his car inside, he came out and motioned for Owen to pull the bike in.

"Is he serious?" Javier asked.

Owen felt some misgivings, too, but he drove the motorcycle into the unit and parked it behind the car. Griffin waited for them until they were back outside, and then pulled the door down.

"Is this a hide-in-plain-sight kind of idea?" Javier asked him.

Griffin bent down and locked the roller door. "You could say that. Come on, we're in here."

He stepped over to the unit next door and opened it up.

Storage shelves stood inside against the walls, stacked with metal and plastic crates. A worktable sat in the middle of the floor beneath a bare lightbulb, spread with tools, blades, and a few gauntlets reminiscent of the one Varius had worn. There was a computer in one of the far corners, and a cot with a sleeping bag across from it.

"Step inside," Griffin said. "Pull that cord over the table to turn on the light."

Owen did what he asked, Javier just behind him, and then

Griffin stepped inside and pulled the door closed. The unit grew dark, except for the harsh, sideways light thrown by the low-hanging bulb.

"Probably not what you were expecting, is it?" Griffin said, propping his hands against the worktable.

"Not exactly," Owen said.

"Sixteen years ago," Griffin said, "a Templar sleeper agent infiltrated the Brotherhood. He learned our secrets. The locations of all our safe houses and training facilities. Then he murdered the Mentor, our leader, and returned to his Templar masters. We call the time that followed the Great Purge. The Templars initiated an extermination campaign, using everything the traitor had learned. They slaughtered us, and not just the Assassins, but our families, too. Children, husbands, wives. The Brotherhood nearly went extinct. Since then, we've had to change tactics and adapt to survive. No more permanent locations. Now we stay mobile, agile, and invisible. Our numbers have rebounded, but they're not even close to what they were."

"My God," Owen whispered.

"The Templars want the world to see Abstergo as a benevolent corporation. But they are as ruthless as they ever were, if not more so. Those are the people who have your friends."

"What do we do?" Javier asked.

"First," Griffin said, "you tell me where to find the Piece of Eden, and we retrieve it. Then we can talk about a rescue."

"We think it's somewhere around the cottage where Ulysses Grant died."

"Right," Griffin said. "Well, that makes sense. Let's get you fellas outfitted."

He walked over to one of the storage shelves and hefted a black crate onto the table. Then he popped the latches and flipped the lid open. Inside were several smaller cases, which he pulled out and laid on the table.

"There're some clothes in the trunk by the cot," Griffin said. "Grab yourself a uniform."

Owen and Javier walked over to see what he meant, and found clothing similar to what Griffin wore. Military fatigues, boots, hoodie, black leather-and-canvas jackets. Owen found a set of everything that fit and changed into them, while Javier did the same. When they returned to the worktable, Griffin had opened up all the cases.

"We're going to fill your pockets," he said. "First, grenades." He pointed to a series of metal spheres about the size of a golf ball. "These are smoke and these are flash, for distraction and cover. These are sleep grenades, if you need someone unconscious for a little while. These here are EMP grenades. They give off a localized electromagnetic pulse. Templar agents have plenty of computerized countermeasures, but these will knock them out and fry them."

He loaded Owen and Javier up with several of each, which they stashed in the pockets of their pants and jackets.

"Now, weapons." Griffin moved down the table to the next set of cases. "I'm not going to force any of these on you. Take the ones you feel comfortable with, but make sure if you pick it up, you know how to use it."

One of the cases contained a set of throwing knives, and Owen felt one of those bubbles Monroe had talked about expanding in his mind, a Bleeding Effect from Varius. He *felt* as if he knew how to use them, but he wasn't actually certain that he did. He took them anyway, along with a couple of other blades. Javier took a few knives, as well as a crossbow pistol.

"Does this shoot darts?" he asked.

"Yes," Griffin said. "There should be some with it."

"Do we get one of those?" Owen asked, pointing at the hidden blade gauntlets.

Griffin reached over and picked one of them up, turning it over in his hands. It was different than the leather weapon Varius had worn. This one was made of some kind of molded metal, with electronic controls and functions Owen couldn't even guess at.

"You haven't earned this," Griffin said. "The gauntlet is a symbol as much as a weapon. One day, if you decide you want to join the Brotherhood and swear yourself to the Creed, you'll receive one of your own. But until that time, you're not worthy."

"That's pretty harsh," Javier said.

"Harsh or not," Griffin said, "that's the way it is. I spent years watching my grandfather and my father strap on their gauntlets before I was finally able to put on one of my own. It's a matter of honor, and I take that very seriously."

He set the gauntlet back down on the table, out of Owen's reach. "Now," he said, "when you have everything you—"

A soft *ping* came from the computer. Griffin looked toward it and checked his watch. Then he walked across the storage unit and sat down in front of the monitor. A few clicks of the mouse, and a video chat opened on the screen. The man looking back appeared somewhat haggard and gaunt, with thick, graying dark hair, and a beard. The background behind him seemed to be aboard some kind of boat.

"Griffin," the man said. "Status report."

"I have two of the subjects," Griffin said. "We're just preparing to go recover the Piece of Eden. Isaiah captured the other four—"

"I know. Rothenburg has reestablished contact."

"The Abstergo informant?" Griffin asked.

"Yes. The intelligence he's given us indicates the Templars are after more than one Piece of Eden. Rothenburg claims it's the Trident."

Griffin hesitated a moment before responding. "Understood, sir. We're heading to New York. We believe the relic is somewhere near Mount McGregor."

"Go," the man on the screen said. "There will be a car waiting for you in Albany. Recover the piece, but know that this is only the beginning. You'll have new orders soon."

"Yes, sir."

The screen went black, and Griffin slumped back in his chair.

"Who was that?" Owen asked.

"One of the leaders of the Brotherhood," Griffin said. "Gavin Banks. He's in hiding along with the rest of us. We keep our communications with him as short as possible."

"What did he mean by the Trident?" Javier asked.

"He means that there are two other pieces out there exactly like the one you saw, and whoever combines all three together could conquer the world."

Javier laughed, and Owen almost did, but he could tell by Griffin's demeanor he wasn't joking or exaggerating. The Assassin got up from his chair and walked toward the unit's door, grabbing one of the gauntlets from the worktable along the way.

"We need to move out," he said, pulling up the roller door. "Hit the light."

So the three of them left, and Griffin drove them in his car toward a private airfield a couple of hours away, where he parked the car in the same hangar as a small jet plane. It was painted white with a blue stripe down the side, and looked as ordinary as the sedan.

"The Templars have you guys beat on the vehicles, don't they," Javier said.

"There are limits to what the Brotherhood could and should afford without drawing Abstergo's attention," Griffin said.

Shortly after that, they were airborne, flying toward New York. That thought created an odd sensation in Owen, since it seemed as if he had just been in New York earlier that morning. But that was the New York of the past, and he had no idea what they would find in the present.

It was night by the time they landed in Albany, and the car waiting for them was another regular sedan, though it was powerful and fast. They drove north along darkened, tree-lined roads, through several sleeping towns, and reached Mount McGregor less than an hour later. Griffin parked the car some distance from the cottage.

"When we go out there, keep close to me." He turned off the engine. "Templars could be here, too. Keep every sense you have sharp—Bleeding Effects and otherwise. Let's get in, get the relic, and get out. Are you ready?"

"Ready," Owen said.

"Ready," Javier said.

They left the car and stalked into the trees, keeping silent in the near total darkness as they circled wide around the cottage. Owen tried to still the shaking in his hands, which quivered with the pounding of his own blood, and focused on Varius's memories, extending his awareness first through every part of his own body, and then out into his surroundings.

Nothing happened at first. But Owen remained patient, listing, waiting, sensing, and gradually the world entered into a higher definition. Suddenly, Owen could feel the texture of the ground through his boot. He could hear the echoes of his own footsteps off the curvature of the trees. He glimpsed an owl take to silent wing, and he saw the shapes of Javier and Griffin beside him, moving through the wood.

When they reached the cabin, all seemed quiet and still. Griffin led them from the tree line, across an open lawn already wet with dew, and up to a back window, which proved no obstacle for the Assassin. He was soon inside, and Owen and Javier followed after him.

The floorboards creaked beneath Owen's feet when he landed, and the stifled air smelled of old, smoked wood. They had come into a bedroom, but not Grant's bedroom if the size of the narrow bed was any indication.

"It's up to you fellas now," Griffin said. "Do you sense anything?"

"I got nothing," Javier said.

"Hang on." Owen closed his eyes, and instead of looking, he tried to feel for the same energy that had led Varius through the rooms of the Aztec Club to the dagger.

"Anything?" Griffin asked.

"Not yet," Owen said. "Just wait."

"We don't have a lot of time," Griffin said.

"Just wait," Owen said again, stepping away from them. Then he thought he might be getting something, and cocked his head a little sideways, as if to hear it better.

There it was. He had to strain very hard to find it, harder than Varius would have to, but it was there. A subtle hum, a kind of resonance he felt in the bones of his skull, and it was familiar to him, or at least to the part of his mind where Varius could still be found.

"This way," he whispered, and stepped forward.

Javier and Griffin followed him from the bedroom, out into a main living room, which had been converted into a kind of museum, with plaques and pictures and display cases for several artifacts. But the dagger wasn't in there, and Owen kept going, through another doorway, and down a hallway to another, larger bedroom. The resonance led him to a certain spot on the floor, beneath a cord rug.

"It's here," he said.

Owen whipped the rug back, pulled out one of his knives, and dropped to his knees. Then he used the blade to pry up a particular floorboard, but he noticed some fresh nicks in the wood, and how easily the board came up.

Beneath it he found a narrow cavity, and resting within it, a rectangular metal tin. Owen pulled it out, but knew instantly it was much too light in weight, and when he opened it, found only a tarnished medal inside, the military cross of the Aztec Club.

"It was here," Owen said. "I can feel it."

"The medal doesn't leave any doubt," Griffin said. "But someone got to it first."

"It had to be recently," Owen said. "These nicks are new."

"The Templars?" Javier asked.

Griffin shook his head. "I don't think so."

"Monroe, then?" Javier said.

Owen hoped it was Monroe. He hoped Monroe had—

A rhythmic whumping rose up, coming from outside the cottage, overhead, and Griffin looked up toward the ceiling. "Helicopters," he said. "Several of them. Abstergo is here."

"What should we do?" Owen asked.

"We don't engage. You're not trained and I can't take them all by myself. We go back to the car, and we get out of here. Understood? Do not engage."

Owen and Javier both nodded.

"Stay close," Griffin said. "Let's move."

He raced from the bedroom, back through the cottage's main hall, where blades of floodlight pierced the windows and sliced up the walls. They ducked back into the smaller bedroom and left through the same window.

Out on the lawn, Owen could see the black shadows of the helicopters hovering overhead, three of them, their rotors stirring up powerful gusts of wind that flattened the grass and threatened to knock Owen over. Smaller black shapes descended from the aircraft, agents sliding down ropes to the ground.

"Move!" Griffin shouted, and the three of them broke into a full sprint, scattering and dodging the roving spotlights, ropes, and the agents who had already touched down.

"Target acquired!" one of them shouted within his helmet, lifting the barrel of an assault rifle toward Javier just a few paces ahead.

Owen reached into his pocket for one of the EMP grenades,

and he threw it. Nothing happened that he could detect, but the agent suddenly stopped in his tracks as if he'd gone blind, grasping at his helmet. That gave Owen another idea, and he stopped running.

"What are you doing?" Javier shouted back at him.

Owen pulled out another EMP grenade, armed it, and hurled it up at the nearest helicopter. It hit, and instantly the pilot seemed to lose control as the engines whined and the rotors slowed. The aircraft swerved through the air as if someone were shaking it, dragging all the agents still roped to it along the ground, plowing them hard into one another. The failing helicopter collided directly with another one, and with a deafening crash they both careened wildly toward the ground.

"Run!" Javier shouted.

Owen sprinted after him toward the trees just as the first helicopter hit the ground and exploded. The force of the blast threw Owen forward off his feet, face-first into the grass where he lay stunned for a moment. But then he felt someone's hands on him, and began to thrash against them, thinking it was an agent, until he rolled over.

"Get moving!" Griffin shouted, hauling him to his feet.

A second explosion followed them into the trees, and Owen glanced back to see the other helicopter had crashed on the far side of the cottage. The three of them raced through the forest, bounding over boulders and fallen trees just as Owen had over the rooftops of New York City in the simulation, and a few minutes later, they reached their car and scrambled in.

"That was insane!" Javier said to Owen, panting hard.

"Save it for the plane!" Griffin barked, turning the key.

He whipped the car out and sped down the road, back the way they had come, his headlights off for the first few miles so they wouldn't draw the attention of the one remaining helicopter still up there in the sky.

Once they were a safe distance away, Griffin took a deep breath and seemed to relax a little. "What were you thinking?" he asked. "I gave you a direct order. Do not engage."

"I know," Owen said. "But I took out two—"

"I'll tell you what you did!" Griffin said. "You got damn lucky! You could have gotten all three of us killed with a stunt like that!"

"I'm sorry," Owen said, even though he wasn't sure if he meant it. "I—"

"Listen to me!" Griffin said. "And listen well. I do not give second chances. If you want my help learning anything about your father, from now on you will do exactly as I say. Do you hear me? Because I am your one shot at knowing the truth, and I will not hesitate to leave you questioning and wondering until the day you die."

Owen closed his mouth, the adrenaline in his body finally dissipating. If Griffin had leveled any other threat against him, he would have ignored him and told him to shove it. But the truth about his father was the one thing Owen couldn't ignore, and wouldn't risk jeopardizing, no matter how angry or wronged he felt.

"Have I made myself clear?" Griffin asked.

"Yes," Owen said. "Perfectly."

"Good," Griffin said.

"What do you mean, from now on?" Javier asked.

"I mean we're not done," Griffin said. "There are still three Pieces of Eden out there, one of which has already been found, and it seems Abstergo believes you and your friends are the key to finding the others."

"Do we have a choice?" Javier asked.

"Of course you have a choice," Griffin said. "You have your own free will, and believe it or not, I would die defending it."

"Then maybe I want out," Javier said, turning to Owen.

But Owen didn't want out. Not yet. Not as long as there was a chance he could find the truth. "I need to know," he said. "I'm all in."

CHAPTER TWENTY-FOUR

atalya sat by herself, away from the others, looking out from their glass cage into the trees. Sean and Grace had told Isaiah everything, and there wasn't anything she could do to stop them. Isaiah had left then, and Victoria had followed him not long after. That had been a couple of hours ago, and the four of them had been left in that room to wait since then. She'd finally let herself eat something, after realizing that refusing their food was an ineffective form of protest. But the apple and bagel hadn't been sitting well in her stomach.

"Hey," she heard Sean say, and through the subtle reflection in the window, she saw him wheeling over to her. "Are you okay?"

"No," she said.

"How come?"

"I can't believe you did that."

"Did what?"

"Don't act dumb," she said. "You know exactly what I mean."

He leaned back in his wheelchair and gripped the handrims. "It made sense to me. I think it was the right thing to do. What, you think Isaiah lied to us?"

"I don't know." Natalya could only shake her head. "That's the point. *I don't know.* Don't get me wrong, Sean. I found him convincing, too. But I would never just hand everything over to him without thinking about it and talking to you guys."

"You're right." He leaned forward in his chair, and something in his movement brought back a sudden memory of Tommy. Natalya blinked it away. "You're right," he said. "We should have discussed it first."

"Doesn't do us much good now," she said.

He wheeled his chair a bit closer, looking over his shoulder as if to see where the other two were. "Hey, I've been meaning to ask you—" But he didn't finish.

She waited a few seconds. "Meaning to ask me what?"

"I just—" he said, and then his cheeks flushed.

Natalya thought she probably knew where this was going, but hoped not. "You just what?"

"I don't know. The Animus. It's just a weird situation. We were . . . you know."

She was right; he was talking about Tommy and Adelina. Natalya didn't want to hurt Sean's feelings, but it seemed as though that was going to be inevitable.

"I mean," he said, "it was them, but it was kind of us, too, and I was just—"

"Sean, it's really not that complicated. Adelina loved *him*. Not you. And Adelina isn't me."

"I know that."

"So what's the problem?"

"There's no problem," he said. "I'm just . . . Never mind, forget it. I'm sorry I brought it up."

"It's okay," she said. "I'm sorry, too. I'm not trying to be rude. We just can't let things get confused, you know? Do you remember what Monroe said? You are you. We have to keep that straight."

"You're right," he said. "Totally right."

"Okay," she said. "I'm glad we at least agree on that." She added that last part even though she knew they still disagreed on both counts.

He nodded once more and wheeled his chair back toward the others, his head hanging a little low. Natalya watched him go and chided herself. She could have been nicer about that, but then, she often found herself saying that. When dealing with people, her first response was usually to take the most direct route, but that wasn't always the wisest course.

She turned to look back out into the trees.

It was too late to take back the information the others had given to Isaiah. So Natalya would go along with them for now. But in no way was she convinced of Isaiah and the good of the Templar Order. But that didn't mean she bought into the Assassins, either. Her experience in the Animus had shown her that both sides brought nothing but destruction. Individually, but especially when they fought each other, and when they did, innocent people paid the price.

But it wouldn't be smart to get all oppositional with a powerful entity like Abstergo. Not yet. Unlike how she'd just handled Sean, Natalya would wait patiently and watch and figure out what the best move would be. That was how her grandparents had escaped Soviet Kazakhstan, and it was how she would escape the Templars.

"Good news!" Victoria said, walking back into the room. "We've made contact with all your parents. We explained the situation to them, and let them know they were free to come and see you at any time. They're on their way as we speak."

"What did you tell them?" Natalya asked.

"We told them that a former employee at your schools, Monroe, had lured you into some unknown scheme with our stolen equipment, but that we had uncovered it and rescued you."

Natalya thought that an expertly crafted deception, true enough it was hard to argue against it, even though she knew the whole story.

"So we can go home?" Grace asked.

"Well, that's up to you, but there's something we would like to offer you."

"What?" Sean asked.

"As Isaiah mentioned, your DNA represents a singular opportunity. We would like to invite you to stay here, at the Aerie, to continue our research. We plan to discuss this very possibility with your parents when they arrive. I suspect they will be quite receptive."

"They will?" Natalya asked. Her parents were mistrustful of most people, but especially those in power or those with money.

"Well," Victoria said, smiling with her big teeth. "Naturally, we will offer a significant financial incentive for participation in the study."

"So what's the catch?" David asked.

"No catch," Victoria said. "But we do have two more Pieces of Eden to find before Monroe does, and we could use your help. We've done some more digging in your DNA, and identified another place of high Memory Concordance that may represent a second prong of the Trident." She turned to look directly at Natalya. "Have you ever wanted to experience China?"

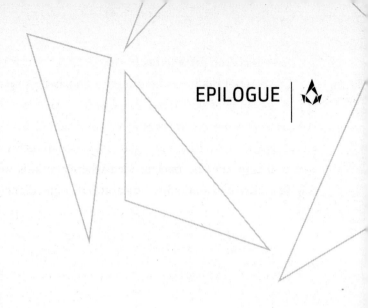

Monroe had driven a few hundred miles since escaping the Templars, and his hands were still shaking. He gripped the steering wheel hard to control it, turning his knuckles white. His eyes had trouble focusing. He'd been up for thirty-six hours, he'd hardly eaten anything, and the road stretched on and on into the pale flat of the desert as the sun rose before him.

He hadn't meant for any of this to happen. At least, not this way. Not like this. But he also couldn't say exactly what he *had* meant to happen. His mission had begun so long ago, and taken so many turns, he sometimes felt as if he'd lost track of it. In those moments, he went back to the beginning, back to where it had started, and he remembered why he was doing all of this.

And who he was doing it for.

This Piece of Eden had been a detour from his primary purpose, but one he absolutely couldn't ignore. He wouldn't allow the Assassins or Templars to get their hands on another Precursor relic. There was too much at stake. The Ascendance Event had already begun, and he had no idea where the kids were now. The Templars had undoubtedly captured some of them, if not all. But it was also possible a few of them had escaped. Owen and Javier stood the best chance, but Grace would likely have some strong skills Bleeding through, too.

Monroe looked down at the passenger seat, where the Animus core rested. At least he still had that. He still had their DNA, and only he had fully decoded what it meant.

The tremors in his hands grew worse, and he realized he had to give his body some food and some rest. He just hoped he had made it far enough away that he could risk stopping.

He ended up pulling over in the next town, a desert nest with one gas station and a population of three hundred and twenty-six. There he refueled the bus, bought a burner phone, ate a shrink-wrapped turkey sandwich, and slept for three hours.

When he woke, he felt a bit more clearheaded.

Even if he had the DNA he needed, he refused to leave those kids in the hands of the Templars. It was his fault they were in danger. His blind carelessness had led the Templars right to them, and so it was his job to get them out. But he wouldn't be able to pull it off on his own. He needed help.

Monroe pulled out the phone he'd just bought, staring at the glowing keypad for a long time before he dialed. It was a number he'd been given a long, long time ago, one he'd committed to memory without knowing if he would ever have cause to use it. He had cause now, though he wondered if it would even still work.

But then it rang.

And someone answered.

"It's Monroe," he said quietly. "We need to talk."